Summer of Dragonfly Changes

Book Two in Loon Lake Series

JOAN GABLE

ISBN: 1490388052
ISBN-13: 978-1490388052

With love to Scott—my Jake.

PROLOGUE

Samantha McGreggor put the final touches on what would be her last article for a while. This brief article, "Dragonfly Changes," was the final piece in a series about strange and unusual insects.

The dragonfly generally lives most of its life as an immature dragonfly or nymph in the water, constantly escaping predation. It usually lives as a nymph for one to three years—on rare occasion up to four years. After its nymph stage, it transforms to the winged insect we all recognize as the dragonfly.

Following this transformation, a dragonfly will live and fly only a few more months, long enough to mature and reproduce. How long it lives depends on the weather. If it transforms during dry, warm weather, it may live as a dragonfly for as long as six months. If it transforms in wet, cold weather, it may live only a few weeks.

Its life cycle is reflected in the dragonfly's symbolism, which is change, especially change in perspective—in self-realization. It represents the kind of change that comes from emotional and mental maturity. And since the adult dragonfly has only a few months to live, it symbolizes living in the moment.

So, when you see that dragonfly at the lake, pond, or pool this summer, take notice of its iridescent wings, its beauty, its flight. Appreciate its life, as it will be over by summer's end. Remember the difficult life it lived as a nymph to become that glistening flying insect. Live this summer like the dragonfly: relax, enjoy, and live life to the fullest. After a long, challenging year, it's time for a summer of dragonfly changes.

CHAPTER 1

"Sammy, it's Jake. I need your help. Please call me back."

Sammy played the message on her voicemail for the fifteenth time. Listening between the lines, of which there were only three, she tried to glean a hidden message.

Playing the message the first time, she thought she heard, "Sammy, it's Jake. I need you. Please come back." But her ears deceived her.

For each of the next fourteen times, she heard the message correctly, but couldn't figure out how he could possibly need her help.

Her heart pounded in her chest causing her ears to ring from the excess blood flow; she worried she might have a heart attack. "Of course," she said to an empty room, "what a perfect way to end Friday, April thirteenth."

Acting on her first impulse, she immediately called her assistant, Kelly.

Kelly picked up on the first ring. "What's up Sammy? I just left you an hour ago."

"I know, I know, sorry to bug you right away. But guess who left me a voice mail at home today? Jake." Sammy delivered the news without giving Kelly the chance to speculate.

"What? Jake? Yay. What'd he say?"

"He needs my help and to call him back."

"What'd he say when you called him back?" Kelly asked, sounding like a curious teenager.

"I haven't called him yet. I called you instead," Sammy replied.

"Certainly, because his message said to call Kelly first, gush like a school-girl, and then call him back, right?" Kelly loved nothing more than to tease Sammy.

"Ha, ha, ha, Kelly. Okay, okay—you're right. But I'm nervous. What in the world do I say?"

"It doesn't sound like you have to say anything, except that you're returning his call. When's the last time you heard from him anyway? Did you ever make firm plans to go back to Minnesota and see him this summer?" Kelly asked.

"We talked a few times last fall. Remember he wanted to come out here to Arizona after Christmas, but his dad broke his leg. I talked to him after New Year's. We've messaged back and forth since then, but…" Sammy started flipping through her calendar pages.

"But right after New Year's was the last time we spoke. I never finalized any summer plans with him."

Sammy met Jake the previous summer at a lakeside resort in northern Minnesota where she'd gone to escape Arizona's summer heat and—more importantly—to reunite with her three sisters. Jake owned and operated the resort with the help of his younger sister, Dana.

Over the summer, Sammy had become good friends with Dana and Jake. Actually, if she had to admit it, she had a sizeable crush on Jake by summer's end. But the timing was off for them. They hadn't been able to get their schedules to sync since last August.

"When's the last time you talked to Dana?" Kelly interrupted Sammy's daydream.

Sammy had to think about it. "Around Thanksgiving, I think. Her aunt was sick or something. Wow, I didn't realize it's been so long. We've e-mailed a few times. But come to think of it, she never replied to my New Year's e-mail either. I wonder if something's wrong."

"Sammy, I'd say something's wrong. You're wasting precious time here. The man is the sweetest guy, so handsome—well, not quite like his cousin, Vince—but he's perfect for you. Call him." Kelly always was the voice of reason.

"What would Greg think if he heard you talk about Vince like that?" Sammy teased.

"He does hear me. He's lying in bed with me right now," Kelly said.

Sammy then heard Greg's voice and imagined him leaning into the phone from the other side of the bed."Hi, Sammy. I saw pictures. Vince is pretty handsome. Any man or woman with eyes can see that."

"Kelly, why didn't you tell me you're in *bed*? I'm so sorry for interrupting."

"It's not what you think. I'm nine months pregnant; *that* hasn't been happening for a few weeks now," Kelly said.

"Too much information, Kell, but really, only weeks? Not bad. But seriously, I'm sorry I interrupted. Tell Greg hi. I'll call ya in the morning."

"Wait, wait, wait…you call me as soon as you talk to Jake. Tonight! I won't be able to sleep until I know what's going on. And trust me, you're not interrupting. Greg's just rubbing my back while we enjoy the quiet of our home. We know that quiet won't last much longer. Call me back."

"Okay. Talk to you soon." Sammy hung up. She swore her palms were starting to sweat—they had never done that before. She couldn't remember the last time she felt this nervous or excited. Taking a deep breath, she dialed his number.

After several rings, Sammy was ready to hang up when she heard a sleepy-sounding "Hello?"

"Hi, Jake. It's Sammy McGreggor." She rolled her eyes. Why did she say her last name? *That sounded so stupid*, she thought. "Did I wake you?"

"No, no, Sammy McGreggor." She loved the way he said her name. It made her feel warm and fuzzy inside.

"You didn't wake me. I was reading a book in bed with Ginger and I left my phone in the kitchen." Sammy could picture him shirtless in bed reading, his dog at his feet. She blushed.

Jake continued. "I'm so glad you called me back. How are you? It's been a while."

"I'm good, Jake. Yes, it has been a while. But your message sounded important. What's up? What can I help you with?" There was so much more she wanted to say, but didn't know where or how to start.

"Sammy, I don't want to dive right into that first. I feel like we need to talk about some things. But I don't know what. Do you know what I mean?"

"Yes, I know what ya mean. I feel like we've left some loose ends with us too, but I don't know what to say either."

She fumbled to find the right words. "So let's not worry about that right now. I know that's not why you called me. What's up?" She was dying to know how she could possibly help.

"George left Dana. She's devastated. I don't know what to do for her—"

"Oh, poor Dana. When did this happen?"

"Right after New Year's. I thought I could help her deal with it, but it's already April and I'm still useless. My dad continues to go to physical therapy for his leg that he broke in December. He's had numerous surgical complications. My mom's been a mess with his situation, mostly because my aunt's also so sick. And to make matters worse, Dana hasn't even told my parents yet." He took a long pause, giving Sammy time to let it all sink in.

"Didn't George know how lucky he was to have her? Oh, what a…" She stopped herself. She didn't want to be too vulgar on the phone with Jake. "What an idiot. And I suppose he cheated on her?"

"How'd you know?" Jake sounded surprised.

"There could be no other reason, Jake. I never really liked him. He was too cute, too smooth, and too young. They got married way too quickly after meeting each other. What was it? Six months?" Sammy couldn't recall. But she did remember that George was about seven years younger than Dana. She knew the age gap could work and that wasn't the problem, per se. She'd only met George a few times last summer, but there was something about him she didn't like or trust. She couldn't put her finger on it then. Now she knew what it was; he was a cheater.

"It was actually only about five months. We all liked him, though. I encouraged it. He adored her so much. She was thrilled with how wonderful he treated her." Sammy heard guilt in Jake's voice.

"Okay, okay, enough about George. What about Dana? How can I help?" Sammy felt sick. She'd grown so fond of Dana last summer. She found Dana to be incredibly giving and kind. Sammy couldn't imagine George crushing her like that. She didn't even like saying his name. *George.*

Letting out a long, heavy sigh, Jake answered, "I'm not sure what I expected you to do, Sammy. But just talking to you makes me feel better. I've missed you."

Whoa. His comment almost made Sammy swoon.

"Jake, I've missed you too. I was so disappointed when you couldn't come out to see me in December. I completely understood about your dad and all, but I can't even tell you how much I was looking forward to seeing you." There. She said it.

"I wanted to see you too. And I would have if it was only my dad's broken leg, but my aunt was so sick on top of it. Even though my mom and aunt are sisters-in-law, they are as close as real sisters. I couldn't bear to leave my mom under the circumstances. Growing old has suddenly become quite complicated and stressful for my parents."

I wouldn't know, Sammy thought, with a familiar twinge of pain. Her parents had died in a car accident over two decades ago, so she no longer had any parental worries.

Jake continued. "And then after the New Year, Dana and George's split was a done deal and Dana insisted on keeping it from my parents until my dad was back on his feet—literally. She's been staying in one of my cabins here at the resort, but since this is where George courted her, I think it has too many painful memories for her and may not be the best thing—"

"Jake, please stop." Sammy gently interrupted. She could hear the distress in his voice. "What can I do?" she asked.

"I don't know," he replied.

Sammy wanted him to ask her to come see him. She wanted him to ask her to come see Dana. She wanted him to *ask.*

If he didn't ask, she had to be strong and help from afar. She didn't want to force herself on him or Dana. She waited for him to say something. He didn't.

"Jake, are you still there?"

"Yes. Will you come to the lake? I want to be with you and I want you to help Dana if you can."

Again, she practically fainted from his response. "Yes, I'd love to come see you and Dana." Her reply was quick and enthusiastic.

Too enthusiastic, she worried. So, she tried to sound slightly indifferent by calmly asking, "What would you recommend?"

"I don't know, Sammy. How about you check over your schedule for the next month? Do you have anything that might keep you from coming to visit for a few weeks?" he asked.

She did, but she didn't want to tell him about that yet. "I'm not sure. Let me look at my calendar and see what I can come up with. Do you have a cabin I can stay in?"

"You can stay with me, in one of my guest rooms," he answered awkwardly. "I want to take care of you while you're here. Would that work?"

"That'd be nice. I'll call you tomorrow."

"Thanks for calling me back, Sammy. I can't wait to see you again."

"Me too, Jake. Good night."

Sammy was beyond thrilled. She could hardly stand the last

few minutes of the conversation—it was what she'd been dreaming about for months now. But it was real.

Even though she was devastated for Dana, she couldn't deny her own happiness.

As promised, she called Kelly back.

Again Kelly answered on the first ring. "What'd he say?"

Sammy laughed. "You've been waiting, haven't you?"

"Yes, I've been cooking up all kinds of scenarios to Greg here. I think he's as curious as I am now. What did Jake want?"

"George left Dana." Sammy braced herself for Kelly's reaction. Kelly stayed with Sammy at the resort for a few days last summer. She had met Dana and instantly connected with her. Sammy knew Kelly would be upset.

"That bastard! What an idiot! So what floozy did he cheat on her with?"

"I don't know. I didn't get all the details."

"How's Dana taking it?"

"Obviously not very well, if Jake's calling and asking me to go there to help."

"What? He asked you to go there? Interesting turn of events. What did you tell him?"

"I told him that I could, of course."

"Sammy, this is better than any scenario I imagined. When are you going? What are the details?"

"I don't know. I need to consider a few things—like the birth of your baby in a few weeks. That's something I can't miss," Sammy said.

"Don't worry about that. This baby will know you love her whenever you meet her. And Greg will take such wonderful care of me—no need to worry about that. This is your life, my friend. You can't let some lonely old woman steal Jake's heart this summer." Kelly sounded ready to launch into one of her pep talks if need be.

"You're right, Kelly. The only lonely old woman stealing his heart this summer will be me," Sammy answered.

"Atta girl, Sammy! Now, I need to get some sleep. Let me know when your plans develop."

"Will do. Sweet dreams, Kell."

As they hung up, Sammy replayed her conversation with Jake. She loved how he wanted her to stay with him and not in a separate cabin.

She dug out her date book and checked her calendars and deadlines. The only thing keeping her in Arizona was Kelly's baby. Even though Kelly meant every word she said, Sammy really wanted to meet that baby when it was born. She would figure it all out, somehow.

***

It didn't take Sammy long to finalize her plans. As a freelance writer, her schedule was what she made it. She was up to date with all her deadlines and had already cleared her calendar for the next two months in anticipation of helping Kelly with the newborn. Her freedom was one of the few benefits of being a single thirty-nine-year-old woman.

She and Jake talked a few times over the weekend, making plans. By Monday morning she'd booked a flight to see Jake and his sister the following Friday, one week after he'd left a voice mail on her phone.

"Wow, one week and you're flying out to see him? Boy, are you easy," Kelly said as she waddled into Sammy's office Monday morning.

Sammy blushed and laughed, choking on her coffee. "Seriously, I know! I'm so ridiculous, aren't I? I have no shame. I really like him and can't wait to see him. I don't think I'll be able to sleep until I see him."

She took another sip of coffee and continued. "And look at me. I haven't lost that five-pound Christmas present I gained. I almost did, until that girls' club showed up with their cookies. How much weight do you think I can lose in four days?"

Kelly burst out laughing. "I can honestly say I've never seen you, Miss McGreggor, act so in love. You didn't even act this way when you came back last August after the 'big kiss.'

But look at you now. You're like a teenage girl in my best friend's body, like some *Freaky Friday* kind of thing. I love it."

Kelly kept laughing. "Man, I almost peed. I have no bladder control with this big belly. I'll be back." She waddled off to the bathroom.

"Saved by the pee," Sammy muttered. *Maybe I am acting like a teenager, because I feel like a teenager. Is that so wrong?*

Kelly returned, wiping tears from her eyes. "Oh, you kill me. But seriously, you look gorgeous. Those five pounds look great on you. You're all curvy and a little bustier, though not quite as curvy and busty as me." She proudly stuck out her belly and chest. "But you look great. Jake will be a horndog around you."

"Kelly!" Sammy feigned surprise. "What in the world's gotten into you?" It wasn't unlike Kelly to talk that way, just not toward Sammy.

"You know it's true. He'll be all over you. And I'm sorry, but this is how I am right now. I'm so hormonally juiced up. Sex is very confusing to me right now."

Sammy put her fingers in her ears. "La, la, la," she said quietly.

Kelly continued without a care, "I want to do it all the time, except physically right now it's pretty gross; plus I'm so tired and the size of a house. It's so strange. I think about it a lot. I'm like a seventeen-year-old boy." Kelly started to fan herself with the morning mail. "See? I'm getting hot and bothered just talking about it."

"Okay, then, really let's *not* talk about it. I'm uncomfortable with this conversation," Sammy said.

"Prude," Kelly whispered with a smile.

A smirk and a shake of her head was the only response Sammy gave Kelly. Sammy knew better than to continue the banter. It could go on for hours, and they needed to get a few things done before she left on Friday.

"Okay, Boss, what do you need me to do these next few days?" Before Sammy could answer, Kelly added bitterly, "I really think George is a shit for treating Dana the way he did.

Do you know any more details yet?"

"Not really. Jake only told me a few basic things. The divorce papers were final last week and that's when she took a turn again and why he called me."

"They're divorced already?" Kelly asked.

"Yes, they split up over the holidays. It shouldn't have taken as long as it did. George and Dana didn't have much stuff to split up. George wanted her out, and she wasn't going to fight him for anything. Jake said she had no fight in her. She was pretty devastated," Sammy rambled on as she organized items on her desk.

"Well, I say good riddance. She can do so much better. And she's been staying at Jake's cabin?" Kelly asked.

"Not with him, but in one of his rental cabins. I actually have no idea what her situation will be like. She hasn't even told her parents. I don't know how she could keep something that big from them," Sammy said, adjusting the window blinds.

"She and George lived in a small house in town, which I think they rented. As far as I knew, she only worked for Jake. I can't imagine she has much money and she might not need much there. But I doubt she'll want to stay in that town."

"Where would she go, then?" Kelly asked.

"I have no idea. My mind goes 'round and 'round when I think of her situation. But I'll know more when I see her. And don't worry, you know I'll give you daily updates on what I learn, Gladys." Sammy showed her age by using a *Bewitched* reference, but it fit the situation so well.

"Hey yeah, you can start a blog while you're at it," Kelly teased right back. Sammy was one of the most technologically resistant writers out there. She had no interest in a website, blog, or social networking. Kelly had done her best to push Sammy into the new millennium, but Sammy remained ten years behind the rest of the world.

"Why you smart aleck…" Sammy tried to sound offended, but her genuine smile gave her away.

"I hope that baby gets your sense of humor," she said.

"She will." Kelly paused and then continued more somberly, "I can't believe I'm going to be a mom in a few weeks. Sammy, I'm scared." She started crying softly. "And I have no idea why I'm crying."

Sammy rushed to her side with a tissue and hugged her. "Hey, hey, it's okay. What are you scared of?"

"Having a baby at my age." Kelly never admitted her age, but Sammy guessed her to be around forty-three. "Something in me has a bad feeling. Like something's going to happen. Greg says it's healthy and natural to be scared. He's so sweet. But sometimes I feel like something's wrong."

Sammy became concerned; she'd never seen Kelly like this. "With the baby?"

"No, the baby's fine. I've been going to the doctor twice a week for monitoring and nothing seems amiss. It's something else. I don't know what. I'm just scared." Kelly wiped her tears away and straightened herself up. "Sorry. This is the last thing you want to witness before you leave."

"You're right—this is the last thing I want to see. I can't leave you like this. I'll cancel my plans and stay here with you."

"Absolutely not! This is just my hormones talking. Besides you can't do anything that Greg isn't doing. He's taking perfect care of me and this baby. We're fine. It's just something I can't explain. Maybe all women go through this before birth—the unknown is scary. Bringing a new, wonderful, sweet baby into this sometimes creepy world is scary," Kelly said and quietly blew her nose.

Then she waved her hands as if pushing her thoughts aside. "I can really get worked up sometimes. I'm sorry. You are sticking to your plans. You're going and telling me everything. I will live vicariously through you."

Kelly grabbed Sammy by the shoulders, lightly shaking her for effect. "You go live this adventure. Dana needs you"—her voice dropped into a seductive tone—"and Jake *wants* you."

"There you go again," Sammy said as she pulled away. "You're incorrigible."

Looking at Kelly through squinted eyes, Sammy said, "I'm going to keep my eyes on you these next few days and if you continue to give me doubt, I'll have no problem changing my plans. So you better shape up. Now, can we please get some work done?" Sammy attempted to change the mood.

"Yes, Boss. Now what can I do for you these next few days?"

They went about sorting their business tasks and developing a plan for the summer. This was their last week in the office together for a few months. They needed a solid plan.

CHAPTER 2

Friday arrived in a flash. Sammy felt unprepared. A one-way ticket to Minneapolis and a one-week rental car reservation was as far as she'd gotten. Whatever happened after that was anyone's guess, which added to her adventure.

Gazing out the airplane window en route to Minneapolis, Sammy thought back to almost a year ago when she arrived at Hunter Lodge on Loon Lake. She remembered the day she met Dana, a petite blonde woman with a nice, youthful tan. Dana was genuinely sweet and full of life. Sammy laughed at how she mistook Dana as Jake's wife at first.

And *Jake*. He was handsome and friendly. Her cheeks blushed with heat as she thought of him. *And that kiss*. The last time she saw him they shared their first and last kiss, but boy, what a kiss. It had stuck with her for months.

A message from the cockpit brought her out of her reverie. She glanced around to see if anyone was watching her. She was sure the look on her face gave away what thoughts ran through her mind.

She looked at her hands. They deceived her. They looked old. But she felt young, alive, and, worst of all, *nervous*.

As the plane touched down, she said a small prayer to protect and care for Kelly and her baby while she was away, give herself the strength and guidance to be of real help to Dana, and allow herself to enjoy Jake and have fun.

This time will never come again, she told herself. *It's time to live in the moment, like a dragonfly*. She thought of how the dragonfly lives only a few quick months as an adult—just long enough to live, reproduce, and fly. Sammy felt that way too, like she had only a few months to make something happen.

***

Stopping in Saw Mill, the last town before Loon Lake, Sammy picked up some provisions: a few bottles of wine, Jake's favorite beer, her favorite coffee, along with some chocolates, snacks, and a stack of gossip magazines for girl-time with Dana. Sammy chuckled as she saw a tiny photo of her sister, Cassandra, and her twin babies on one of the magazine covers.

At four o'clock she finally arrived at the lake. That first glimpse of the water overwhelmed her with excitement and happiness just as it did every time. It happened over twenty years ago, last year, and again today. She thought of the many times her family stayed at the lake when she was young.

Once more, she had a flashback to her arrival last year, as well as her departure at summer's end. She blushed.

She parked the car and headed toward the lodge to find Jake.

Zipping her jacket up to her neck, Sammy thought about how today's arrival was much different from last year's when Dana greeted her that sunny day. Back then she was overwhelmed by the thrill of the unknown.

Today it was cold and cloudy. Everything was wet. The dreary cabins were dark with vacancy. Then she saw the smoke and smelled its fragrance coming from the chimney on Jake's lodge. It was a welcome sign and one that made her imagine romantic things in front of Jake's fire. She was even more excited this time, but not by the unknown. She knew *who* excited her.

Just as she was about to knock on the door, it opened. There in front of her was the man of her dreams—literally. She had dreamed of Jake for months and only now realized how foolishly she wasted time. She didn't know how to greet him. But it didn't matter. He made the first move.

"Sammy, you're a sight to see. Hello," he said in a low voice as he slipped his hands around her waist and pulled her toward him.

Before she could answer, there it was: that kiss she'd been dreaming about. She felt it in every ounce of her body, even in those five extra curvy pounds.

When they parted, she smiled at him with a quiet, "Hi."

"Hi." He smiled back. "You look beautiful, even more gorgeous than I remembered."

She thought the exact same thing. "Thank you."

"Come in. Come in. How are you? Tired? Hungry? Thirsty? How was the flight? How was the drive? Can I take your coat? Let me take that bag." He fussed over her and she loved it.

"I'm fine, Jake, really. This is awkward, isn't it?" Sammy asked nervously.

"Yeah, it is a little. But it's so great to see you. I'm excited that you're here. I just regret that it took Dana getting a divorce to finally get me to ask you to visit. Would you've come if she didn't…if she wasn't a mess?" He fumbled for the right words.

"I would've come anytime you asked. I thought about you a lot." She couldn't take her eyes off his.

"So, no new boyfriend this past year?" He kept his eyes locked with hers.

"No new boyfriend this year." She offered a half-smile but held her gaze. "No new girlfriend this year?" she asked with raised eyebrows.

"No new girlfriend this year." His eyes smiled now too, never leaving hers.

"Good." She finally looked away, feeling too exposed to continue their game.

"Good." He pulled her close and gave her that kiss again. She gave in, letting her kiss say all the things her words couldn't.

When the kiss ended, he kept her face cupped in his hands. "I'm so happy you're here."

She smiled. "I am too. I wish it was under different circumstances," she said as she broke away. "How's Dana? Is she around?"

"She's not so good. She isn't here tonight. She's in town with a friend seeing a movie and then staying at her friend's house. I didn't tell her you were coming. I wanted you to surprise her, but mostly I wanted a night of you all to myself."

"I like the way you think. What's new with you? How's your dad? And your mom?" She wanted to know everything.

"All in good time, Sammy. Let's get your things out of the car. Another thunderstorm is on its way in and we should get you settled in before it hits. We've had several storms this week and I've lost power three nights already. I'm almost sure if the winds get as high as they're expecting, we'll be powerless again tonight."

I already am, she thought to herself. "That might be fun."

She covered her thoughts by quickly changing the subject. "And where's Ginger?" Sammy noticed Jake's German shepherd wasn't around.

"She's got a boyfriend down the road, a golden retriever. And she's smitten. She should be home soon, though. As soon as the thunder starts rumbling, she'll want to be here with me." He looked out the window. "We'd better hurry."

They unloaded Sammy's car, and as Jake had predicted, Ginger met up with them shortly after the first rumble. "Perfect timing," Jake said as large rain-drops began to kick up mud. They made a run for it.

***

Sammy unpacked her bags and settled into one of Jake's guest rooms. Neither she nor Jake presumed otherwise. She definitely needed her own space and wanted to take things slow with him.

As she walked past the mirror in Jake's guest room, she caught a glimpse of her reflection. Upon closer examination, the woman looking back at her looked younger than Sammy remembered. Jake did that to her.

She found Jake in the living room adding logs to the fire.

"I turned off several lights, hope you don't mind. I want to be ready if we lose power." He lit a few more candles.

"Why would I mind? It looks beautiful," she said as she wrapped her long, fuzzy, lavender sweater tighter around her.

"So do you, especially in that sweater. It makes your eyes reflect the same purple color." He gazed at her and quickly added, "Wine or beer?"

"Whatever you're having…whoa." A loud crack of thunder shook the cabin. "That was fantastic!"

Jake laughed as he handed her a glass of red wine. "Come, sit here with me." He sat down on the worn leather couch, which was the color of dark chocolate, next to the fireplace. From here they would have a view of the lightning storm over the lake.

She noticed Jake had set out cheese and crackers. When she sat, he wrapped a blanket around them both.

"This is perfect," he said as he held out his glass toward her. "Cheers."

"Cheers," she said as the glasses clinked. "You're right. This is perfect, Jake. If anyone told me a week ago that this is what I'd be doing tonight, I wouldn't have believed them."

"And I can't imagine doing anything else right now, Sammy."

She leaned into him this time and kissed him. She wasn't going to play games or be coy or walk on eggshells. Not this week. She was going to go for whatever she wanted, say what she wanted, and do what she wanted.

"Okay, Handsome, I think we need to play a little game of catch-up tonight, don't ya think? Where do you want to start?" She smiled at him.

"You know where I want to start," he said, raising his eyebrows up and down.

She laughed. "Okay, let me rephrase that. What do you want to talk about first?"

"Your novel. What's the status?"

"My editor and I are still working on it. Next question," she said quickly.

"Kelly and her baby?" he fired back at her.

"It's a girl, due in two weeks, if not sooner. Next question."

"Cassandra and the twins?" He didn't skip a beat.

"All three healthy and beautiful. Next question."

"What happened with Alex and Vince?" He was good at this game.

"Ah, rats. You got me. That's a tough one." She laughed. "I don't know much. Alex said it was a summer fling and that it ended. Sadly, my sister's always been like that. She gets close to a man or somewhat serious and then puts on the brakes. What has he said?"

"Well, you know my cousin. He's very casual about things too. Except I think his mom's condition complicated things for him." Jake said the last part quietly.

"Yeah, about that…This is awkward, but Alex never said anything about Vince's mom, and you didn't either the few times we've talked since last fall. I remember Dana mentioning your sick aunt around Thanksgiving and you've brought it up a few times now. Can you elaborate a bit for me? I can make some assumptions, but I'd rather know the facts."

"I'm sorry. I guess I thought Vince said something to Alex, but maybe things ended with them before he found out. His mom was diagnosed with cancer last October. It's been a horrible thing for Vince, his family, and my mom. It's just been tough. Her prognosis is bad. That's the main reason why my sister doesn't want to tell my mom anything. She doesn't want to burden her more."

"Oh, poor Vince. I feel so bad for him. I know Alex ended things last September and hasn't kept in contact with him.

She's been busy getting settled in a new city and is actually seeing a therapist for some emotional issues." Sammy wondered briefly if she was betraying her sister by telling Jake about the therapist. But Sammy didn't want Jake to think her sister was a terrible person. Sammy was proud of Alex for tackling her problems head-on.

"I remember Vince said that was one of the main reasons Alex ended things. She started therapy and wanted to be fair to him and keep him out of her problems."

"Wow. That surprises me," Sammy said, genuinely shocked. It made her even more proud of her sister. She knew Alex was right and needed to tackle her issues without a new relationship in her life.

She found herself thankful that Vince didn't have to concern himself with Alex while dealing with his mom's illness. *Things work out the way they're supposed to*, she thought.

Nonetheless, Sammy was curious about Vince's impression of Alex. "So, do you think Vince was okay with things ending? Did he like her? Did he want to see where things could go?"

"I know he liked her a lot. But she made it clear to him that she was interested in her new career and needed to give it one hundred percent. He understood that." Jake sipped his wine, looking pensive.

"But I also know Vince, and know that he wants something different for his future: more stability, a family…He hasn't ever really said these things to me outright, but I've known him my whole life and I knew Alex wasn't the one for him."

"What about you, Jake Hunter? What do you want?" Sammy asked.

"Besides you? And this?" he asked, sincere and direct.

"I guess I mean after this. You're a winter hermit up here in the woods. Do you want something different for your future? More stability, a family…"

"Those are good questions, Miss McGreggor. Ask me again in a few weeks." He smiled wide. It took her breath away.

He's more handsome than ever, she thought. His chiseled jaw line and cheek bones softened when he smiled. The candlelight made his gray eyes sparkle. The gray hairs starting to show through the sandy-blond looked good on him.

"Can I have more wine, please?" she asked as she snacked on a piece of cheese.

"Of course." He topped off both glasses. "So back to Cassandra, did they write her off the show?"

"Do you watch it now?" Sammy asked, referring to the sitcom that her sister starred in.

"I started to after I met her last summer. I wanted to see how they addressed her pregnancy, but she wasn't on anymore. What happened?" he asked.

"Ah, so you don't read the tabloids," she teased. "They had her character marry a boyfriend from a few seasons ago and move away. She's sort of on an indefinite leave for as long as she likes. They've offered her a spin-off show if she wants it or she can return whenever she's ready. Apparently they didn't want to have her character get pregnant and they didn't want to try to fool the audience."

"That's cool," Jake said. "Is she considering retiring from acting?"

"I don't know about that. I know she's happy to have this time with her babies. And I think in the back of her mind, she questions the longevity of the show. I doubt she'll do anything until after the fall and the start of the next season."

"Good for her. I'm glad it worked out so well," he said as he held out his hand. "Come with me. I need to show you something."

She took his hand and walked with him to the back door. "Now close your eyes," he said. She obeyed as he helped her step out the door.

She heard him flip some switches and felt the cooler air.

"Okay, open them."

Sammy opened her eyes to a beautiful screened-in deck that twinkled with strings of holiday lights. Jake flipped another switch, and soon she heard the bubbling of a hot tub.

"Jake, this room is amazing," she said as she scanned the wooden deck and the short stone wall that surrounded it.

Large overstuffed chairs and lounges and stained-glass lamps created intimate sitting areas. There were dozens of plants in every shape and size. The twinkling glow of the light strings gave the room a festive atmosphere.

"When did you do this?"

"We worked on it in early November and then after Christmas," Jake said as he pointed to two overstuffed chairs.

They sat and he continued. "After Vince's mom was diagnosed, I saw something change in him. He switched his teaching position to a job-share—where two teachers share the same position. It's unusual in his school, but he looked into it, got it to work out, and took some time off to be with his family. I knew he needed another outlet or project, if you will.

"So I enlisted his help and we worked on it a few days in early November, building the frame. We were lucky that there wasn't much snow then. But we froze our butts off finishing it after Christmas," he said with a shiver.

"I bet you did." Sammy sipped on her wine and gazed around the room.

"But it was really great to have the time to work with Vince, to talk and *not talk*. Then, in January, after Dana's separation, she needed something to do. So I let her decorate the whole room," Jake said with a smile.

Sammy noticed the love and pride he had in his voice. It was a beautiful room and a great amenity for him. But more so she loved the reasons he built it. He mostly did it for them, not himself. She knew how hard he worked and that he wasn't really a hot tub kind of guy.

"It's beautiful. It's a wonderful reminder of the love you have for your cousin and sister. Do you feel that love in here?" Sammy asked.

Jake smiled. "Uh, I've never really looked at it like that." He looked at her squarely then. "But that's one of the reasons I like you so much. You have a unique way of seeing things."

Another loud crack of thunder interrupted the moment.

"We'd better go back inside," he said as he quickly turned off the hot tub and lights.

They found themselves back by the fire just as the power went out.

The candlelight and crackling flames in the fireplace lit the room right up. Sammy thought it was the most romantic spot in the world. They stayed up late talking, drinking wine, cuddling, and kissing by firelight. They talked like old friends.

Sammy went to sleep that night thinking about their friendship—how they were building everything on that foundation of friendship. She hoped that meant their relationship had a chance.

CHAPTER 3

Still on Arizona time, Sammy woke late the next morning to rain and thick gray skies. She stayed in bed listening to the rhythm of the rain on the roof. Knowing the temperature was already in the nineties back home, Sammy thought about how much she missed these kinds of mornings. Spring never really comes to Phoenix.

Listening to the rain, she recalled her childhood summers in the Midwest: the warm, rainy mornings when her sisters and she would wake, put on swim-suits, and play outside in the rain and puddles. She could picture her mom in front of the kitchen window with her mug of coffee and robe, laughing and waving at her girls.

The lake, the resort…both had a strange effect on Sammy. She had flashes of memories that she hadn't recalled in ages. Sammy began to think of it as the "vacation effect," where random thoughts and flashes of memories enter her vacationing mind that otherwise has no room for such thoughts during her everyday life. She called these memories her "firefly memories."

As she continued to enjoy the rain, she listened for Jake. She smelled coffee and the fireplace, but heard no sound of him. All she heard was the rain and the distant call of a loon.

She checked her cell phone for messages and e-mail—nothing important. Pure relaxation seeped into her whole body as she happily climbed out of bed.

After freshening up a bit, she tiptoed out to the kitchen and silently watched Jake, who hadn't heard her get up. He sat by the fireplace with Ginger at his feet, sipping a steamy cup of coffee while reading the news on a tablet. She made a mental note to remember this image, calling it "Early Morning Jake and Dog." She was falling hard.

Just as Ginger raised her head slightly, ready to announce Sammy's presence, Sammy spoke up. "Well, I see technology has improved around here. I remember when we were young and could only get two radio stations here, *on AM*, not even FM." She laughed to herself at the thought as she poured a cup of coffee.

"Ah, yes, I remember those good old days too," he said with a smile. "The lack of newspaper delivery in the winter really got to me this year. I finally broke down and bought myself one of these gadgets for Christmas. These things are amazing. I can even use them for a few hours when the power goes out. Which, as you can obviously tell, is back on. How'd you sleep? You look refreshed." Jake smiled at her.

"I slept better than I have in ages. I think it was all the rain and fresh air. What a great morning. I love this gray and rain," she said as she dreamily gazed out the large window toward the lake.

"Yeah, I figured you would. Dana's on her way. She should be here soon. I asked her to pick up some pastries and deli meats, cheeses, and bread. She has a wonderful older woman friend who owns a bakery in town. They have the best pastries ever. Breakfast should be a real treat," he said.

"That sounds delicious." She sat down next to him. She didn't know what to do or how to act.

He leaned over and kissed her gently on the cheek. "Good morning."

"Good morning." She smiled. Lucky for her, Jake made the moves and she needn't worry what to do. "So what do you usually do on days like this—or any day in the winter for that matter?"

"If you weren't here today, this is what I would be doing this morning. Later in the day, I'd walk down the road and visit with the neighbors who are here. In wintertime, I'd see if anyone needed help with any projects or needed firewood," he said, putting away his tablet.

He snuggled in closer to her as he continued. "We become a very social group over the long, cold winter and help each other out. Seems someone always has a project they need help with: a roof needing repair and sometimes shoveling, some firewood cutting, those sorts of things."

"What about for fun?" she asked enjoying the intimacy.

"We usually get together once or twice a week for dinner and card games. And often times we look after the homes of the folks that aren't up here over the winters. That can be fun," he said with a chuckle, as though recalling a humorous incident. "We check for intruders, animals, or possible wind and snow damage. And there are sometimes hunters and ice fishermen to visit with."

"Ice fishing? They do that here? That sounds cold. *Brrr.*"—Sammy furrowed her brow—"I can't imagine such a lifestyle. It seems like I'm always in a hurry at home. Plus, I can't imagine not seeing Kelly every day or even on a regular basis. What about Dana? What's she been doing these last few months?"

"I'll let her answer that question for you. I think you'll be surprised. Don't get me wrong, she's had plenty of days when she did next to nothing but cry and sulk. But she's been busy with a few things."

"Hmm, you speak in tongues. I'm intrigued," Sammy said.

"Well, you'll learn soon enough. Sounds like Dana pulled up. And just in time—I'm starving."

A few moments later, Dana burst through the door dripping wet. "What's up with the rental car in the parking lot?" Her arms were loaded down with bags and boxes.

Sammy hardly recognized Dana, who was but a shadow of the woman Sammy met last summer. Dana was practically skin and bones. She looked as though she'd shrunk in size, as if someone stuck her in the hot wash and dry cycle and she came out a few sizes smaller. Her eyes were missing their twinkle and were a bit swollen and red. She looked sad and broken, which made Sammy want to hug her—which was exactly what she did the second Dana locked eyes with her.

"What in the world…" squeaked out of Dana's mouth as Sammy squeezed her. Sammy was careful not to hug Dana too tight. She was afraid she might break her fragile body.

"Sammy, what are you doing here?" Dana asked.

"Who knew your brother was so romantic? He called me last week out of the blue and invited me. Kelly's baby is due soon, so I had to come sooner than later. I got in last night and we had a wonderful evening catching up." Sammy smiled and noticed the look of appreciation from Jake. She figured Dana didn't need to be privy to the real reason for the invite.

Dana gave Jake a light smack to his shoulder. "Why didn't you tell me she was coming, or that you even talked to her for that matter?"

"I thought it would be a fun surprise for you. Plus, I wasn't sure she'd actually show up." Jake blushed with that last statement.

"Why wouldn't I come?" Sammy was quick to ask.

"I don't know. It's been a while and I didn't know if you were seeing someone else." As he said it, Sammy could tell he regretted it.

Dana physically flinched at the words. Sammy could see the pain in her eyes even though Dana continued to smile, keeping up a front.

Sammy pretended she didn't notice the awkward tension in the room. "It's so wonderful to see you, Dana. I can't wait to catch up. But first let me help you unpack all these goodies. They smell *so good.* Jake said you have a friend with a bakery." Sammy had successfully changed the subject: Dana seemed to relax a bit.

"Yes, Greta. She's a dear old German woman, and she owns a bakery in town. She uses wonderful European recipes for pastries, breads, and sausages. She's a sweetheart, but she always says whatever's on her mind, no matter how shocking. It's refreshing—sometimes painful, but always honest, and very German of her," Dana said with a laugh.

As Sammy and Dana continued to chat and set up the breakfast buffet, Sammy watched Jake prepare Dana's coffee to her liking without asking: a dash of half and half and one packet of sweetener. It was a small, simple act on Jake's part—but it made Sammy more smitten.

With their plates piled high with the bakery goodies, they settled down for their breakfast feast. The rain continued to come down and the wind began to pick up.

Out on the lake, the wind created rough waves that washed up tree debris on the shore.

Jake's phone interrupted the sound of the rain and he walked to the other side of the room to answer it.

The women tried—unsuccessfully—to eavesdrop on Jake's phone conversation.

When he hung up the phone, he noticed they were both still trying to listen in. "Sounded interesting, huh?" he teased.

Returning to the table, he filled them in. "That was Dave down the road. He had some large pieces of driftwood, the size of logs, wash up on his beach this morning. His teenage sons thought it would be fun to make a fort with them."

Chuckling, he continued. "The boys made a homemade crane, which, long story short, was a bad idea. Two logs and a homemade crane crashed through their living room wall of windows. He has the supplies to fix the damage, but he was looking for some help. I offered to help him in a bit if that's okay with you two. Give you some girl-time?"

"Certainly," Sammy said.

"Can we see it?" Dana asked.

"Sure, we can walk down there after breakfast and check it out," Jake said. "When he was telling me this story, I could honestly picture my teenage self and teenage Vince doing something just as ridiculous. Why is it, the older we get, the less we think we can do?" He shook his head.

"I agree. We all start out as artists and experimenters when we're kids. But as more and more adults in our lives tell us we can't do these things, we stop trying, don't we?" Sammy had often thought about that.

"It's true. I wanted to be an artist most of my childhood and ended up going to college for design. And now look at me," Dana said sadly as she shrugged her shoulders.

Sammy could tell how fragile Dana was, that she could easily see the doom and gloom in things. "It'll be fun to have some girl-time together. How long do you think you'll be down there?"

"I should be back in time for dinner," Jake said.

"Sounds perfect. We'll just have to start happy hour without you," Sammy said, winking at Dana.

"I'd expect nothing less," Jake said, shaking his head.

They continued their breakfast with friendly chitchat: the recent news of their dad's physical therapy, their aunt's latest update.

After breakfast, the three walked down the road to see the big hole in the wall. Sammy cherished the walk in the rain. She and Jake held hands under a large umbrella.

Dana, covered in rain gear, walked with Ginger who kept rubbing up against her for a petting. Sammy thought maybe the dog sensed Dana's sadness and longing.

Sammy looked forward to visiting with Dana that afternoon. She hoped that Dana would appreciate someone new to talk to. She also hoped that she could figure out how to be of actual help to Dana.

CHAPTER 4

Sammy and Dana left Jake behind and headed back to the lodge. After meeting Ginger and her boyfriend along the way, the women happily chatted about puppy love—literally—the rest of the walk home.

With her foot barely in the door, Dana got straight to the point. "Okay, so what's my brother told you? *About me*, I mean."

"When he called me last week, he said that you and George were divorced and that you hadn't told your parents yet to spare your mom the additional concern. I didn't get any real specifics. He asked me to come visit him and see if I could cheer you up." Sammy wanted to be straight with Dana and not hide her real intentions.

Before Dana could react, Sammy rambled on. "How are you? You don't look so good…That came out wrong…Even though you're nothing but skin and bones, you're still cute as can be…But you look sad and heartbroken…Which I'm sure you are. Why wouldn't you be? But really, how are you?"

"I'm doing better, which isn't saying much. I was really in the dumps for a while…*a long while*. Then I was insanely mad at a lot of things, myself in particular. Then I was mad at him again and the other woman. Did Jake tell you there was another woman?" Dana almost spit the words out of her mouth. "See? It makes me so angry."

"You should be angry. I assumed there was another woman. Jake confirmed my suspicions, but he didn't elaborate. Do you want to tell me about it? By the way, it's almost noon on a Saturday, and, according to my aunt, it's an acceptable time for a glass of wine—or a whole bottle. And this particular conversation may require it. Will you have a glass with me?" Sammy grabbed a chilled bottle of Chardonnay from the fridge.

"Yes, that sounds good." Dana grabbed two glasses and a corkscrew. "Bring the bottle with you."

They settled down in the comfortable chairs on the screened-in deck. Dana handed Sammy a soft blanket in exchange for the wine, which she proceeded to open and pour into their glasses. Sammy couldn't help but think, *Dana's done this a bit more frequently since last summer.*

It had finally stopped raining but remained cold and gray outside. The smell of wet pine trees triggered some distant feeling in Sammy. She slowly breathed it in, enjoying the scent.

"What are you doing?" Dana asked as she handed Sammy a glass of wine.

"I was inhaling the scent of the wet pine needles and trees. The smell reminds me of something, but I can't picture it. Something with my dad, I'm almost certain. But I'm not sure what." Sammy shook her head slightly as if trying to clear her mind.

Straightening up in her chair, Sammy said, "Okay, I need to understand what you've been through with George. Can you please start from the beginning? And don't leave a thing out, or sugarcoat anything, or try to say things other than what you're feeling. Okay? I'm *your* friend here. I care. I want to help if I can."

"Oh Sammy, it all just sucks. I'll start with how it all began to end. Last October, early October, Aunt Jeannie was diagnosed with cancer practically everywhere, very advanced. We were all devastated: my Uncle Joe, Vince, my mom and dad, Jake and I, and poor Aunt Jeannie. She was blown away. Everyone's hearts were breaking. We were numb. We did whatever we could do to deal with day-to-day life." Dana wiped a tear from her eye and took a long sip of wine. "Mmm, this is nice wine."

She continued. "Obviously Jake's resort was closed by then, so I worked at Greta's bakery a few days a week doing her books. I also helped at a few other stores in town. I enjoyed working with different people every day and doing different things. It was actually fun and I didn't want to find a permanent position, because…" Fresh tears stung her eyes.

Dana looked away. "Oh, it's so hard to say this next part." She paused again, the words caught in her throat.

"Because I'd been thinking seriously about getting pregnant. I had gone off birth control and was mentally preparing to get pregnant. Can you believe I thought of having that jerk's baby? Oh, when I think of it, I feel sick to my stomach."

Sammy could sense Dana's pain and shared it. The thought made Sammy sick too. "Go on," she said gently.

"Anyway, I wanted to go to Chicago and help my mom with things for two weeks. This was the last week in October. My aunt was having all sorts of tests. They also live in the Chicago area. Vince found someone to temporarily take over his teaching and coaching positions." Dana's random thoughts spilled out as they came to her.

"I felt I needed to be there to support my family. George was fine with this. Kevin, George's old high school buddy, moved back in town last September, so George was happy to get to spend more time with Kevin while I was away."

Dana's tone took on a disapproving edge. "As a side note here, I wasn't crazy about Kevin. They acted like they were still in high school when they were together. I'm not saying there's anything wrong with being young at heart, but they acted immature and irresponsible. I didn't recognize George when he was with Kevin. He wasn't the man I married."

Regaining her composure, she returned to her story. "Anyway, I was too worried about my family, all of them, and too sad myself, to worry about George too. He said he'd be fine and it never crossed my mind that he would cheat on me—never. So I left." Dana's voice broke.

"I used to think, 'If only I'd never left—things would still be fine and perfect.'" Tears ran down Dana's face. "But then I see things for how they are and know that I needed to find this out about George. I need him out of my life. I need to find me again."

Sammy listened to Dana and then to the silence. It wasn't her time to speak yet. She quietly sipped her wine. It went perfectly with the painful conversation.

"I was at my mom's for two weeks. And then Thanksgiving was right around the corner, and my mom really wanted me to stay through the holiday. I thought about driving to see George for a weekend and then driving back, but we had a lovely little early winter snowstorm, so I stayed put.

"George told me he missed me, but was having fun with Kevin. They were going out every night, having a great time. He told me that I should stay through Thanksgiving." She stopped just long enough to sip her wine.

She started speaking again, this time with more disdain. "Again, foolish me, I thought he was being so thoughtful and understanding and so great to let me stay with my parents."

Her attitude softened as she thought of her aunt. "In fact, we actually had the nicest Thanksgiving as a family. We knew it would probably be my Aunt Jeannie's last so we made it as special as possible." Fresh tears rolled down her cheeks, but this time because of her sadness for her aunt and her family's impending loss.

Sammy put her hand on Dana's.

Dana continued. "It was too much. I was so sad about Aunt Jeannie and to see my Uncle Joe deal with it. But you know what the hardest part was?" Dana finally looked in Sammy eyes.

Sammy quietly shook her head in response.

"That Vince changed before my eyes. You know Vince, the happy-go-lucky son-of-a-gun. Ever since he was a little kid, he was lit up from within. Everyone loved to be around him. He was just fun—funny, smart, and so handsome. He was always good-looking and gets better looking every year, just like Rob Lowe."

She turned away. "But when he found out that his mom was sick and dying, that light inside him didn't just dim a little. It went out. He physically looked different.

"And not like me. I know I look like hell, but that's because I've hardly had the will to take care of myself.

"But Vince? Losing that glow changed how he looks. He's still the wonderful, sweet, charming guy you met last summer. But he's changed. You'll see. I'm sure he'll be up this summer. Oh wait, how long are you here?" It was as if Dana finally snapped out of a trance. She was so into her own story and pain that she forgot about Sammy's story. She noticed Sammy was wiping tears from her eyes too.

"I don't know yet. Kelly's due to have her baby in a week or so, so I need to be home for that. There isn't much else planned for the summer. I recently spent several weeks with Cass and her adorable twins. I would love to see Vince, but I just don't know what to expect with your brother." Sammy blushed. This was the first time she acknowledged that there was something going on with Jake.

"He's crazy about you, you know. He was really bummed that he couldn't see you in December. I tried to convince him to visit you in January, but I think he was much too worried about me to leave me here alone. And honestly, I'm thankful he didn't. I was pretty deep in despair some days. So, where did I leave off?" Dana asked as she refilled both wine glasses.

"You enjoyed a lovely Thanksgiving with the whole family and had been away from George for almost a month," Sammy recounted.

"Yes, I was away from my dearly devoted husband for over a month by then. I finally went home, so thrilled to see him, excited to make a baby, and I had plans to see my family for New Year's. I got home to find he had moved out. Can you believe it?" she asked.

"He left a note asking me to call his cell phone when I got in. I called; he came home and told me he wanted a divorce. He told me flat out that he had met another woman and they were in love. He didn't love me anymore. He wanted to marry her.

"I lost it. His news blindsided me. It was such an incredible shock. It all gets fuzzy from then on," she said, as if trying to recall the events.

"I don't really know what happened next. He left. I stayed in the house for two days crying and packing my things up. I finally called Jake. He picked me and my stuff up. I've never been back to that house since.

"I met George a few days later at a coffee shop. He simply told me that he'd met a woman. She tended bar at a place he and Kevin went to every night that I was gone, even Thanksgiving. He didn't even spend Thanksgiving with his parents. He's such a loser!" Dana said with contempt.

"Oh, it makes me so mad to think of all the wasted time our relationship was. I was a fool. I can't even find any good in our marriage." Dana looked out the window and wiped away tears.

Sammy knew by the way Dana was talking on and on about her saga, that Dana *needed* to say it all out loud.

"I stayed with Jake a few days and then my dad broke his leg. So I returned to my parents' house to help my mom and stayed for Christmas and New Year's. I think I kept hoping there was still a chance George and I would get back together. It was New Year's Eve that I finally accepted our break up and really talked to Jake about it.

"The divorce was final a few weeks ago. He filed right away; there was nothing to sort out, nothing to fight over. All I have is my car, clothes, and a few belongings. Luckily, I was smart enough to have my own savings account, because he drained our joint savings account.

"He even tried to get some cash out of my account at Christmas, that son of a bitch. That's when I really knew we were over. Thank goodness the bank didn't let him. But I only have like four thousand dollars to my name. I always thought we were so poor in money, but rich in love. I was such a fool."

Sammy knew the blame game could go back and forth for ages. She knew how that break up teeter-totter goes: You love him; you hate him. He was the best; he was the worst. She wasn't sure what to say to Dana to make her feel better.

"Dana, no. He was the fool. He was the one who had your unconditional love and trust. He blew it. He didn't cherish you or your love or your relationship enough to protect it. You were suffering a great pain. It was his job as a husband to be with you in your time of need. He should've been with you, comforting you, giving you strength. That's what husbands do, or at least are supposed to do, not that I know," Sammy said quietly, unsure she should be giving this advice.

She continued anyway, "Just because you were away comforting your family doesn't mean he could take a vacation from your marriage. Oh, I'm so angry with him. And you should be too."

Sammy got more worked up. "It's too soon for you to forgive him. Be angry and use that anger to make yourself happy. You deserve to be so happy, Dana. He failed you. That's how it is. You did nothing wrong. I'm so sorry. I wish you didn't have to go through that and continue to go through it. I'm so sorry for Vince, for your whole family. George is the fool, not you."

She wanted to give George a piece of her mind. She wondered if Jake chewed him out or heck, even punched George in the face, because if someone deserved a punch in the face, it was George. And Sammy never liked the idea of men fighting. But George? She thought he deserved a good ass-kicking.

"Okay, now you know all the gory details. After my dad broke his leg, my mom was a mental wreck by then. I didn't have the heart to tell her about George at that point. Since I hoped we still had some sort of a chance, I didn't want to tell her about his infidelity because she would never forgive him. Now that it's been so long, I'm not sure how to tell her.

"She'll be so mad at me for keeping this secret, but seriously I didn't want her to worry about me, on top of my dad's physical therapy and Aunt Jeannie's condition, which is getting worse. I don't think her treatments will work. Well, actually, we all sort of knew they wouldn't work; the cancer was extremely advanced. We just hoped it would prolong her life, which it has. But still, some days I feel hopeless."

Sammy tried to imagine the weight of it all as Dana continued.

"It's been terrible staying here too. But I don't have anywhere else to go. That's another thing that makes me so mad at George: he's ruined this place for me."

"What do you mean?" Sammy thought she understood, but wasn't sure if something else might have happened here at the resort.

"I mean that when I look around I see all these stupid memories I had with him. I remember our first kiss on the swing, our first swim off the dock, our first boat ride, and the many times we camped in a cozy little tent. I think of us cuddling next to the weekly bonfires, and going fishing with him. I remember how handsome and cute he was working on the boats and motors and how he pursued me relentlessly," she said with sadness.

"I see these visions and memories around here. I no longer see the fun times I had with Jake and Vince or even you and your sisters last summer. All I see are pieces of my past that have me aching for the man he was. I miss that person. And now it hurts to see these memories everywhere. This is where we fell in love. What do I do with that? You had all those memories come back to you last summer that made you sad—how did you deal with it?" Dana asked.

Sammy shook her head. "My memories were bittersweet and still are. These lost memories continue to be here. When I pulled in yesterday, they were here waiting for me."

Carefully choosing her words, she continued. "It's a different pain. Yes, they make me sad, but they also make me happy. I think enough time has passed since my parents' deaths that it doesn't really hurt or make me angry anymore."

Sammy paused for a moment, deep in thought. "If my aunt had brought us back here right away the summer after my parents' accident, I'm sure our memories would've been too much to take. But even then, they wouldn't be like how your memories are now." Sammy didn't know how to make her friend feel better.

Dana sat back and added, "I haven't worked in town since October. I visit with Greta once in a while. She's really good at making me feel better. She hates George and has lots of fun German sayings about him. But I don't feel like myself in that town. I feel like the poor pathetic ex-wife of a local boy. How's that for a feeling?"

"What about here at the resort? Aside from the memories of *him*"—Sammy couldn't even say his name—"do you feel like yourself here? Does it help to be around Jake? And what have you been doing to stay busy up here?"

"Jake didn't tell you?" Dana lit up a little bit.

"Tell me what?" Sammy asked.

"What I've been doing around here to stay busy?" Dana asked.

"No," Sammy whispered to add to the mystery. "He kept quiet about it and said he'd let you tell me."

"Ha, that's cool. Okay, come with me. Grab your jacket." Dana walked back inside the lodge, grabbed her jacket, and headed for the door.

Sammy had to hurry to keep up. "Where are we going?"

"You'll see. Not far." They stepped outside and Dana led Sammy to a cabin. "I've been staying in the same cabin you stayed in last year." When they got to the porch door, Dana commanded, "Okay, close your eyes."

Sammy obeyed. "Again?"

"What do you mean by 'again'?" Dana carefully led Sammy through the front porch to the main cabin door.

"Your brother made me close my eyes last night when he showed me his new deck." Sammy took baby steps and waved her arms out in front of her. "I'm afraid of walking into something."

"You're fine. I wouldn't let that happen. Okay, open your eyes," Dana said.

"Holy moly," Sammy exclaimed as she looked around the cabin. "Dana, it's beautiful. You did this?" She didn't recognize the cabin. It was completely redone.

There were new wide-plank pine floors. The cream-colored walls were accented by brightly colored paintings. The kitchenette had new granite countertops and new appliances.

The decor was modern and clean and yet remained warm and woodsy. The new furniture was a mixture of textures and woods. It was all so natural looking. The ceiling beams were refinished and installed with new lighting and a fan. Plants were tucked in spots throughout the room, adding to the natural feel.

"Jake helped me install the flooring. That was a pain in the *you know what.* And obviously I had contractors install the appliances, countertops, and bathroom fixtures. But the rest I did myself. Check out the bathroom." Dana beamed with pride.

Sammy looked in the bathroom and was amazed. "It's gorgeous!"

Everything from top to bottom was new and looked high-end. The old creaky shower was replaced by a Jacuzzi tub and rainfall showerhead. "How does that tub fit in here? Did you move that wall?"

"Yup. Jake was slightly freaked out by the idea, but I moved all three bedroom walls a bit to make each room larger. It didn't take much effort, because they weren't structural. We shifted them before redoing the floor, so it all fit. Jake was impressed."

"I am too. If I hadn't been here last year, I would never guess that those aren't the original walls. What do the bedrooms look like? Is there any storage?" Sammy couldn't imagine that there was any room left in the bedrooms.

"Yes, take a look. I know that storage is a huge issue for guests." Dana grinned from ear to ear. Sammy took notice that this was the happiest she'd seen Dana all day.

Sammy peeked in the bedroom to find a queen-size bed, an overstuffed chair, and a deer antler floor lamp. The room was spacious. The wall that had been moved was now essentially floor-to-ceiling shelves and drawers. "What in the world?"

"Isn't it cool? I saw it in a European design magazine. The storage pieces basically create the wall. There's a thin layer of high density insulation in there and no electrical wiring so it didn't need to be thick. Isn't it brilliant? Every bedroom has one and I added lots of extra shelves in the kitchen and under the seating areas in the living space. What do you think? Does it still capture the feeling of the lake?"

"Yes, somehow it does. The accessories are still woodsy and yet everything looks clean and updated. Amazing. How much did all of this cost you?"

"I was able to do all this, in this cabin, for around twelve thousand. Does that seem like a lot?

"Jake gave me a fourteen thousand dollar budget per cabin. Some came in under, some over. I did most of the labor myself and found all materials at bargain prices. But in the end, I was within my budget. I was savvy," Dana said with pride as she put her hands on her hips.

"You did all the cabins?" Sammy asked in disbelief. "In less than four months?"

"I did. It was so fun." Dana grinned like an innocent child and added with a shrug of her shoulders, "Besides, I had nothing else to do."

"Dana, this is really an accomplishment. I think you found your calling."

"What? Redecorating family member's cabins?" Dana asked.

"Not only family members. Redecorating, restoring, renovating, whatever you want to call it. You're gifted. Lots of people can decorate, but you maintained the personality of the cabin and the natural surroundings. You've elevated the feel of the space. We both know that the folks who stay here just want to fish and relax, but now that this cabin is so nice they'll never want to leave."

"That's the point. Did Jake tell you about the bakery?" Dana asked enthusiastically.

"What bakery?" Sammy was confused. What *did* she and Jake talk about?

"I was talking to Jake about redoing the bar area in his lodge to include a bakery café. I thought about bringing in treats from Greta's bakery on the weekend mornings and have a cool café area. I wanted to create a place for the women to get together and share coffee and treats and the fishermen can sit around and talk about their catch and the daily hot spots." Dana's eyes twinkled as she spoke.

"That sounds like a beautiful idea. I absolutely love it. What does Jake think about it?"

"He keeps saying, 'We'll see.' I think he's doing all this to humor me. And it worked: these cabins have been a fun distraction. But now they're done. What do I do next?" She sounded deflated again. The highs and lows of heartbreak were at work.

"Did Jake pay you to do this?" Sammy wondered what his philanthropic projects were costing him.

"No he didn't. But he's given me a free place to stay and buys everything I need for now. So, it's been a blessing for me. Besides, all these renovations have cost him a pretty penny. I know he's not a wealthy guy, but he does a good job investing his money. I don't think he's even increasing his rental rates this summer. But I'm not worried about him. He's a financial genius sometimes.

"But I do worry about what I'll do next. He needs me out of this cabin in a few weeks. The summer season starts soon, as you might recall. I can't go back to Chicago to stay with my parents or any old friends there. It's sad to say, but I've lost contact with so many of my old friends in such a short time."

"Dana, don't worry about that. You have a few weeks; we'll figure something out. Can we go find Jake and see how they're doing fixing that window? This has been a great afternoon and I've loved catching up with you. I'm sorry you've been so sad, but after seeing what you did to this cabin, my faith in you is beyond restored. We'll find your future. I'm good at figuring out what other people should do, just not so talented at showing myself the way." Sammy smiled.

Dana hugged her. "Thanks, Sammy. Let's find Jake. I'm hungry."

"Me too." The girls walked arm in arm down the wet, muddy road. Sammy noticed Dana had a little bounce in her step that was missing earlier that morning. She knew then she could help her friend.

They met Jake on the road. "Hi ladies, I was just on my way to get you. Dave tossed some chicken on the grill and his wife's been busy in the kitchen for the last hour. You ready for some dinner?"

"We sure are." They answered in stereo, making them giggle.

"Two peas in a pod—just like last summer. I like it." Jake slowly took Sammy's hand. The two walked hand in hand down the road.

They ended the evening with good food and company. After dinner, Jake and Dave finished the repairs and Sammy and Dana helped Dave's wife clean up while they talked about movies, TV, books, and the latest Hollywood gossip.

The three walked back to the resort with Ginger in tow. The night sky was dark, and the clouds were starting to clear. A few bright stars twinkled between the clouds.

Jake and Sammy walked Dana to her cabin, wished her a good night, and quietly walked back to his lodge, holding hands and rubbing shoulders. Sammy was happy.

"I'm pretty beat," Jake said as if asking Sammy a question.

"I'm sure you are. You worked your tail off today. I'm tired too and ready to call it a night. I'll see you in the morning," Sammy answered his unspoken question.

Jake opened the lodge door for her. "Do you need anything before bed?"

She stepped inside. *Besides you?* she thought. "Just a kiss."

He kissed her tenderly.

"Sweet dreams," Sammy whispered as she walked away.

"After that kiss, you better believe it," Jake answered. "Good night."

They went to their separate sleeping quarters. Sammy tossed and turned for over two hours. When she wasn't thinking about Jake, she was thinking about Dana and how she could help her friend. She came up with a fantastic idea. She couldn't wait to tell Jake about it in the morning.

As she tried to fall asleep, it dawned on her what the smell of wet pines earlier in the day reminded her of: the Christmas tree farm she and her father went to for years. In snow, rain, or shine, they always picked out the tree together. She longed to walk among the pine trees with him again. But in her dreams, she could.

CHAPTER 5

Sammy woke early the next morning, excited to tell Jake her idea. She found him in the kitchen enjoying his morning coffee.

"Good morning. My, you look bright-eyed this morning," Jake said as he rose to greet her with a gentle kiss.

She had grown to love his new greetings.

"Good morning. I *feel* pretty bright-eyed and bushy-tailed this morning. My mind was going crazy last night and there are a few things I want to talk to you about," she said.

"Like what?" He poured her a cup of coffee.

"Like Dana," she said.

"Here"—he pulled out the chair next to where he was sitting—"sit, have some breakfast, and tell me what's on your mind."

Sammy took a long sip of coffee, eyeing the spread of breakfast treats leftover from the day before.

She began, "Well, after talking to Dana yesterday, I learned she is quite miserable here, and for good reason. All she has is memories of when George was courting her here and them falling in love. She can't even recall her fond memories of your youth here. She needs to get away from this place for a while."

"I agree. But where? She doesn't really know where to go." He absentmindedly reached for Ginger, who came to him for an ear-scratching.

"Well, she can come home with me." Sammy grinned from ear to ear.

"With you? I thought…" He didn't finish his sentence.

"You thought what?" Sammy was intrigued.

"I guess I hoped you would stick around here for a while. Can't you help her from here?" He looked at her pleadingly. It made her smile.

"You're adorable. Is this your way of asking me to stay?"

"I guess, yes, if you need me to ask. Will you please stay a while?" He batted his eyes to sweeten the deal, making her laugh out loud.

"I would love to, but I can't. Kelly's baby is due any day now and I really want to be there when she's born and see her when she's a brand-spanking newborn. They grow so fast," Sammy said.

"You want to take Dana with you to Arizona? And then what?" he asked hesitantly.

"Yes. Well that's only part of it. I figured it would be good for her to get away for a while. See Kelly, the baby. Are you ready for the best part?" Sammy moved her eyebrows up and down for effect, this time making him laugh.

"Let 'er rip," he said as he leaned back in his chair, smiling, elbows out, and hands behind his head.

"Well, I was in California a few months ago, when Cass had her babies. Aunt Kathy was there. You remember my Aunt Kathy, right?" Sammy asked as she thought back to last summer when her aunt breezed into the resort for a few days bringing loads of wine and fun with her.

"Of course. Who could forget Aunt Kathy?" he said with a smile.

"Well, she was there for several weeks helping Cass with the babies. We were all having a wonderful time. I hated to leave. But anyway…Aunt Kathy mentioned how she and Hank were building a new guest casita. The only thing 'casita' about it is its adobe exterior. It's actually a rather large house, with a huge great room and gourmet kitchen, study, two half-baths, and six master guest suites with master baths."

Sammy looked to Jake expectantly. *Nothing.*

She continued. "I think she has visions of hosting all us girls next Christmas, which would be fantastic. But she was also toying with the idea of running it like a bed and breakfast. She was worried about tackling such a project on her own. And last night—"

Jake cut her off. "You were thinking that Dana could help her."

"Exactly!" Sammy sat back, feeling pleased with herself.

"You're pretty proud of yourself, huh?" he said.

"Yes, I am. You cannot make me feel otherwise." She crossed her arms stubbornly.

"Fair enough. That's a good plan. One question: would Kathy be on board with this idea? Aren't you getting a little ahead of yourself or her?" he asked.

"I won't know until I ask. I need to wait a few hours to catch up to her time zone and I'll call her. What do you think Dana would do? Would she want to go to California?" Sammy asked.

"Seriously? *I* want to go spend the summer in Napa in Aunt Kathy's casita on a vineyard. What's not to love about that plan? I think she'll jump at the chance. Especially since she somewhat knows your aunt. I think that'll at least make her feel like she has a friend there and not totally alone," Jake said as he reached out to Sammy, pulling her to his lap.

She happily cuddled with him. "But she needs to tell your parents about her and George first. How can she not say anything? Isn't that weird to you? Kind of immature? Or is there something more I don't get?" she asked softly, not wanting to offend him or his sister. She didn't want him to get defensive.

"No, I agree with you one hundred percent. I think she should've told my parents months ago, when it all started. But I think in Dana's heart, she was hoping it would all work out with George, and she didn't want our family hating him when they got back together," he said.

"I can understand that. But they're divorced now. Doesn't she need her mother's comfort?" Sammy shook her head, trying to grasp the thought.

"Normally, yes. But sadly, my mom is also the one in need of comfort right now. It's a mess. I agree. I know Dana probably handled it all wrong. But what's done is done. I do agree that she needs to go see my mom before she leaves. When did you want to leave?" he asked.

"Well, if she wants to drive her car, we'd need to leave in a few days."

"And then what? How long would you be in Arizona? Would you drive with her to California? Would you be able come back here?" He bombarded her with questions.

"I'm not sure about the logistics. But I figured she has nothing but time, and my schedule is clear right now and for as long as I wish. I would like to drive with her to California. I love cross-country road trips. And I wouldn't want her to be alone with her thoughts.

"And then, yes, after I know she's happily settled in Napa, and Kelly and baby are fine, I would like to come back here to see you, probably in about a month. How does that sound?"

He took her hand in his, rubbing it lightly with his thumb. "It sounds pretty incredible. Dana and I are lucky to have a friend like you."

"Will you be okay without her help this summer? She seems to do a lot for you up here." Sammy was suddenly concerned for him.

"Relax. I'll be fine. Yes, she's a tremendous help to me and I'll miss her help, but mostly I'll miss her company. I can hire a few folks to help around here, and I've always let Dana do my bookkeeping merely because she enjoyed it. It'll be fun to take that task back over myself. I'm thrilled she can have a real adventure on her own and I know she'll be a huge help to Kathy."

"Do you think I should ask Dana first before I get Aunt Kathy's hopes up?"

Jake shook his head. "No, you better work out the details with Kathy first. Dana doesn't have anything else to do. She can't refuse."

"Okay. It's so beautiful and sunny out this morning. Do you want to go for a walk with me to kill some time before I call Kathy?"

"You bet."

They walked hand in hand in the crisp morning air. The rain clouds were gone. The trees sparked a bright, clean green. Ginger trailed behind, zigzagging off on her own route smelling her way.

***

When they returned from their walk, Sammy called Aunt Kathy. Jake watched lovingly as Sammy talked to her aunt. He heard most of their conversation and Sammy filled him in on what he didn't catch the moment she hung up.

Kathy "just 'bout busted with joy" at the idea of hosting "Sweet Dana" for a few months. These were Aunt Kathy's words and Sammy told Jake as much.

Turned out, the timing of her call couldn't have been better. The construction of the casita was completed last week.

Now, Kathy was focusing her attention on the renovation of their courtyard and the construction of the pool, hot tubs, saunas, and other water features.

Kathy hadn't begun any of the interior design work yet and was planning to hire some designers. Luckily, Sammy called when she did. After Sammy explained how Dana renovated and decorated all of Jake's cabins, Kathy insisted that Dana help her design the casita from head to toe, that is, if Dana wanted to, of course.

Sammy knew this would be the icing on the cake for Dana.

Aunt Kathy promised to e-mail Sammy some photos of the completed casita for Dana to start thinking about. Sammy was so excited for her friend and her aunt. She knew they would be in for a wonderful summer together and knew that Aunt Kathy would help Dana mend her broken heart.

The plans were set. As long as Kelly's delivery was uneventful, Dana and Sammy would arrive in Napa in a few weeks.

"Here comes the devil now," Jake said as he noticed Dana leave her cabin and head their way.

"I'm nervous," Sammy whispered.

Dana knocked quickly and let herself in. "Hey, what's up? How you guys doing this morning?"

Sammy noticed Dana already looked happier than she had the day before.

"Good," Jake and Sammy replied in unison, both slightly embarrassed.

"Oh, nice. You're going to be one of those couples." Dana teased them with a smile and a fake roll of her eyes. "But, seriously, what's up? You two look like you're up to something."

"I have a proposition for you, Dana." Sammy dove right in; she was too excited to beat around the bush.

"Er, uh, okay. I'm listening," Dana said as she threw Jake a suspicious look.

"I just talked to my Aunt Kathy. You remember her, right?"

"Of course. Who could forget Aunt Kathy?" She gave Jake's exact response.

"Anyway," Sammy continued, with a slight shake of her head, "I saw her a few months ago at Cassy's after the babies were born—"

"Oh, I bet that was fun," Dana interrupted.

"Yes, yes, loads of fun." Sammy moved her hands as if waving the topic away like a fly.

"Anyway, she was telling me about how she and Hank were building a new guesthouse and she was thinking about running it like a bed and breakfast type of place. So, last night I got to thinking maybe she was ready for some help."

Sammy paused for effect. "I just called her. She's hoping you'll summer there, help her decorate the whole guesthouse, and then figure out what to do with it from there. Okay, guesthouse is probably an understatement, but anyway, she wants and needs help with all the decorating, furniture, window treatments, towels, bedding—you name it, she needs it. And she's hoping you'll help her do all that." Sammy finally stopped for a breath.

Dana could barely speak. She stared at Sammy, looked to Jake questioningly, and back to Sammy with her mouth slightly open. Words escaped her.

"Did you hear me?" Sammy asked as she glanced to Jake for help.

"Yes, yes, I heard you. I just can't believe you. Are you serious? This is amazing. I would love to do that. What a dream come true. Oh my goodness…" Dana put her hands over her mouth and started laughing. She smothered Sammy with a hug. "Thank you, thank you, Sammy. You're such an amazing friend."

Sammy hugged Dana, gently feeling Dana's bones poking out of her back. She hoped her aunt could do something about that too. But she knew her aunt would.

Dana suddenly pulled back. "She really needs help, right? This isn't a pity party project is it?"

"Of course not. She really does need help. She wouldn't ask if she didn't need you. She certainly would let you stay as long as you wanted to visit, but she plans on putting you to work while you're there. I hope you don't mind," Sammy said hesitantly.

"I'll let the two of you figure out the reimbursement details. But she mentioned definitely including room and board in your wages and she has big plans of putting you to work for as long as you want to stay. But, there's more…"

"What?" Dana's worry showed in her furrowed brow.

"I assumed you want to drive your car out to California to have it there. And I wondered if I could ride with you, with a brief stop in Arizona first?" Sammy asked hesitantly.

"Road trip!" Dana yelled with a fist in the air like a cheerleader.

"Okay, then." Sammy laughed. "That's a 'yes,' right?"

Dana laughed and answered her with another hug. "Yes, it's a yes. When do you want to leave?"

"In a few days, if we can. Kelly's baby is due any day now and I really want to be there when she's born," Sammy said.

"That's perfect. That gives me enough time to go see Mom and Dad. I need to tell them everything before I leave."

Sammy was pleasantly surprised and noticed by the look on Jake's face that he was too.

"But what about Aunt Jeannie and Vince?" Tears began to well up in Dana's eyes. "How can I say goodbye to Aunt Jeannie, knowing I might never see her again? Or not be there for Vince when he needs us the most?"

Jake finally broke his silence, as he walked to Dana and gently hugged his younger sister. "You have to do this for you. Both Aunt Jeannie and Vince will understand that. I know it'll be hard to say good-bye to Jeannie, but every time it's hard to say good-bye. We never know if it'll be the last time. And in a painfully lucky way, at least we get the chance to say good-bye to her."

Sammy winced at those words. She had to turn away so they couldn't see the look on her face. She never got to say good-bye to her parents. And even though it had been more than twenty years, that fact still caused her pain, longing, and sadness. She quickly wiped tears from her eyes.

"I know you're right. It's just going to be difficult." Dana was wiping tears from her face too. "I think I'll go call Mom now and let her know I'll be there late tonight. I'll get packing too and head out by noon. I want to spend a few days there. Is it okay if I come back on Wednesday?"

"Sure. Is that enough time?" Sammy didn't like having to rush Dana, but she really wanted to get back to Kelly.

"Yes, that'll be enough time. We can leave here Thursday morning, then." Dana perked up after saying that. "I'll see you two on Wednesday."

"Perfect," Sammy answered. "If we drive with only a few stops, we can make it home by Saturday."

"Good luck with Mom and Dad," Jake added as he hugged his sister again. "You'll feel a great sense of relief after you tell them. They'll understand."

When Dana left, Jake wrapped his arms around Sammy from behind and whispered in her ear, "Wednesday, huh? That doesn't give us much time, does it?"

"For what?" Sammy whispered back as she turned to face him.

"For this," he said as he kissed her passionately—hungrily. Gone were the gentle kisses of affection. He kissed her with intention and she understood that intention. She willingly kissed him back and answered his unspoken question.

He easily lifted her up and carried her to his bedroom, never taking his mouth from hers. He stepped into his bedroom and painfully stopped the kiss.

He looked eagerly into her eyes as if asking permission to proceed. Her only answer was a shy giggle as she gently kicked the door shut behind them.

This was exactly how she dreamed her first time with Jake would be—only it was better.

***

Sammy and Jake spent the better part of the day in bed. Sammy woke up that morning knowing she loved Jake. But now, she was *in love* with Jake. She was in deep—not just ankle- or knee-deep, but oops, big drop-off up to your chin deep.

He was the perfect fit and made love to her like no man before him. As far as she was concerned, there were no men before Jake. She felt as though her life started anew that moment.

"I'm so sorry I said what I did about telling Aunt Jeannie good-bye," Jake said tenderly, snapping Sammy out of her dreamlike state.

He continued softly, "I wanted to take back the words as

soon as I said them. I saw your reaction; I could feel your pain. I was so, so sorry, Sammy." He kissed her tenderly on her neck.

"It's okay. You were right, though, and you were just trying to comfort Dana. You shouldn't have to filter your thoughts or comments around me. It's been over twenty years. You'd think I wouldn't react like that still." Sammy was almost embarrassed by her reaction.

"I'm so sorry," Jake quietly repeated. "And I'm incredibly thankful. I was watching you sleep a while ago and thought about how lucky I am and my sister is to have you in our lives. I can't believe you single-handedly solved Dana's problems. Thank you."

"Okay, first off, you're welcome. Second, I'm not doing it single-handedly. You called me, remember? And I reached out to Kathy. It takes a village here. And finally, her problems are far from over," she said as she reached for his hand.

Observing her hand in his, she continued. "Dana's going to need time to forgive herself for marrying George. I know she feels that's her number one mistake. And she'll not forgive herself easily. Kathy and the vineyard will be wonderful distractions for Dana. But only Dana can solve her problems."

"You're so sweet," he said as he kissed her gently on the cheek. "And smart," he added with a kiss on her forehead. "And sexy." He smiled.

"Shhhh, I'm too tired to talk," she whispered as she put her finger to his lips.

"Then what do you suggest we do?" he asked eagerly.

Her response was a hungry, passionate kiss and a sparkle in her eyes letting him know she was ready for more.

***

That night, Jake and Sammy found themselves relaxing in the hot tub, soaking in each other's company. Sammy was on cloud nine and didn't plan on getting off it anytime soon. She wanted *this* for the next three days straight.

"This was by far the best day I've had in a long time." She smiled and laughed at how casual she made it sound.

"Oh gee, thanks." He laughed as he splashed her lightly. "It was my best day too. I have a confession to make. Do you want to hear it?" he asked shyly.

"I don't know. Do I? Please don't ruin my best day."

"Do you remember that day last summer, when we spent the day on the rafts with Vince and your sisters? You were wearing a bright-blue bikini, looking gorgeous."

She blushed. "Yeah, I do remember that day. It was fun."

"Well, I've wanted to do *this* with you ever since that day." He laughed nervously.

"Really? Why didn't you ever do anything last summer to let me know?" she asked.

"I was stupid, that whole 'don't fraternize with the patrons' sort of thing. Dumb, I know. I should have given the resort to Vince."

"Or I could've stayed elsewhere," Sammy replied with a sly smile. "So, are you going to tell Vince that we did *this*?"

"Oh, most definitely. I'll wait until the timing is right." He smiled proudly. "What about you? Are you going to tell anyone we did *this*?"

"Oh yes. I'll call Kelly tomorrow morning. Any later and she'd have my head." Sammy smiled.

They continued to soak and talk the night away.

CHAPTER 6

The next few days flew by as Sammy had Jake all to herself. The two made good use of their time together and alone. Their days were magical and dreamy, and Sammy hated leaving them behind. She knew that when she returned in a month, the resort would be up and running, forcing her to share Jake with his guests.

Thursday morning, the morning of the cross-country road trip, arrived before she knew it. After long good-byes, hugs, and kisses, Sammy, in her rental car, and Dana, in her beat-up SUV, drove away from Jake and Loon Lake. The two women shared the same mix of emotions—excitement and sadness—but for very different reasons.

Sammy was sad to leave Jake, especially right when things were so hot and heavy. She felt like one of those clichéd teenage girls who couldn't live without her new boyfriend. Sammy knew she *could* live without him, but it was just so much fun right now she didn't *want* to.

But she was excited to see Kelly and, soon, the new baby, and to enjoy the road trip with Dana. Three days on the open road would give her and Dana plenty of time to really get to know each other, and Sammy hoped she would be able to better judge Dana's ability to cope on her own in California.

After dropping off Sammy's rental car and stopping in town so Dana could say good-bye to Greta, the road trip began. About two hours into the trip—that is, two hours of singing and sampling most of the snacks they brought with them—the women grew quiet. Each had her own thoughts rolling around in her head.

"Will people think I'm a failure since I'm divorced?"

"Have you ever thought someone was a failure because they were divorced?" Sammy asked, already knowing the answer.

"No. But that doesn't mean others don't."

Sammy paused before continuing. "Well, of course I can't speak for *everyone*, but Dana, half the world is divorced, so we know that half won't think you're a failure. Most everyone else knows how hard it is to keep a relationship or marriage together these days. There are so many external influences on relationships. I sometimes think it's a miracle as many people stay married as they do."

Sammy knew that wasn't the answer Dana was looking for. She pressed on cautiously. "Dana, it's okay for you to feel like a failure. We all feel that way sometimes, over a relationship, a friendship, a job…There's always something we could've done better."

"What about you? Did you ever feel like a failure?" Dana asked.

"Yes. Last summer I felt like a failure. I was really disheartened by the work I was doing. Writing about environmental problems all the time started to really get to me. I'd been doing it for so long, and nothing seemed to change or improve. I took that as a reflection on what I was doing and felt like I was failing. So, yes, I definitely know what it's like to feel like a failure.

"And even on a relationship level, I was crazy about a guy in college. I saw a future with him. He broke up with me only to date a good friend of mine. That was a big heartbreak for me. I felt like a failure then too. I became really guarded about relationships after that."

"I feel like a huge failure right now," Dana confessed. "And not even just that my marriage didn't work, but look at me: I'm thirty-seven years old, with hardly any money to my name, and I'm going to be living off the generosity of your aunt for who knows how long. What a loser!" Angry tears sneaked out the corners of her eyes.

"Seriously? Is that how you see this?" Sammy asked.

"Sometimes," Dana replied shamefully.

"And other times?"

"I see it for the wonderful opportunity that it is." Dana couldn't look at Sammy.

"Well, you certainly must know you're not the first thirty-seven year old that doesn't have much money and that tons of people get a break because of *who* they know and not *what* they know. And besides, Aunt Kathy is going to work you to the bone, I should know." Sammy laughed as she remembered the first time she asked Aunt Kathy for some financial help.

"What's so funny?" Dana asked.

"Oh, I just remembered a time when I was in college and I asked Aunt Kathy for a loan so I could go to Greece with my friends over spring break. She gladly lent me the money, but I had to sign a contract saying I would pay back every dime at five dollars an hour doing work of her choosing. It sounded like easy money to me at the time. But I had to work my butt off the following summer at the house."

Sammy laughed again as she continued. "I painted the outside of the house—two stories, mind you. I helped her build a new shed and lots of other crazy yard projects. I worked in her office making copies, filing, and cleaning. I even had to ride with Alex, who was driving with her learner's permit. I can't remember what other forms of torture she bestowed on me, but trust me there were more."

"You went to Greece with your friends in college?" Dana asked in awe.

"Is that all you got from that?" Sammy shook her head and chuckled.

Dana laughed. "No, no, I heard the other stuff too. It just

doesn't sound like it was hard work. Really, it sounds fun."

Sammy looked out the window, remembering when she made poor Alex drive through a fast food drive-through. Sammy smiled. Alex had scraped the whole passenger side of the car along a post and was mortified. "Well, of course, now looking back on it, I know it was cool of Kathy to make me do some of those things."

A thought dawned on Sammy. "So, we never really talked about what you did in Chicago before moving to Loon Lake with Jake. What made you want to pick up and leave Chicago and live on a lake out in the middle of nowhere? I know why Jake did it. But why did you?"

"We never talked about it? Well, I wasn't really doing much in Chicago when he decided to buy the place. I went to college for design, both interior and graphic. When I got out, there wasn't anything special that was driving me. I worked at an ad agency for several years and didn't like it. There was a lot of backstabbing and everyone took credit for others' ideas. It was a cutthroat atmosphere. I think I learned too late that it's not necessarily like that at every ad agency. At the time I thought that was the case.

"Then I was at a PR firm and had some fun there. I was good with client and media relations, and had a little advertising work again too, but it wasn't something I *loved* either. Except when I started dating a guy in the office, and *that* was love. However, we broke up, which made my job uncomfortable—borderline miserable—and I ended up quitting that job.

"Then I found a sales position at an art gallery." Dana sounded happier with each recollection. "I really enjoyed it. I would say that position was my high point in job satisfaction in Chicago. I loved the artists there and loved selling their work. Unfortunately, there was still something missing. Is this boring you?" Dana asked suddenly, interrupting herself.

"No, no, I love it. Go on."

"Anyway, I felt like there was something missing in my life. Jake started talking about buying and running the resort and *that* spoke to me. I could see his vision and I wanted to be a part of it. Turns out, I loved it. I loved everyday life at the resort: working with my brother, visiting with guests, helping him run the place, and dealing with simple daily operations. It was, for lack of better words, 'good, clean living.' I didn't miss the city. I was happy.

"Then George came along the second spring we were there, and it all happened so fast. That's my big regret; I got caught up in the fire with him. Not like you and Jake." Dana glanced at Sammy with a grin. "You two are perfect for each other and are taking it nice and slow."

Sammy tensed up, which Dana was quick to notice. "What? What did I miss?"

"Nothing. You missed nothing," Sammy quickly replied, blushing.

"You had a strange look on your face." Dana looked at her again. "No! You didn't? Oh my, you did! When?" Dana started laughing.

"The other day when you left the resort," Sammy answered shyly.

"I can't believe I missed this. I'm so in my own little world. Well? How was it? No details please, he *is* my brother after all. But, how was it?"

"Dreamy. Wonderful. Amazing. What other words am I missing?" Sammy answered softly.

"Oh, wow, that's so cool. I'm so happy for you. He hasn't been with another woman since he met you. I was beginning to worry about him. And here I am dragging you away from that. I'm sorry. You could've stayed. I'm a big girl; I can make it to California by myself."

"I know you can. But I need to see Kelly and her baby. And the truth is I've never been out to Aunt Kathy's place yet. It's been thirteen years. It's a shame that she felt like she had to build a big fancy guesthouse so her girls would finally visit her. But that's not the case, really. I've been busy…" Sammy trailed off, asking herself, *What have I been doing for thirteen years?*

"But the reality is," Sammy continued, justifying something else entirely and not necessarily to Dana, "Kathy and Hank travel all the time. Whenever I had the time, they had extravagant travel plans. Anyway, I can't wait to go to Kathy's with you. I'll be back at Loon Lake soon enough and be with Jake. I feel some changes happening for everyone this summer." *Dragonfly changes*, Sammy thought.

***

The next morning, as the women headed out on the second day of their road trip, Sammy noticed the rear passenger tire was low on air. Luckily, both a garage and a coffee shop were blocks away from their hotel.

When they pulled up to the shop, a young, handsome man started walking toward their car.

"He's cute," Dana whispered out of the corner of her mouth.

"Agreed," Sammy said with a smile.

"Can I help you ladies?" drawled the handsome mechanic. He was clean shaven with a crew cut and a tan. He even smelled good. His green eyes sparkled above perfect cheekbones and dimples. He looked to be in his early thirties and wasn't wearing a wedding ring.

"Yes, please," Dana answered with a smile. "The rear passenger tire looks low this morning. We're passing through to Arizona and still have two long days ahead of us. Can you check the tire to see if there's a problem?"

"Most certainly. We don't want ya driving that far on a bad tire. Just pull up in that side of the garage." He pointed up ahead. Dana and Sammy both admired his tan, muscular arms and strong-looking hands that were unusually clean for a man of his profession.

"Thanks," Dana added with another smile.

"He's darling. What's a cutie like him doing here?" Dana asked herself rather than Sammy.

"Seriously, I feel like we're on some hidden camera show. He's adorable. He looks like a tennis instructor or something." Sammy saw the mechanic approaching Dana's car door again. "Act cool, Dana."

He opened the door for her. "My name's Mike and I should be able to tell you what's wrong with the tire in a jiffy. And I can tell right now, that luckily we have those tires in stock in case we need to replace it. So you'll be on your way soon. There's a waiting area inside. Let me know if I can get you anything."

"Okay. Thanks, Mike," Dana said with a flirtatious tilt of her head. "My name's Dana if you need me."

The women walked toward the waiting area. When they were out of hearing range, Sammy started teasing Dana. "What was that little head-tilt thing? You little flirt. 'If you need me.' Nicely played, my friend. There's that coffee shop across the street. Why don't you go find us some coffee and pastries and a little something special for Mike. I'll wait here with the car."

"Good idea," Dana agreed.

Sammy watched her friend practically skip to the coffee shop. She hoped maybe Dana would appreciate her single status sooner than later. If this little meeting with Mike was any indication, Dana might bounce back quickly.

Moments later, Sammy caught a glimpse of Dana leaving the coffee shop and noticed that Dana had rolled her shorts up a little higher and unbuttoned an extra button or two on her blouse. Sammy chuckled. She was so fond of Dana and enjoyed watching her in action.

Dana dropped off two iced lattes and doughnuts and headed out to the garage to find Mike. Sammy watched as Dana gave an iced coffee and bag of goodies to Mike. She continued to keep an eye on them as the two talked, smiled, laughed, and flirted with each other. Dana was beaming when she returned.

"What's the verdict?" Sammy wondered.

"He's changing out the tire. He said he could repair it, but I'm worried about driving across country and through the hot desert with a patched tire. He should be done in about an hour." She smiled and bit into a doughnut the size of her fist.

"That's it?" Sammy asked, waiting for more on Mike.

"What? What else is there?" Dana asked blankly.

"What did you and Mike talk about?"

"Just that. He's sweet and super cute, and it's fun that he's the one fixing my tire instead of a smelly, old geezer. This is really a perfect little road trip distraction. What? Seriously? You think I'm gonna shack up with him in the greasy garage or something?"

"No, of course not." Sammy laughed at the ridiculousness of it. "However, I'm sure someone has done that with him."

"Sammy, please. Get your mind out of the gutter. He's a sweet man. Shame on you," Dana chided.

"Hey, you're the one that brought it up." Sammy said in defense. The two continued their banter over their doughnuts and coffee.

The tire was replaced and they were back on the road. Time and scenery passed by. They occasionally teased each other about Mike the Mechanic and what he really wanted to fix. Dana was right: he was the perfect road trip distraction.

That night, in their hotel room, Sammy showed Dana the photos of the casita that Aunt Kathy had e-mailed her. They both *oohed* and *ahhed* at the beautiful new home.

Dana's excitement skyrocketed. Her racing mind prompted her to scribble out shopping and to-do lists as well as ideas and sketches.

Sammy snuck away to call Jake. After that she phoned Kelly, who claimed to feel "strange"—that was the only way she could describe it. Sammy hoped she could make it back to Kelly in time.

The two women went to sleep that night with visions of their own near futures dancing in their heads.

CHAPTER 7

Sammy's ringing cell phone woke her at 5 a.m. the next morning. It was Greg.

"Hello? Greg? What is it? Is it time?" Sammy surveyed the dark room, assessing the pack-up time.

"Yes, Sammy, it's time. Kelly just started having contractions, but her doctor said she wanted to see her regardless. We're heading to the hospital now," Greg replied. Sammy could hear the anxiety and excitement in his voice. The news *really* woke her up.

"Okay," Sammy said as she hopped out of bed and opened the drapes a bit to let the early-morning sunlight in.

"We're in Albuquerque. We might be able to make it there in about seven hours." Sammy dug out some clothes to change into.

"Well, drive safely, Sammy. We'll see you soon."

"Tell her I love her and to wait for me!" Sammy laughed at what she knew would be Kelly's comment to that and hung up the phone.

By then, Dana was awake and looking for a change of clothes too. "Baby coming?"

"Yup. She just started having contractions. We might make it. She isn't due until next week. Darn, I thought I had more time." Sammy rummaged through her bags.

"We'll make it. Most first times are over twelve hours or so," Dana said reassuringly.

"No, I know. Chances are good we might make it. But let's hurry." Sammy ducked into the bathroom.

They were on the road in less than a half hour, record timing for two women and one bathroom.

***

When they arrived at the hospital almost eight hours later, they found Kelly looking worn-out but radiant and holding a sleeping, pink bundle of joy.

"Oh, I missed it. I'm so sorry." Sammy leaned over and kissed Kelly on the forehead and then peered in on the wrapped infant."She's the most precious thing I've ever seen. She's so tiny."

"When?" Sammy asked.

Greg piped in. "At 1:15 p.m. You missed it by about thirty minutes."

"But, seriously, you didn't need to be here for *that*. Wow—the things I did. I'm kind of an exhibitionist now," Kelly said with a proud laugh.

"Only you, sweetheart, would think such a thing. And don't go getting any ideas." Greg instructed his wife and then said sweetly, "Can I get you anything, love? Or you ladies, do you need anything?"

"No I'm fine, hon," Kelly answered with love in her eyes.

"I'm fine too," said Sammy. "Oh, where are my manners? Greg, this is my friend, Dana. Dana, this is Greg, the proud papa."

They exchanged greetings and Greg excused himself to make a few phone calls. Kelly and Dana greeted each other with hugs.

"She's absolutely precious. Now you can finally tell me her

name." Sammy was dying to know. Kelly had been holding out on her.

"Maxie Bella. Maxie, after Greg's dad. She may need therapy later in life over it, but Greg really liked the idea."

"Maxie Bella Carter. It's perfect for her. A perfect fit. How could I have missed her birth? I'm so sorry I wasn't here for you." Sammy's disappointment was genuine. They went through so much together throughout Kelly's pregnancy.

"It's fine, Sammy. It was meant to be. It was actually a really smooth and easy delivery. Pretty unbelievable—only about eight hours from first contraction to birth." Kelly looked down at her daughter. "The perfect work day,"

"I wanted Greg to call you right away, though, in case you were able to make it. Then I worried that it was a false alarm and had visions of you driving frantically. Then the contractions came on full blast and I knew you'd likely miss it. But I was content knowing you were with me mentally," Kelly said as she adjusted the bundle in her arms.

"And Greg was perfectly wonderful through it all—not the best coach, mind you, but the sweetest husband and daddy. And you're here now. I can't tell you how happy she makes me. She's so little. Obviously I've never held a newborn like this. I don't ever want to let go."

"Well, lucky for you, you don't have to," Sammy replied quietly. "And it's weird, but I'm gonna miss you being pregnant."

"Well, maybe it's your turn next," teased Kelly.

"Yeah, maybe not. I think you need to work on a sibling for Maxie. What do they call those babies born within a year? Irish twins? Have those."

Kelly laughed. "Let's see how I do with this little one first," she whispered.

The three women sat in silence for a few minutes, watching the newborn sleep. Then Kelly recapped the whole labor and delivery in detail. Sammy took notes to help Kelly write about it later in the baby book. Next, Sammy and Dana told Kelly about Mike the Mechanic.

At some point, Greg interrupted. "Sorry to break this party up, ladies. But the nurses need to give Maxie a little look over and Kelly needs to rest."

"Yes, of course," Sammy said. "I need to take Dana back to my place anyway. I'll be back in a few hours with dinner for you two. Okay?"

"That would be wonderful," Kelly answered with a smile.

"Thank you, Sammy. We're so happy you're here with us now," Greg added appreciatively.

"See you both soon," Sammy said as Dana waved her good-bye too.

"They're so cute together," Dana said as they left the hospital room.

"Yes, mama and baby are awfully sweet."

"No, I meant Kelly and Greg."

Dana's comment stunned Sammy. "Oh, you're right. Does that make you feel weird or envious or sad?"

"Not really any of those things. I'm happy for Kelly to have that love. When I see it, and try to imagine me and George with a baby like that now…I can't picture it. He hurt me so much, that I cannot picture that 'what if' anymore," Dana said.

"Good. That's progress, Dana, and healthy that you can admit it and see that now." Sammy happily tapped the elevator's down button.

The elevator doors opened on an older woman and younger child, obviously a grandmother and granddaughter. The two stepped out as Sammy and Dana stepped in.

When the elevator doors shut, Dana asked, "What about you? When you see grandmothers with grandchildren are you envious or sad?"

"Yes, I always am and always will be. I miss my mom every single day of my life and wish she could be a grandma to her grandkids. I wish I could say otherwise, but I can't."

"I get that. I really understand it now and worry about Vince in the same way." Dana paused a moment before quietly saying, "I'm sorry."

"Don't be. I'm just being honest, my friend," Sammy said as the elevator doors opened on the main floor. "I'm looking forward to going home."

***

The women arrived at Sammy's home just outside the city. Dana claimed it was nothing like she imagined.

She pictured green grass and palm trees. Instead Sammy's yard was covered in rocks with a hundred different desert plants in all shapes, sizes, and colors.

"Your yard is so cool. And your house! I love the Southwestern architecture," Dana said.

"Thanks." Sammy showed Dana to her guest room, and Dana seemed to love the inside of the house as much as the outside.

They settled in a bit. Dana unpacked while Sammy checked her snail mail and voice mails.

The day was warm for the end of April—already in the high nineties—so Sammy and Dana went for a swim in the late afternoon.

As she sat on the steps of her pool, Sammy said, "I'm heading back to the hospital in a bit. Do you need anything before I go?"

"Nope, I'm good," Dana said as she floated around Sammy's pool on a raft. "I feel a strange sense of relaxation and relief. Two feelings I haven't had in a long time."

Sammy smiled. "Good, that's what I was hoping for. I thought maybe getting you away from Loon Lake and Saw Mill for a while might help change your perspective. Sometimes, the best thing we can change about a situation is our perspective."

"You're a wise woman, Sammy. I hope I can be as smart as you when I grow up."

"Thanks, I think," Sammy said with a laugh.

She climbed out of the pool and dried off. "I'll put a delivery menu by the phone in the kitchen. It's to a great pizzeria nearby. Please be sure to order dinner, or else I'll feel like a terrible hostess. I have plenty of drinks in the fridge. Help yourself to anything you find. I should be back in a few hours. I just want to check on Kelly and the baby and bring her and Greg some dinner."

"You're such a good friend," Dana said.

"It takes one to know one," Sammy replied. "I'll say goodbye before I go." She headed inside, leaving Dana to float around the pool some more.

***

Sammy walked in on Kelly nursing Maxie.

"Sorry for the lack of discretion on my part, but breastfeeding a newborn is not as *natural* as everyone makes is sound." Kelly sounded frustrated.

Sammy laughed. "Oh, please. I spent a few weeks with Cass and her twin babies. There were boobs everywhere. She had such trouble with the twins too. Ginny was a good little eater; she wanted to nurse all the time, which is a problem in its own right. And Jill was difficult to nurse right from the start. So you just keep at it. It looks like Maxie's getting the hang of it."

"Yes, let's hope her mommy does too. Can you believe I have a baby?" Kelly asked in disbelief as she tried to burp Maxie.

"It does seem a little surreal, Kell. I love it. You look beautiful and natural with her there. How do you feel? Have your concerns subsided?" Sammy asked.

"Yeah, for the most part. It's still too new and I'm too tired to think about them. She's done eating. Do you want to hold her?"

"Yes, I've wanted to get my hands on her since I met her," Sammy said as she gently lifted Maxie from Kelly's arms.

"She's so tiny, so precious. I'm in love," Sammy said as she looked down at the sweet baby.

"With her or Jake?" Kelly asked seriously.

"Both, I think."

"Wow, really? That's exciting—" Kelly didn't quite finish her sentence as Greg walked in on the three.

"Well, you're a natural there, Godmother," Greg said to Sammy.

"Godmother?" Sammy asked.

"Yes," Kelly and Greg said together.

"We'd like you to be Maxie's godmother. Will you?" Kelly asked more formally.

"Of course I will. Hello, my little goddaughter," Sammy said as she gently kissed the baby on her forehead and rummaged around the blanket for a tiny little hand.

Greg fixed Kelly and himself plates of the food Sammy had brought. The three chatted as Kelly and Greg ate and Sammy held the baby. It was a lovely evening, and Sammy was sad to leave them, but knew they all needed their rest.

"Please let me know if you need anything, okay?" Sammy reminded them both.

"Okay," Greg said. "We'll be checking out tomorrow night as long as Maxie's pediatrician gives her a clean bill of health. So we shouldn't need anything."

"Good. I'll just come by and check on you tomorrow around noon. Let me know if you need anything before then, anyway. Love to you all." She gave hugs and kisses to all three, with extra kisses on the new baby's knitted cap.

Sammy never knew how much she loved babies until she spent time around Cass's babies, Jill and Ginny. Now Sammy couldn't seem to get enough of them.

***

Sammy returned home in time to have dinner with Dana, who went to bed early, giving Sammy the chance to call Jake. The two talked on the phone for hours. Sammy recapped the road trip and described Kelly's baby. He told her about his recent talk with Vince and that he was going to visit his parents, Aunt Jeannie, and Vince in the coming week. They talked long into the night, like old friends and new lovers.

***

As promised, Sammy returned the next afternoon to see Kelly and Maxie. Greg took the opportunity to run to a nearby coffee shop and return some work e-mails.

"How's Dana doing?" Kelly asked as she handed the baby to Sammy.

"She's getting better every day. You should've seen her last weekend when I arrived at the resort. She didn't look like the woman we met last year."

"Well, yes, I can see that now too. She looks worn out and heartbroken. We all recognize that look." Kelly nodded and continued. "She's so lucky to have you *and* the opportunity to go help Aunt Kathy."

Kelly gingerly changed positions in her bed. "That would be so fun to decorate a guesthouse in a vineyard. Admit it: you're a little envious of that, aren't you? What about your sister, Gabby? Won't she be bummed that she isn't the one helping Kathy?"

Sammy cringed. "Oh no…I never thought about Gabby. You're right, though. She won't take this news well. She loves to paint rooms and decorate stuff."

She quickly shook her head, as if answering on Gabby's behalf. "But, honestly, how would she have the time? Her three boys are always on some sports team or in some camp or into other activities. She spends her summer days driving them around to different functions."

As if arguing with herself, Sammy continued. "Oh, she isn't going to like this. On the other hand, she also met Dana last summer and liked her so much. Certainly she'll understand Dana's situation and know she needs this right now."

Sammy practically whispered as she admitted sadly, "But you're also right about me. I'm a little envious of Dana's opportunity to go shop and work with Kathy. I would love that time with her."

"But?" Kelly added expectantly.

"But, I would rather go spend some time with Jake this summer. I feel like this is our last chance to see if there's something between us. And man, there are some major sparks right now," Sammy said.

She began to fill her dear friend in on all the juicy details of their intimate time together. Sammy didn't normally kiss and tell, but this was not her normal kiss to tell. And Kelly thrived on this kind of information.

"I hate to leave you this summer, Kelly," Sammy said, abruptly changing the subject.

"You have to. There isn't really anything you can do for me. Yes, of course I'll miss you tons and want to see you and have you watch Maxie grow. But I do understand this thing between you and Jake and I want you to pursue it. He's worth it."

"But—"

"But nothing! How can I be so selfish as to want you to stay here with me, when Jake will need you too? It won't be all fun and games for him like last summer. He's there without his sister, who's been up there with him from the beginning. And he's likely going to watch poor Foxy Vince go through some shit when his mother dies."

Sammy couldn't argue with that. "No, you're right, and so wise, Kell. I hadn't looked at it that way. I was sort of thinking about how Dana helped him a lot but forgot about the everyday companionship that she obviously gave him."

She looked down at little Maxie and kissed her gently on the head, before continuing. "And poor Vince, I can't even imagine what he's going through. Yes, I feel in my heart that I'm supposed to be with Jake this summer, to see what happens. Are you sure you'll be all right?" Sammy still worried about Kelly.

"Of course. My mom's coming next week and Greg's mom will always be around. I'll have these sweet grandmas with me to hold the baby and help change diapers," Kelly said, wincing as she changed positions again.

"I'm going to be one of those spoiled new moms that have

their house cleaned and meals cooked by others so I can rest when the baby rests and be ready to feed her at her every beck and call. It will be delightful. And we will have the rest of our lives together, when you and Jake figure out how the heck you're going to make your relationship work."

"That sounded great up until that last part. Gee, thanks for the encouragement," Sammy teased.

"You're welcome. Just doing my job."

"Speaking of jobs, let's not worry about anything until August, okay?" Sammy had worked her butt off the past several months to finish the rewrites for her novel, and wrote a year's worth of articles in half the time, so that she and Kelly could take a few months off.

"Sounds good to me," Kelly agreed. "So when are you heading to Cali?"

"Probably next weekend. I want to hang with you and Maxie a little bit before I go."

"Perfect. I'm excited for you and Dana."

"Speaking of Dana, I better go check on her now. Are you still heading home tonight?"

"Yup, so far that's the plan."

Maxie started to squirm around in Sammy arms.

"Good. You get some rest. I'll be over tomorrow around noon to bring you and Greg lunch. Okay?"

"Sounds wonderful. I'm so happy you're here," Kelly said with a drowsy grin. "Can you put Maxie in her little crib there? I think I better nap while she does."

Sammy happily tucked Maxie into her crib and hugged her friend good-bye.

As she closed the door to Kelly's room behind her, she felt a new sense of peace. She hadn't realized how worried she'd been about Kelly's pregnancy until that moment.

***

The following week was filled with excitement and scary little diapers. Sammy spent some time each day visiting with Kelly and Maxie. She wanted to get as big a dose of them as she could and that meant she was there to help with lots of diaper changes.

When she wasn't with Kelly and baby, she was in her office or pool with Dana. She had set Dana up with a key to her office so Dana could scour the Internet for design ideas, make notes, and print out all kinds of examples for Kathy.

By the end of the week, Dana had three big binders full of ideas and information for Kathy. She also had a nice tan and looked like she put on three much-needed pounds.

Sammy took the time to not only visit with Kelly and Dana but also to carefully pack for her return to Loon Lake. She had no idea how long she was going for or what to expect when she got there.

She caught up with all of her sisters. Cass was doing wonderfully; the twins were almost three months old and doing great. Their baptisms were scheduled for October.

She had long talks with Alex about Vince. Alex was shocked to hear about his mom and felt terrible. She explained that they ended their relationship as mature adults. She hadn't acted rashly or foolishly, and she felt she handled everything openly and honestly.

Alex didn't feel guilt or regret, only genuine sadness for Vince. She asked Sammy if she should contact him, but Sammy assured her it wasn't necessary. Sammy doubted Alex could be of any comfort to Vince, though she kept that thought to herself.

Her conversation with Gabby surprised Sammy the most. She expected Gabby to be somewhat disappointed at the missed opportunity to help Aunt Kathy. But just as Sammy suspected, Gabby had her hands full with her three boys and husband, Eddie.

Gabby was sincerely happy for Dana to have the chance for a fresh start and was happy for Aunt Kathy. She knew Aunt Kathy missed her girls and would dote on Dana as much for herself as for Dana. She said it was a win-win for the two.

Sammy felt more at ease with everyone's situation with each passing day. Things were magically falling into place. It was almost too good to be true and this caused a slight worry in the back of Sammy's mind. But she didn't dwell on it. She wanted to enjoy the peacefulness and the excitement. Everything was good in her world.

***

"California, here we come!" the women exclaimed as they headed out on their next road trip. Compared to their previous road trip, this one would be much quicker, only two short days of driving. They started out Saturday morning, May fifth, one week after Maxie was born.

It was just over three weeks since Jake left Sammy a voice mail. One month ago, Sammy would've never imagined this is where her life would be.

Here she was driving to her aunt's house in California with her boyfriend's sister. It felt funny to think of Jake as her *boyfriend*, but at this point they were definitely more than friends. She looked forward to seeing him in a few weeks; however, she had a feeling her time with Kathy and Dana would be moments to remember.

CHAPTER 8

The drive to California was quiet and serene. The women were more pensive, often drifting off in their own thoughts. Sammy could sense that Dana grew more relaxed with each mile driven.

The California scenery was having a magical effect on both women. Sammy looked out the window, thinking about when her aunt came to live with them, twenty-one years ago. *Aunt Kathy was so young then, only forty-six*, Sammy thought, letting out a small chuckle.

"What?" Dana asked as she heard Sammy laugh.

"Oh, I was thinking about when Aunt Kathy came to live with us and I just thought how *young* she was, at forty-six. I guess when you're closing in on forty like me, forty-six is still young."

"What was she like?" Dana asked.

"When? Back then?" Sammy figured Dana might want to know as much as she could about her new benefactor.

"Whenever you want to start. We still have about an hour. Tell me about her." Dana straightened behind the wheel, becoming more present.

"Well, okay. I'll start from as far back as I can remember," Sammy said thoughtfully. "My grandparents, Kathy and my mom's parents, met and lived in Minneapolis. My grandmother lived in Saw Mill as a child."

Dana interrupted. "Is that how your family found Loon Lake?"

"Yeah, my parents actually found the old resort when they were looking for a nearby place to honeymoon."

"They honeymooned there?" Dana asked.

"Yeah, can you imagine? They vacationed there every summer after that, up until the year they died," Sammy said.

"Anyway, that's way ahead in my story here. Since my grandmother was from northern Minnesota, she dreamed of living somewhere warmer. So after my grandparents married, my grandfather took a job from an army pal in Atlanta, Georgia. My grandmother loved the mild winters and happily had her two daughters there, Kathy and Virginia, my mom," Sammy said with a distant smile.

"They grew up in Atlanta?" Dana asked.

"Yes, until the girls were young teenagers. That's how Aunt Kathy developed her Southern drawl, which is now a strange mix of Southern and cowgirl."

"I wondered where she got that. Did your mom talk like that too?"

"Only a little bit. She was younger than my aunt, so I think when they moved she had more time to lose the drawl. But Kathy was apt to use her Southern charm to her advantage."

"Where'd they move to?"

"While my grandma loved the weather, she couldn't bear the racial tension and segregation in the South. They ended up moving back to Minneapolis and lived one block away from my dad's house where he grew up. My parents became instant neighborhood pals, and as soon as the hormones kicked in, they were first loves."

"That's so sweet," Dana said, "but what about Kathy?"

"Kathy and my mom were really close. So when my parents married and moved to the Cincinnati suburbs for my dad's job, Aunt Kathy moved there too."

"Is that where you grew up? In Cincinnati? Near where Vince lives?"

"I don't know exactly where Vince lives. But yeah, we grew up in the suburbs. Anyway, back to Kathy…That's where Kathy met her first husband, Stan. She married Uncle Stanley when we were young. I'm not sure how they met. I only found out last summer that she couldn't have children, which ultimately ended their marriage." Sammy noticed the look of horror on Dana's face, she quickly added, "It was *her*, not him, who ended things."

"She was one of the few divorced people that I knew when I was growing up. And she also worked for herself as a real estate agent. In our young eyes, she was this awesome 'woman of the eighties.' She was successful, rich as far as I knew, and attractive. She had dark-brown hair, bright-green eyes, and seemed to always have a tan. Her body was always fit and trim, which she attributed to a lack of child-bearing. And she's always had her hearty laugh that was contagious."

"Yes, I remember her laugh," Dana interjected. "Alex has the same sort of laugh, doesn't she?"

"Yes, Alex does. I try to remember if Alex had that laugh before Kathy moved in with us or not. I can't remember…"

"Anyway," Sammy said, coming back from memory lane, "Kathy was smart and, now that I look back, quite sexy. I don't know why she remained single. Well, until she got stuck with us girls that is. I could understand why no man would want a single woman rearing four teenage girls that weren't even her own. Do you really want to know all this?"

"Yes, yes. So far, I love it. It explains so much. When I met her last year, I thought she had this powerful presence about her, a force to be reckoned with. I was awestruck."

"Yes, she was, and is, all of those things. I think when my mom died something inside Kathy wanted to change. It's hard to explain. I think she wanted to be softer—less aggressive, less bossy. I think she wanted to be sad and miss my mom. But she was stuck with us kids and had to be strong for all of us. It enhanced that natural strength in her."

Sammy was suddenly overwhelmed with emotion and had to stop talking. Wiping tears from her eyes, she continued. "Sorry about that. I just suddenly envisioned myself losing one of my sisters right now and that's how Kathy was when she took us in. I can't imagine trying to do that for Gabby's boys right now. Granted, they're quite a bit younger than we were, but my mom was forty-four when she died and Kathy was forty-six. So, it would be exactly like Gabby and me in seven years. I couldn't imagine taking over her life and caring for her three sons."

Attempting to sound less somber, she continued, "Oh, and don't get me started on living past forty-four. Cassy was freaking out about that last fall, reaching the age my mom was when she died. It's so weird to outlive that 'mortal number,' if you will." Sammy was unexpectedly saddened by where her mind was taking her. She stopped talking.

After a long pause, Dana asked, "Are you okay? Is this too much to talk about?"

"It shouldn't be, should it? It was so long ago and I'm getting all confused in my mind—talk of my mom and Kathy, old and new. I'm sorry I'm suddenly so emotional. And look at the scenery. It must be these miles and miles of nature. It's getting into my psyche." Sammy gazed out the window at the rolling hills and distant mountains. It was all so beautiful, it literally made her cry.

Dana suddenly laughed quite inappropriately. "Yay," she said and handed Sammy a tissue. "It's so refreshing to see someone else have an emotional breakdown besides me right now. Thank you for that."

Dana patted her friend's hand. "I've been such a train wreck and can fall apart at the slightest thought of my recent past. It's great to feel like maybe I'm normal, huh? I forgot most people get sad once in a while. I'm sorry for laughing. I was laughing at me, really, not you, by the way."

Sammy smiled shyly. "No, no. Go ahead and laugh. Dana, you and I are stuck on this emotional journey for the next few weeks at least. I feel very vulnerable, as I know you must feel too. We're bound to say some freaky stuff to each other. But I know we'll both be happier and healthier when it's all over. Where was I with Kathy?"

"She was forty-six and moved in with you girls," Dana said, prompting her.

"Yes, she was only a few years older than Cass is right now—and your brother." It suddenly dawned on her that Jake was the same age as Cass.

"Could you imagine if Jake had to take in four kids, two of which are young teenagers? Cass can barely handle her babies, let alone try to handle a teenager suddenly," Sammy said.

"Jake would probably be really good at it," Dana said thoughtfully. "He's always been good with kids of all ages."

That information stunned Sammy. She never really saw or pictured Jake interacting with children. Now, her mind was distracted with the intriguing images.

"Hello, in there…" Dana said, snapping Sammy out of her daydream.

Sammy blushed. "Anyway, yes, Kathy moved in and helped us all survive those tough first years without my parents. Cass and I were both out of the house mostly, but Gabby was in high school and Alex just started high school. Those were such emotional and drama-filled years." Sammy thought back to the previous drama-filled summer with her grown sisters at Loon Lake.

"Fast forward a bit to about thirteen or fourteen years ago, when Alex started off to college the first time around. Aunt Kathy began traveling with some close friends. It was Alex's second fall out of the house away at college when Kathy and some girl friends came out here to Napa Valley for a wine tour."

Her tone changed suddenly, matching her enthusiasm. "They were in a little local bar one night and Kathy got to chatting with a 'handsome cowboy,' as she described him. They talked all night, danced a bit. She thought he was a 'local yokel,'—her words. She didn't really know anything about the wine world at the time and was merely having fun sightseeing.

"She claimed to have fallen in love with Hank that night on a bar stool. He was the man of her dreams. The one she'd waited her whole life to meet. She was fifty-four years old.

"She found herself in a long-distance relationship. They talked every night on the phone. She went back out to see him the Friday after Thanksgiving and found out he owned a vineyard. He'd never mentioned it before."

"That's so romantic," Dana said.

"Isn't it? All of us girls were home that following Christmas. That's when she told us more of the juicy details. She was in love and wanted to marry him. None of us met him, but seeing as though she never had a serious boyfriend the whole time she was living with us, who were we to stand in her way?

"They eloped that New Year's Eve. None of us girls were there, and we were okay with it. She wanted a small, intimate ceremony with just Hank at his vineyard. And we could absolutely not deny her a thing. She gave us so much.

"Besides, Gabby was pregnant with her first baby then. Cass had started dating Phillip. We were all very self-centered at that time in our lives. We did have a big reception back at our house afterward. Cass flew in for it, but Gabby had to miss it since she was already home at Christmastime.

"That spring, Kathy sold our family home and moved out here to live happily ever after with Hank. All three of my sisters have been out here to stay with them—Alex has even lived with them a few times—but this is my first visit. I've had plans in the past, but something always came up.

"Kathy comes to Arizona to visit me every winter. Hank comes with her sometimes. We meet up at my sisters' houses or other places, like last summer at the lake. So, it's not so strange that I haven't been to their house. But I'm super psyched to see her and Hank at their home."

"That's quite a story. She's had quite a life, huh? Can I be honest with you about something?" Dana asked hesitantly.

"Of course," Sammy said with concern.

"I'm kind of scared to start this adventure out here. I feel so out of my element. It's beautiful, for certain, and looks like a wonderful place to visit. But, for me, it feels sort of final, like that first day off to college—the unknown, the loneliness. On the one hand, it's exciting and new; but on the other, it scares the heck out of me." Dana gulped.

"Can I be honest with you about something too?" Sammy asked her in return.

"Yes, please do," Dana replied.

"I'm scared to be alone with your brother this summer. There, I said it out loud. I'm scared to put myself out there with him, to have nowhere to escape to if things go south. I'm scared to let myself be that open and vulnerable. But also, I'm more excited about this than anything I can remember." Saying it all out loud made Sammy's heart pound.

"Fair enough. Here's to a scary, exciting summer: a summer of changes," Dana said with conviction.

"A summer of changes," Sammy agreed. *Dragonfly changes.*

"I think we're getting close to the valley. Where are those directions?"

Sammy dug out the directions and proceeded to help guide Dana to the vineyard.

***

They drove up the dusty, winding road lined with old oak trees to Hidden Peaks Vineyard, arriving as the sun set.

"Oh my goodness…" Dana was rendered speechless at the sight of Hank and Kathy's home.

Sammy had seen pictures and heard all about it from her sisters, so while she was mentally prepared, she was nonetheless impressed. "It's gorgeous, isn't it?"

"It looks like a super swanky dude ranch," Dana said excitedly.

The home was a rambling stone ranch. A large redwood portico in front of the main door covered the drive, welcoming guests to the home. The gorgeous wood and the stone walls enhanced the ranch's earthy and natural look. The setting sun, hills, and surrounding vineyards made the estate look magical.

"Seriously, if I saw fairies fly around right now, it would not faze me one bit," Dana said matter-of-factly.

Sammy laughed. "It does look a bit surreal, doesn't it?"

Kathy burst out the front door as the car pulled up under the portico. Sammy noticed how radiant she looked. Her aunt was wearing a flowing lavender dress with a long white sweater and her usual cowgirl boots. Her salt-and-pepper hair was tied back with a matching lavender ribbon.

Age and gourmet dining had transformed Kathy's young fit body to a thicker womanly figure, appropriate for a woman of sixty-seven. But she was still tan and beautiful. Love and Napa Valley had aged her well.

Sammy hopped out of the car as fast as she could and ran to her aunt. Kathy gave Sammy one of her famous bear hugs, squeezing the air right out of her niece. Sammy loved it. She remembered Kathy's scent: fresh yet earthy, and fruity with a hint of red wine.

"Aunt Kathy, you look dazzling. I'm so happy to see you." Sammy beamed.

"Aw, Sammy, look at *you*. How did y'all get so grown-up? I swear just yesterday you were this sweet little pip-squeak off at college. What happened?"

"You went off and got married, Aunt Kathy. What was I left to do but grow old?" Sammy teased.

Something happened when these women got together. They spoke a secret language that would make an English professor cringe. Kathy's cowgirl dialect had grown exponentially with her time with Hank.

"Well, now. I guess it's my own fault, then. And where is my Sweet Dana, my handy-girl, my worker bee?"

Dana had stood aside quietly, allowing Sammy and Kathy a proper greeting. "I'm here, Kathy. It's so great to see you again." Dana awkwardly put her hand out.

"Aw, that's not Dana Hunter. That's merely her skin and bones. Whaddya do with the rest of her, Sammy?" Kathy asked as she gently pulled Dana in for a tender bear hug.

"I know, Kathy, right? I'm hoping you can do something about that," Sammy was caught off guard by Dana's maiden name.

Sammy met her as Dana Keller and it never dawned on her to ask if she changed her name back. Of course she had, but Sammy never thought about it. Leave it to Kathy to know what it's like to be a newly divorced woman.

"Thank you so much for this opportunity, Aunt Kathy. Is it okay if I call you Aunt Kathy?" Dana asked shyly.

Noticing that Dana was asking her as well as Kathy, Sammy nodded her approval.

"You betcha," said Kathy. "And I want to thank y'all for agreeing to come here and help an old gal. I can't wait to get started. Now, come in, come in. I'll show y'all to your rooms and let ya freshen up. Hank's out walking around the fruit and should be back soon for dinner. I'll have the fellas take your stuff to the rooms. Does everything come out of the car?"

"Yes," both women answered together.

"Okay, then. I'm pleased as punch to have to you girls here. I can't believe you're finally here, Samantha. Oh, I'm so happy, I'm gonna cry or bust or somethin'." She gave Sammy another squeeze.

Kathy led the women through the main house, talking nonstop as they walked. She pointed in the directions of all the rooms and other amenities. As they walked out the back door, they found themselves by a courtyard still under construction. Kathy continued to explain the plans for the courtyard, pool area, and other features.

"Here she is: Escondido." Kathy spread her arms wide, presenting the new guesthouse to the women. "Isn't she a beauty?"

"She is," both women agreed.

"Why 'Escondido'?" Sammy asked.

"It's Spanish for 'hidden,' like in Hidden Peaks. We wanna put some fancy climbing plants and vines around it eventually and set some outlandishly big rocks in front, so it really does look hidden in here. We also want the outside to look like it's been here for ages. Maybe you can help me figure that out, Dana. But for now we need everything around it clear for construction and other nonsense." Kathy spoke with such pride and joy.

Kathy let them inside and showed them the guesthouse. The entryway opened up to a large, high-ceilinged great room with wooden beams on the ceiling. In the center of the back wall, framed by windows, was a floor-to-ceiling stone fireplace.

"Is that redwood?" Dana asked, looking up and admiring the beams.

"Sure is. California redwood. Might've even hid a Bigfoot once upon a time," Kathy said with a dreamy little grin.

"You believe in Bigfoot?" Dana asked.

Sammy laughed loudly, knowing too well her aunt's strong beliefs in the unbelievable.

"I most certainly do. I'll take y'all on a day trip up to see some redwoods. It'll make a believer out of you. And don't laugh at me, Sammy, I know you believe too."

"No, no, you're right. I totally believe," Sammy answered seriously.

"Really? But I thought you're a scientist," Dana said, as if it made all other information null and void.

"So? There are plenty of scientists studying and looking for Bigfoot. There's a lot in this world that science can't explain. And there are many scientists who believe in the unbelievable. We know how miraculous some things in nature really are. Plus, growing up with this woman, it's hard not to believe in such things." Sammy shrugged.

Kathy continued to reveal the features of the open kitchen and attached wine bar. She showed the women the den and two half baths on the main floor, and then proceeded to tour them through the six master suites on the second floor.

The house was completely finished. The walls were primed but not painted and everything was bare of décor. It was a complete blank slate: a decorator's dream.

"I want to do the six bedrooms in a series within a theme, but I don't know what exactly. I wanted to do the seasons, like one room for each season, but then that leaves two extra rooms. And then I thought of doing each room for a different wine. But I'm not sure we could make each different enough…" Kathy thought out loud.

"Anywho," she continued, "that'll be our first task, Miss Dana. I'm so excited. And that den is going to be your office this summer. I have a temporary desk, chair, filing system, and some bookcases in there right now for ya. But I'll need ya to make it look professional. Sound good?"

"Sounds amazing," Dana said.

The women settled into the only two bedrooms, next to each other, that had beds and dressers.

"And the beds and furniture are also temporary. Oh sweetie, I can't wait to get cracking on this with y'all. And dang it, I'm tryin' hard not to say 'y'all' all the time. I sound like a bumpkin. I'm not doing a very good job at it, am I?" Kathy sounded genuinely frustrated.

"Why, Aunt Kathy? It's endearing to hear you talk like that," Sammy said, and she meant it. She couldn't remember the last time she heard anyone use the word *bumpkin.*

"Aw, to you maybe and that's so sweet," she said. "I just noticed I talk a little more country out here with Hank. Then we go to places where everyone is so sophisticated. And there are oodles of Europeans here with these gorgeous accents. I've suddenly become a little self-conscious of what I sound like."

"I know exactly what you mean, Kathy," said Dana. "During my time in Saw Mill, I found myself using the local slang and getting a little Minnesotan accent. There's absolutely nothing wrong with that, but it wasn't me. I was picking up these phrases and sayings from George and his folks. I became very aware of how I talked these last few months and I basically had to reprogram myself."

"Yes, that's exactly how I feel. Everyone says they love how I talk; it's just sometimes I don't quite like it. Oh well, ya know what they say about old dogs and new tricks." She quickly changed the topic.

"Anyway, I'll give y'all, er, *you girls* some time to freshen up. We'll have drinks and snacks in the dining room at the house when you're ready. You might want to change; it's cooling down out there." Kathy left the women to settle in.

***

Walking back to the main house for dinner, Sammy thought about Dana referring to her in-laws earlier in the bedroom. "Hey, Dana, I remember last summer you did a lot of stuff with George's parents. Even Jake helped them out a bit. You seemed close. How have they been through *this*?" Sammy knew she sounded awkward but didn't know the proper way to ask.

"Through the *divorce*? It's okay, you can say the word," Dana said with a tender smile.

"The truth is they were on my side. They saw how wrong George handled everything. I really cared about them, and we grew to love each other. Last summer, we were a family. We were in it until death do us part, all of us.

"George ruined that. I think he even helped himself to some of their money after he couldn't get his hands on mine. He's in a downward spiral, and I'm afraid they're going to be hurt by him. It's sad. It was sad to say good-bye to them. But that's what I did—said good-bye. And I don't plan to keep in touch. They understood that. They were sweet. But I need to start with a clean slate." Dana took a deep breath.

"I liked hearing your aunt use my maiden name," she said. "It feels good to be Dana Hunter again. I saw the look on your face. Hearing your aunt say it out loud took me by surprise too. It still sounds weird some days. Other days, it sounds refreshing."

Kathy met them at the back door as if she'd been waiting for them. "I heard y'all coming. Come in, come in. Miss Dana, please meet the love of my life. This is Hank Van Dyke. Hank, this is Dana Hunter, our newest employee."

Hank broke away from his hug with Sammy and gave Dana a gentle but strong handshake. "Welcome, Dana. So nice to meet ya, darlin'. I'm lookin' forward to ya helpin' Kathy this summer. Lord knows she can use a hand with our grand plans."

Sammy marveled at Hank. She always thought he looked and talked like Jimmy Stewart. Sammy had loved Jimmy Stewart from the first time she saw *It's a Wonderful Life*. She noticed the resemblance the moment she met Hank and had put him up on a pedestal ever since.

"And look at you, Sammy. So gorgeous. Hard to believe Kathy didn't give birth to ya—such a resemblance," Hank said with a wide grin.

"Oh please, don't insult the poor girl." Kathy gave Hank a playful swat on his rear end. Sammy and Dana exchanged raised eyebrows.

They settled down in the formal dining room. The foursome chatted and enjoyed a feast of wine, local cheeses, and breads made by the ranch's chef. A young man named Mateo politely waited on them all night.

They talked about the girls' cross-country drive. Now that the women were with Kathy and Hank, they were referred to as *girls*, not women. And neither one seemed to mind.

"So, Mr. Van Dyke, how did you come to Napa Valley and start a winery?" Dana asked.

"Oh my, that's a long story, and please, call me Hank. Where do I begin?" Hank asked as he refilled the wine glasses.

"Tell the girls *all* of it, starting from those great-great-great-grandparents," Kathy said.

"Lordy, that'll take all night," Hank replied.

"We have plenty of time," Sammy said. "Please tell Dana. She'll love it." Sammy recalled how moved she was by Hank's story the first time she heard it.

"Okay, remember, y'all asked for it," Hank said with a smile. "All my ancestral information I'm about to tell ya I heard as a young child from my grandmother. I might mix up some of the years and I'll skip all their great-great-titles, cuz it can get confusin'. But just know these are my ancestors' stories of how they came here and what led me back here later in my own life. I've written a lot of it down to remember, so you can always read it for a little more detail if ya ever have an inkling to."

"I'd like to read it sometime," Sammy interrupted.

"Great, darlin', I'll dig it out for ya one of these days," Hank said with a wink.

Dana laughed quietly just as Mateo brought in dinner, which distracted Hank and Kathy.

The distraction gave Dana the chance to whisper to Sammy. "Right now, when Hank winked and called you darlin', I swear he looked like Vince in thirty-some years."

Sammy raised her eyebrows with a grin and whispered back. "He did, didn't he?"

As they enjoyed dinner, Hank told his story. He told of how a young man named James Closson came to Napa Valley from Missouri in the 1830s. Hank enchanted the women with stories of James being friends with the local Mexicans and Native Americans and how James fell in love and married a beautiful Native American woman, having three sons with her. She ended up dying from smallpox a few years later.

About the same time, Hank explained, Mexico was disposing of its California property, and since James had done a great deal of work for a Mexican general, the general granted James some land to start a farm. James later remarried a family friend from Missouri and they had two daughters together, one of which was Hank's grandma's grandmother.

Hank continued to tell colorful tales of the new European immigrants that saw the start of the Gold Rush in the late 1840s. He explained that this brought the demand for wine in California and that wine-making in Napa really took off in the 1850s. The story continued with James and his sons learning wine-making and becoming one of fifty recognized vintners in Napa Valley by the 1860s.

There was a special sparkle in Hank's eyes as he explained that in the early 1870s, after finishing the transcontinental railroad, many Chinese laborers came to Napa Valley and built some of these large stone wineries that still stood today, along with the hillside caves used as storage cellars and the stone walls that meander across Napa's hills. James' sons hired Chinese laborers to build cellar caves that still stood on Hank's property.

He told of his grandmother growing up on the vineyards and how she told wonderful stories of wine-tasting parties and the harvest. He explained that after Prohibition in 1919, few wineries survived and that through the Crash, Depression, Dust Bowl, and World War II, the family ranch was sold off bit by bit until it was completely gone by the 1940s.

Then Hank's story finally included him and where he grew up and how he got into the construction business in Texas.

"Growing up, I would spend my summers visiting my grandma in San Francisco. She always told me fantastic stories of the vineyard and handsome James that married a beautiful Native American woman. I dreamt of these visions when I was a kid.

"I followed in my pop's footsteps with construction. I met my first wife a few years after college. We married. She miscarried two years in a row and died of leukemia the third year," Hank said quietly.

Dana was blindsided by this part of his story. "I'm so sorry," she said to Hank. She glanced toward Sammy in search of more words.

Sammy looked at a loss as well. Based on Hank's demeanor, Sammy could see that even after all these years, the memory and loss still caused him great pain.

Kathy reached over and lovingly held Hank's hand.

Hank looked at Dana and replied, "Thank you, darlin'. But God had a plan for me. I was sad about losing her and the family I never got a chance to have. I moved to Southern

California, started my own construction company, and dove into work. I made lots of money as this state grew quickly.

"After several years, I felt like I needed something more in my life. I was content as a young bachelor and not having children. It was obviously meant to be that way. It was January 1974 when I read an article in the newspaper about the wine-making industry making a comeback in Napa.

"I instantly had a vision, almost as if God sent me a message. I drove my car up here the next day. Drove out to where my grandmother had taken me several times. Again, as though God was answering my question, a dusty For Sale sign swung at the drive's entrance," Hank said with a smile.

Sammy got goose bumps as she listened.

"I bought it that day. It was in pitiful condition. I had to build a temporary house to live in while I rebuilt this main ranch house. Tore down most outer buildings and started over. Brought up one of my construction crews to live here and help me.

"We developed the vineyard by working long days removing stones by hand. We had to put in drainage, reshape and grade the land. I had to plant cover crops the first few years to aerate and restore the organic quality of the soil. We laid out where the vines were going to go, put in the trellises, planted the vines, irrigated, cultivated—all the while learning wine-making techniques."

Hank laughed. "Folks have some romantic vision of grape farmers in wine country. But it is the hardest work I've ever done. I was rewarded in the early nineties with my first bottle of wine and then rewarded again the night I met Kathy. One night with her, I knew we were meant to be together." He smiled at Kathy.

"And you continued your construction business while you grew the vineyard?" Dana asked.

"Yes. I lucked out with the fellas I hired over the years. I kept my business in Southern California with a new manager who I trusted completely. He continued to grow that business very well, allowing us to enter into a partnership. I continue to see the benefits from that partnership.

"I brought my best crew here. Some stayed to help my construction group expand here in Northern California, while others took personal interests in the vineyard and wine-making. We've become one large family."

He looked lovingly at Kathy as he continued. "I wasn't blessed to have my own children, but I've had countless blessings from my extended work family. If a worker is sick, I make sure someone gets him to a doctor. If a wife has a baby, we throw a party and make sure the family has everything they need for the little one. I try to help in any way I can," Hank said.

"This place is not just a vineyard or winery to me. It's more than my home or mine and Kathy's home. It's a living land, full of memories of people who once lived here. The reason I love the caves that are still in the hills here is because I think about the Chinese laborers when I walk inside them. Sometimes, when I roam the hills, I can picture James and his wives and children working and playing in the fields.

"The grape fields are tended to by hundreds of people, not just me. We are all vested in its success, its growth cycle. I'm blessed to be a caretaker of this land until I can no longer care for it. Its dirt is in my bones, the wine is in my blood, the memories are in my dreams still." Hank was attempting to sound stoic. "Sometimes, I can feel my grandmother here."

"Wow, that's an amazing story," Dana said.

Sammy wiped tears from her eyes and said with a smile, "Thanks for telling us your story, Hank."

"No, thank you, girls, for humoring me and listening to an old man. And now you're part of this land's future, Dana. We're so happy to have you. Welcome." Hank held up his glass for a final toast as he said this. Everyone responded with a raise of their glass and a drink.

Dana proceeded to ask a dozen questions. Sammy and Kathy enjoyed watching Dana interrogate Hank.

Eventually Mateo came in and announced, "Dessert is ready in the other room, whenever you are."

Kathy replied, "Thank you, Mateo. We could listen to Hank talk all night. I know I could." She smiled and winked. "But we should really go enjoy dessert before it gets too late."

They all agreed and Kathy directed the group back to the less formal sitting room.

As soon as they stepped into the other room, Kathy, Hank, and Sammy cheered in unison, "Surprise! Happy birthday, Dana!"

A cake with lit candles and wrapped gifts were waiting for her.

"How'd you know?" Dana asked with her hands covering her mouth.

"Jake told me," Sammy said. "He was sad to miss your birthday and asked me to make it special. I wanted to say something all day, but thought this might be a better surprise."

"This is wonderful. Thank you. What kind of cake it that? Is that…" Dana asked.

"Your favorite poppy seed cake with custard on top?" Kathy was clearly proud of herself. "Yup, Jake e-mailed me the recipe that he got from your pal Greta. I made it today, *by myself.*"

"You? You never bake." Sammy was impressed.

"Correction, I never *used* to bake. Felicia, our chef here, has me baking in the kitchen with her all the time," Kathy said. "I still don't cook, but I can mix ingredients just fine."

"Thank you so much. I'm overwhelmed. And so many gifts? You shouldn't have," Dana said.

"We didn't do much," Sammy replied. "Some are from your parents and Jake."

Dana looked even more amazed.

"Better blow out the candles before the custard gets it," Kathy instructed.

"Make a wish," Sammy reminded her.

Dana closed her eyes, obviously making a wish to the universe. She opened them and blew out her candles.

They all enjoyed the cake as Dana opened her gifts.

Jake gave her a fancy tablet, the same kind he was so

enamored with. He asked Sammy to buy Dana a nice digital camera for her new adventure; it was a generous gift from their parents. Sammy was given a hefty budget and enjoyed picking out a high-end camera with extra lenses and a nice carrying case.

Dana was touched by her family's generosity, but was blown away by Kathy's. Kathy gave Dana new outfits for her "work in Napa." There were two casual sun dresses, three sexy cocktail dresses, and five pairs of shoes—one for each outfit.

"This is too much," Dana told Kathy. "Thank you so much, but I can't accept them."

"Nonsense, of course you can. Don't be ridiculous," Kathy said casually. "They're just a little something, not nearly as expensive as ya must think they are. Besides, my friend's daughter opened a new boutique in Calistoga and I had to patron her shop, of course. Then she gave me a generous discount on top of it. So really I'm simply stimulatin' our local economy."

"Well, if you put it that way." Dana went to Kathy and gave her a long hug. "Thank you so much. You have no idea," Dana whispered in Kathy's ear.

"Looks like there's one more gift," Kathy replied.

"What in the world?" Dana read the card and looked up at her friend. "Thank you, Sammy." She opened her last gift. It was a pair of butterscotch cowgirl boots, with small swirls of turquoise, hot-pink, and bright orange.

"They're gorgeous. I love them." She hugged her friend and proceeded to try the boots on. "A perfect fit."

"Perfect for trompin' around a vineyard, don't ya think, Kathy?" asked Sammy.

"Agreed," Kathy said with a nod.

"This has been such a fantastic birthday. A few weeks ago, I actually thought this would be the worst birthday ever. But thanks to you three, it'll be up there among my most memorable. Wow, what a wonderful start to a new year. Thank you all so much for everything."

"You're welcome, dear. Now we got to kick you girls outta

here, so Hanky Panky and I can get some rest. I've got big plans for us gals tomorrow. Y'all sleep in and we'll start out when we start out. Breakfast will be ready in the dinin' room whenever you are. So just find Mateo and he'll help ya out."

They said their good nights and Sammy helped Dana carry her birthday haul to the guesthouse.

"This was really too much, Sammy," Dana said as they left the main house.

"Please, I didn't do anything but a little shopping. And seriously, Kathy has plenty of money, so don't feel guilty about her generosity. I'm sure she really did it as a favor to her friend's daughter just like she said; you merely happened to luck out by it. Are you okay with it?"

"Yes, I think you're right. But it was so generous. I imagine she's like that with everyone. Do you think Hank is okay with her spending his money like that?"

"He seems more than okay with their life. Besides"—Sammy's voice dropped to a whisper—"I have a hunch that she has more money than him, although I've never asked her."

"Really?" Dana whispered back, flabbergasted.

"Yeah, you'll have to ask her sometime this summer. And then let me know if I'm right." Sammy opened the door to the guesthouse.

"That was such a cool story Hank told about his family's history here. It was fascinating. It's the kind of story that will stick with me for a long time, ya know?"

Sammy agreed. "It is—it mesmerized me. I wonder how far back he has photographs of this place. I don't know my family history past my grandparents. I wonder how much Aunt Kathy knows."

"Same here. I know where my grandparents were all from, but my knowledge ends there."

Sammy bid her friend more birthday wishes and a good night. There was still so much to talk about, but they were both exhausted and had no idea what Kathy had in store for them the next day. Sammy was staying for another two and a half weeks, plenty of time to talk.

It was much too late for Sammy to call Jake. She was even too tired to dream. She was so happy to be there—with her aunt, Dana, and Jimmy Stewart—that she fell asleep with a smile on her face.

CHAPTER 9

Sammy woke early the next morning to the sun streaming through her window. She called Jake first thing, while she was still tucked in under her covers.

They talked for more than an hour, as Sammy told him all about her and Dana's drive to Napa and about Kathy's house and the guesthouse. She filled him in on all the happy details about Dana's birthday. She hated to hang up, but was eager to start her day.

Sammy found Dana dressed and pouring over the instruction manual to her new camera in the guesthouse den, Dana's office. Dana's new tablet was running, her three big idea binders were unpacked, and her shiny new cowgirl boots were christening her feet.

"You look right at home, Dana," Sammy said as she sat down in the extra chair.

"I *feel* at home," Dana said with girlish excitement. "The lighting in this guesthouse is fantastic. My head is *swarming* with ideas. I can't stand it. I could barely sleep."

"Have you been to the main house yet?" Sammy asked as she spun her chair in a circle.

"No, not yet. I was waiting for you. I read all about my camera and am ready to use it. I have so many exciting ideas. I never knew I had this kind of potential." Dana's excitement was contagious.

"Great! You can tell me about it over breakfast," Sammy said as she headed for the door.

Dana skipped to catch up. The two women gushed about how beautiful everything looked in the early-morning sunlight. They couldn't wait to see what Kathy had planned for them.

"Howdy, girls," Kathy said as they entered the main house.

"Good morning, Aunt Kathy," Sammy said, greeting her aunt with a hug.

"How'd y'all"—Kathy caught herself—"*you girls* sleep last night?"

"I slept like a rock," Sammy answered.

"I couldn't sleep much at all. I have so many ideas rumbling around in my mind," Dana said with enthusiasm.

"That's sounds promisin'. Come tell me all about it," Kathy commanded as they headed to the dining room for breakfast.

There was a buffet set up with scrambled eggs, cheeses, meats, pastries, oatmeal, fruit, juices, three kinds of coffee, and all the fixings.

"Jake told me what your favorite coffee and creamer was, Sammy," Kathy announced with a secretive smile.

"When did he tell you that?" Sammy was confused.

"We've been e-mailin' back-n-forth these last few days, while in cahoots about the birthday surprise. I asked if he knew any particular grocery requests for either y'all.

"He's a keeper," she continued approvingly. "He knew how both y'all took your coffee and some other favorites. What a doll."

Sammy smiled as she recalled how Jake had lovingly prepared his sister's coffee. She almost started to chuckle as she imagined what he would say about him *lovingly* preparing it.

"Is all this food for us?" Dana asked with astonishment.

"No. Sorry, dear, I don't imagine you're *that* hungry. We do this kind of spread every morning for all the estate staff. We have over thirty full-time employees, with usually half here every weekday and twice that many seasonal employees. Hank likes to keep them well fed. And nothin' goes to waste: leftovers are taken home to families."

Kathy nibbled a slice of cheese and then continued—the pride evident in her voice. "We have a kitchen staff that prepares buffet breakfast and lunch every day for anyone who wants to stop in. Some days, we'll have special group dinners if it's harvest time or other such time when everyone works long hours. Hank takes good care of his employees."

Both Sammy and Dana glanced around the room. The dining room appeared to sit about ten people. As if Kathy could read their minds, she swung open two French doors at the end of the dining table. There was a beautiful covered outdoor sitting area with three large dining tables and several smaller intimate tables and a fireplace.

"You girls grab some food and come outside," Kathy instructed as she took a cup of coffee out to a table.

Sammy was the first to join her with her cup of coffee and some scrambled eggs.

"What're you working on?" Sammy asked as she surveyed Kathy's table. There was an opened laptop, a map, a notepad, and three different colored pens. Kathy was scribbling different-colored notes.

"Several things, actually. I made a list of all the stuff I want to do with y'all these next two weeks before you leave. Major work projects can wait until after that. I made some notes about some properties for sale I want to look at this week with *you girls*." She paused and grinned wide. "And I checked the map for some fun Bigfoot country."

"Oh, yay, Bigfoot country," Sammy said with a smile. She felt like a child again. She loved letting go and allowing Kathy to take care of her. It was one of those rare pleasures to let Kathy be Kathy. Sammy could rest her mind and leave the planning behind. She was excited to not have to work on anything the next few weeks except how she was going to get back to Loon Lake.

Dana soon joined them looking intrigued by Kathy's setup. "What's all this?"

"My desk," Kathy said with her hearty laugh. "I like to sit out here in the mornings and plan out my day, week, month, etcetera—whatever needs plannin'. I was just tellin' Sammy that I mapped out some of my favorite Bigfoot spots to take y'all to this week as well as some properties I want to look at."

"Properties?" Dana asked with confusion.

"Yes," Sammy answered for her aunt. "I failed to mention that Aunt Kathy is a real estate mogul." Sammy and Kathy both laughed.

"What?" Dana couldn't tell whether Sammy was serious or not.

"Well, mogul is a bit of a stretch," Kathy said as she sipped her coffee. "But yes, I buy and sell real estate. I was even a flipper several years ago before reality television made it popular. Back then the market was hotter too. But these days are much different."

"And tell her about your and Hank's business partnership." Sammy encouraged her aunt. "This is cool."

"Well, the fellas that worked on the guesthouse and now the courtyard, the construction crew, is one of Hank's own crew. Like he said last night, he started out in construction and always did that along with the winery. He made his living with construction. The winery was his dream. But anyway, when we met, I was doin' real estate and we combined our interests, so to speak." Kathy laughed a suggestive little laugh.

"Ew, Aunt Kathy. Stop. You sound like Kelly."

"Oh, how is Kelly?" Kathy interrupted her story.

Sammy proceeded to tell her about how adorable Maxie was and that she was going to be her godmother and filled her in on Kelly's world.

Dana quietly finished her breakfast, politely waiting to interrupt. "Okay, so please, you were telling me about *one* of Hank's construction crews."

"Oh yes, sorry, dear. Anyway, Hank has his own construction company, and I buy properties. He fixes places up or builds new stuff and we sell 'em," Kathy said casually.

"Wow, that's amazing," Dana said. Sammy could tell Dana became more impressed with Kathy every day.

"So you probably have lots of designers you work with. Will anyone be upset with you for not using them on Escondido?" Dana asked, concerned.

"No, not at all. I do work with several designers, but each project is so unique that I know who to use and who not to use. Escondido has always been my baby, and I hadn't figured out who I wanted to use yet. Nobody seemed right for the job. I'm serious. Y'all were the perfect candidate."

"Are you worried about my capabilities?" Dana asked.

"Nope. Sammy sent me some photos of the cabins ya did and she was convinced that y'all could do this," Kathy said without a hint of concern. "Besides, it's all surface design that can easily be changed later if we need to."

"Well, can I tell you two some of the stuff I was thinking about last night when I was trying to fall asleep?" Dana asked eagerly.

"Please do," Sammy said. Kathy nodded in agreement.

"And don't hesitate to tell me if you think I'm crazy or that I'm off my rocker, but I feel like I'm starting this exciting adventure right now and I want to document the whole thing. I'm not much of a techie, but ever since Jake got his tablet last Christmas I discovered the wonderful world of blogs."

Sammy laughed in response.

"What?" Dana asked, deflated.

"No, no, it's not you. It's just that Kelly's been on me to join the blog world and the social networking revolution. It's become this little joke with us. I know she's right; I just haven't embraced it yet. I know you're on to something, and if you have any questions, talk to Kelly, she's researched a lot of this already."

Kathy nodded in agreement. "Yes. Look here in my inbox. I had my IT guy set up an alert on blogs I enjoy reading. I don't know the techie terms either. There are so many blogs I enjoy: travel, wine, real estate, house flipping. Sammy, you *should* write one. It would be so easy for you. I would love to read yours, Dana."

Sounding more encouraged, Dana continued, "So, I would like to start a blog about this journey. Mostly about decorating the guesthouse, if that's okay with you, Kathy?" She looked at Kathy for approval.

Kathy smiled and nodded with anticipation.

"I'd show all the before and after photos. And then if we do any little projects folks can do on their own, show those too. And of course add anything else exciting around here. I would like to do it professionally, and not really a personal blog about my thoughts and feelings, but only the cool stuff we do at Escondido. Would that be okay?"

"I love the idea!" Kathy exclaimed. "I like the way y'all think, young lady. I know you're goin' to be a fantastic addition around here for certain. And my IT guy can help ya with anything ya need."

"I was so surprised by Jake's and my parents' gifts last night. They gave me the tools to start this journey, and I don't think they even knew it. And you ladies, the gifts you gave me? You gave me beauty and confidence, two things that I desperately needed. I just feel new this morning. Thank you. Thirty-seven feels good."

"Oh, Dana, you're so welcome. Jake actually thought you needed the tablet and camera to start your professional career. He had a plan for you. I know you'll make him and your parents proud," Sammy said.

"Okay girls, nuff business talk. We got all summer for that. Let's get to some fun. Bigfoot country today?" Kathy asked with excitement.

"Bigfoot country today," Sammy and Dana said together.

"Okay, y'all need to pack an overnight bag. We'll be back tomorrow night. I've got to make a few calls and find Hank. I'll meet ya under the portico in an hour." Kathy collected her belongings and headed inside.

Sammy and Dana exchanged excited looks.

***

Six hours later, the threesome found themselves in the dusty parking lot of a Bigfoot museum in Willow Creek, California. Sammy and Dana were as excited as children going to the circus.

A two-story tall Bigfoot statue welcomed them. They took turns taking goofy photos of each other holding its hand. Dana was convinced her photo would be perfect for her blog.

Kathy was greeted by the manager. Apparently, the museum was normally closed on Mondays, but Kathy made a generous donation for a private tour.

The manager showed them several footprint casts and other Bigfoot "evidence." They watched famous video footage of a sighting. The museum was quite convincing. Sammy and Kathy loved all the things they saw and asked dozens of questions. The manager told his own sighting story.

A half hour later, they all climbed back into Kathy's SUV. "I have to admit, it's pretty persuasive stuff," Dana said hesitantly.

"Well, I think so too," said Kathy. "I love the vibe that this museum gives ya. It's all so real…Well, now we're off to see some redwoods. When y'all see these gentle giants, you'll definitely find yourself questioning Bigfoot's existence."

They drove another hour deep into the Humboldt Redwood Forest. There, the women were dwarfed by the giant trees. Sammy climbed on some fallen trees while Dana took more than a hundred photos, enjoying her fancy new camera. The women were silent, almost reverent among the trees.

Sammy was the first to break the tranquil silence. "What do you think, Dana? Do you think some large mammal could live up here among the trees? A large apelike creature?"

"Yeah, I can imagine it," Dana answered. "These trees are so ancient; the things they must've seen. Who am I to say there is no such thing as a Bigfoot?"

"Good 'nuff for me, girls. Back in the car! My friend in Shelter Cove is waitin' for us."

It was a whirlwind of a day, with much time spent on the road. But the women didn't seem to mind. There was always great scenery and even better conversation.

They also had a wonderful picnic packed by Felicia complimented by an assortment of drinks in an accompanying cooler. The only stops they made were for restrooms, gasoline, and, of course, photographs.

Kathy had to make one additional stop at a roadside wood-carving shop, because the carved bears and totem poles out front "spoke" to her. Sammy informed her aunt that the comfy car seats "spoke" to Sammy's butt and Dana agreed, laughing.

Kathy dashed in and out of the shop so quickly Sammy wondered if she had time to find anything. As they drove away, Sammy asked, "Didn't find what you were looking for?"

"Actually, I think I commissioned a piece from the craftsman," Kathy answered vaguely.

"That quickly? What kind of a piece?" Sammy asked.

"I hope so. I think he understood what I wanted. You'll both just have to wait and see. It'll be my secret," Kathy said dreamily as she continued to enjoy the drive.

***

Shortly before sunset, they made it to an inn perched on a cliff overlooking the Pacific Ocean. Inside, Kathy was greeted with hugs by the inn's owners. Introductions were made. Kathy gave them a basket of wine and chatted up a storm.

Sammy and Dana were able to sneak off to their room while Kathy continued to catch up with her friends.

The two insisted on bunking together in a suite overlooking the ocean. The room had two queen-size beds and two lounge chairs on a balcony. It was perfect for their travel-weary bodies. The women collapsed on the balcony lounges and watched the sun disappear into the ocean.

After enjoying dinner with Kathy and her friends, they called it an early night. Back in their room, as they both lay in their beds drifting off to sleep, Sammy mumbled, "I don't know where Kathy gets her energy. I'm exhausted."

"I don't know either. She just goes and goes and goes. I hope I can keep up with her this summer. I'm completely exhausted too, which is a good thing, because I definitely need to sleep tonight."

"Well, good night, then, Dana," Sammy said.

"Sammy? Thank you for all of this. I feel like we're a world away from my old life and I'm actually looking forward to waking up tomorrow. I can admit that there hasn't been many days when I could have said that these last few months."

"We *are* a world away," Sammy said. She felt different too. "And you're welcome. I think I needed it too. I feel a different sense of peace right now. It's been great seeing Kathy and going on this little adventure today. She sure is something. I needed to be reminded of that. Good night."

***

The girls met Kathy and the inn keepers for breakfast the next morning.

"So, girls, I met Linda and Mark here at their inn on New Year's Day, 1999. Hank took me here for our official honeymoon. He was in the middle of a big construction project and couldn't take much time off or go too far away. He took me here and I fell for this place. Y'all just bought it then, didn't ya?"

"Actually, we inherited the inn the summer before from Mark's grandpa. It was pretty run down then, if you recall," Linda reminded her.

"Oh yes, it was a little worse for the wear—a real fixer-upper—but she had beautiful bones. Y'all did an amazing job on her." Kathy beamed. "Hank and I've come here at least twice a year since. It's our own little getaway. And we've become good friends with Linda and Mark." Kathy smiled sweetly at her friends.

"And we are so blessed to know ya, Kath," Linda replied fondly.

"In fact, it was Linda's harebrained idea for me to run a bed-and-breakfast at Hidden Peaks. And Dana, she's agreed to mentor us on any and all aspects of Escondido. Not that you'll need much mentoring with your oodles of experience at Jake's resort."

"Oh, I'm sure we'll have plenty of questions in the next few months. I'm looking forward to your advice," Dana said graciously.

The group enjoyed a lively breakfast filled with talks of Bigfoot, grape harvests, art festivals, and furniture shops. Linda suggested a few new local shops for Kathy to hit on her way home.

The morning got away from them. They said their good-byes and made plans to talk again soon on business matters. The women were heading home, by way of furniture stores and two of Kathy's potential properties.

They quickly found the furniture shop Linda recommended.

"I'm excited to see what it's like to shop with Kathy," Dana whispered as they headed inside.

"It's fun," Sammy whispered back with an ear-to-ear grin.

And it was. Sammy and Dana watched as Kathy practically waltzed through the store. She made comments about everything. Sammy could tell that Dana was taking mental notes of her aunt's tastes.

After taking a complete inventory of the store, Kathy turned to Dana and asked her, "Okay Dana, if y'all could buy only one piece of furniture for Escondido, don't mind the price tag, which one would ya buy?"

Dana furrowed her brow. "Only one? That's tough. There are several unusual pieces in here and nice ones. But if I had to go with only one…" She paused as she surveyed the shop once more.

Dana continued with confidence, "I would go with that gorgeous denim sectional. It's the perfect fit for in front of the fireplace, can sit at least eight comfortably, but it's not too massive. The material is durable and surprisingly soft. It has such a clean look and can adapt with a variety of decor. It would be a nice addition to that room."

Kathy thought for about ten seconds and walked away.

"Did I say something wrong?" Dana asked Sammy in dismay.

"No. I liked the couch too," Sammy answered blankly.

Kathy came back with a saleslady. "I'll take that denim sectional, please. I need it delivered to Napa. Could it be delivered tomorrow?"

"Certainly." The saleslady could not be more agreeable, or pleased with her commission, Sammy thought.

"Good choice, kiddo. I liked that couch too. I wanted it the moment I saw it, but wasn't sure it was the right fit for Escondido. Nice to see we're on the same page." Kathy quickly made the purchase and the three were back in the car traveling along the coastal road.

"Where to next, Kathy?" Sammy asked after about an hour on the road.

"Santa Rosa. There are two properties I want to look at. One's an old horse ranch that just went on the market. I've loved that ranch for about as long as I've loved Hank," Kathy said with a wistful look on her face.

Changing to a more businesslike tone, she continued, "It's pretty beat up and has no vineyards planted on it. It's real range land. We see it every time we leave Shelter Cove. It's never been on the market before. There was one private sale a few years ago. I think they must've foreclosed. It's bank owned now. It'll go quick, I imagine.

"The second property is a hidden gem that looks like the perfect little retreat," Kathy said as her wistful look returned.

The girls eagerly watched out the window for a telling sign of either of the wanted properties.

Within a half hour, Kathy dreamily said, "There she is, up on that ridge." She sounded like a schoolgirl pointing out the handsome quarterback.

Kathy turned off the main road and traveled up the dusty hill. The view was spectacular. But Sammy thought the landscape and vegetation left much to be desired. It was merely pastures and meadows with one small pond.

"A diamond in the rough," Kathy said as though it needed an excuse.

They were met by a real estate agent and shown the entire property, all two-hundred acres. It was prime horse property. The house and buildings, built in the 1970s, were in need of major repairs and remodeling. The sale price was just shy of three million, a real bargain according to Kathy.

Next they stopped at the second property. It was smaller, only eighty-seven acres. But it had a small lake with a dock and boathouse, rather than a pond. It had a fifteen-acre vineyard and a nice little two-bedroom, two-bathroom bungalow. It had been built within the last five years and not in need of a thing. The property was "darlin'," according to Kathy.

The difference in the two properties was this one was less than half the acreage and about twice the price—almost five million.

The girls *oohed* and *ahhed* at each of the properties' attributes and made sure to not say one negative word about either. They could feel it was going to be a difficult decision for Kathy.

Once back on the road, with about an hour's drive home, Kathy was unusually quiet.

"Well, what's it gonna be, Aunt Kathy?" Sammy was dying to know her thoughts.

"Dunno girls. I need to talk to Hank about these. The big property's a mess and I think will have lots of red tape tied nicely to it. But it absolutely breaks my heart to think of a developer snatching it up and developing the heck out of it with a golf course, grocery-mart, and what have you. I want to buy it just to prevent that from happening.

"But that second place, oh how she made my heart go pitter-patter. Did you see that sweet little dock and boathouse? Lordy, I was in love. And the little house, it was such a love shack, wasn't it?"

"Yes, it was," Sammy confirmed. Dana nodded.

"What would you do with them? Buy and sell them?" Sammy was confused. Kathy appeared to be personally invested in these, not just interested in making some money.

"I don't know yet. Like I said, I need to talk to Hank about it," Kathy said distantly.

"Can you afford such properties?" Sammy didn't mean to be rude, but she could always talk money with Kathy. Kathy was the savviest business women she knew.

Kathy laughed. "I think so, and if not, I could take out a loan from that sister of yours, Miss Hollywood herself."

Sammy thought about her sister and imagined she probably had millions stashed away somewhere. She knew Cass always invested in real estate. Sammy wondered how in the world there could be such wealth in her family while she and her other two sisters were so monetarily average.

Over the years, Cass and Aunt Kathy had helped out Sammy, Alex, and Gabby. But only in dire situations. Certainly none of them made a habit of it. Gabby, in fact, had to keep her loans secret from Eddie. He refused to take her family's "handouts" as he called them.

Dana looked like a deer caught in headlights.

"I know, trust me, I know," Sammy whispered.

They finally made it back to Hidden Peaks. The girls were happy to be back at Escondido. That night Kathy and Hank dined out with some friends. Kathy extended the invitation to Sammy and Dana, which they happily declined. The girls were exhausted and wanted to stay in. Again, they wondered where Kathy got all of her energy.

Sammy and Dana ordered pizza from the kitchen—no takeout necessary—and ate on Sammy's bed in the guesthouse.

"What a crazy two days. Don't you think?" Dana asked as she flipped through the photos she downloaded onto her tablet.

"Yeah, fun to see how the other half lives, huh?" Sammy said, looking over Dana's shoulder at her photos. "I never imagined my aunt to be so wealthy or live such an extravagant life. She's so unpretentious. And Hank is like…"

"Jimmy Stewart?" Dana finished Sammy's sentence.

"Yes!" Sammy slapped her knee. "You see it too. Thank you. Yes, he's so down-to-earth." Sammy sat back against the wall.

"I think you're in for a wild ride, Dana," Sammy said as she imagined what the next few months with Kathy would be like.

"I got a hunch you're right," Dana said with a nervous giggle.

CHAPTER 10

The next two weeks were as adventurous as those first few days with Aunt Kathy. She dragged Sammy and Dana along with her everywhere she went. The girls happily obeyed, enjoying every encounter. There were luncheons, wine-tastings, shopping excursions, cocktail parties, and sightseeing trips.

They didn't look at any more potential properties. Kathy appeared to struggle with what to do with each place. She had some ideas, but nothing she would mention out loud.

Hank and his crew showed the girls everything involved in the wine-making process. They took long hikes through the vineyards and watched the men repair trellises, remove the excess foliage, and prepare for summer irrigation.

They even explored the cave cellars that were built long ago by the Chinese laborers.

Sammy began to feel the magical allure of grape-growing and wine-making. She found herself envious of Dana's opportunity to be there for the harvest, or the "crush" as it was called. But her own excitement escalated with each passing day. She couldn't wait to see Jake again.

Sammy made her arrangements to fly to Minneapolis and take a puddle-jumper to Saw Mill's small airport, where Jake would pick her up. She wasn't even going to mess with renting a car right away. Between her road trips with Dana and these last few weeks driving around with Kathy, Sammy was downright tired of driving. She wanted to get to the lake and stay put for a while.

The night before her flight, Sammy, Dana, and Kathy were sitting on the denim sectional enjoying some wine. It was unseasonably cold that night, allowing them to enjoy a fire.

"I'm going to miss you ladies," Sammy said sadly, making a dramatic little frown.

"Aw, I'm gonna miss you too, child," Kathy said as she started to cry. "It's been glorious having y'all here. And don't get me wrong, Dana, I'm pleased as punch you're stayin' on to play with me. But I'm gonna miss my baby." Kathy leaned over and smothered Sammy with a hug.

"I'm gonna miss you, Aunt Kathy." Sammy was openly crying now too.

Emotionally raw as she was, Dana simply joined in on the crying—she couldn't help herself.

"But you're gonna see that handsome fella tomorrow. Don't let him get away," Kathy commanded as she wiped her tears from her eyes.

"I'll try not to. I'm excited to see him," Sammy said wiping away her tears too.

"Well, y'all deserve to be happy and in love," Kathy said.

Sammy and Kathy both noticed Dana tense up and stare into her wine glass.

Kathy gave Dana a pained look. "That goes for you too, Dana. This is how an old gal sees things here. George is a handsome, young man. I repeat: he is *young.*

"He will regret leaving y'all—*leaving you*—someday and in the not-too-distant future. This I'm as sure of as the sun's risin' tomorrow. But y'all cannot wait for that time and you cannot waste any more time on him than y'already have.

"You can choose to be defective, as I know personally that's how ya feel. But by doing so, you give George so much more power than he ever deserves. He deserves nothing more from ya. Y'all deserve so much more in life and you'll find it someday.

"What I wouldn't give to have your young, gorgeous, sexy body. Seriously, do y'all see how my body parts move of their own accord?" Kathy waved her arms in the air, demonstrating how they jiggled. "I have no inkling when that happened. I wouldn't even be able to pick my own bare bottom out of a lineup, that's how much I don't recognize this body."

Sammy let out a small laugh in spite of herself. Dana smiled.

"I'm serious, Dana. Ten years will be gone in a blink of your eye. You have been given the gift to start over while you're young and beautiful. I know it's hard for you to see past this hurt and pain that's consuming you right now, but you will survive if ya choose to."

"I know you're right, Kathy," Dana said. "I feel stronger with every passing day. It still suddenly hits me during random conversations. The truth is I'm worried about being out here in wine lover's country, seeing happy drunk couples falling more in love. But it also feels magical and exciting here. I know I'll be okay. I only hope it's sooner than later."

"Well, I feel much better leaving you here with Kathy's wisdom," Sammy said. "I was a little worried about you staying here all alone. But after seeing how much fun the last two weeks were and how much work you have ahead of you, I feel better now."

"And we're getting started with work right away in the mornin'. We have to have this placed finished by New Year's Eve," Kathy said mysteriously.

"Why? Are you planning to have it opened by then? Or having a party?" Dana asked.

"Well, yes, some sort of party," Kathy said. "Sammy, I'm hoping you, and maybe Jake, and all your sisters and families can come ring in the New Year with Hank and me as we renew our wedding vows." Kathy both asked and announced all at once.

Without skipping a beat, Sammy exclaimed, "Of course we all will! Oh, this makes me so happy. I wouldn't miss it for the world. Now, Jake coming—that's still a mystery. We'll see what happens this summer. But I'll be here for sure." Sammy couldn't imagine a happier occasion.

Dana smiled from ear to ear. "Oh, Kathy, that sounds so romantic. I'll do everything I possibly can to make this New Year's one to remember."

"Wonderful! Now, don't tell the sissies. I want to invite them each personally," Kathy added.

"I won't mention a thing. But you better invite Alex soon. She's been talking about a Costa Rican Christmas already." Sammy rolled her eyes.

"Thanks for the heads up. Now, I better call it a night. Are ya sure you don't mind one of Hank's fellas taking you to the San Fran airport in the morning? I can cancel my meetin' and take ya myself or have Dana take you."

"No, no, no," Sammy insisted. "We've had plenty of time together these last few weeks. You girls need to get to work and Dana should certainly attend your monthly staff meeting. She's one of them now. Besides, I'll see you in October at Cass's and again at New Year's. I'm so excited."

"All right, then, one more hug and we'll say good-bye in the morning." Kathy hugged them both and headed back to the main house.

"Are you sure you're going to be okay?" Sammy asked again, still concerned.

"To be honest, it might be lonely staying in this house by myself. But I was alone in Jake's cabin too. And mentally, I was in such a bad place then. I'm stronger now. I see a brighter future. And I cannot wait to get started on this house. I'm truly excited and thrilled to be here. Thank you for doing this for me, Sammy. I know it never would've happened without you. I will never forget this."

"I'm *really* excited for you too. This place is magical, and I think it'll have a healing power for you. You'll have to stay in touch, everyday. I'm worried I'll be bored out of my gourd at Loon Lake after about a week," Sammy said.

"I'm sure Jake can come up with a project for you. He's good at that," Dana said with a small laugh. "What about writing another novel? Is that a possibility?"

"It is. I have a new idea brewing in my head. I'll keep you posted. I better get to sleep. I have to leave early to get to the airport with plenty of extra time. I'll see you when I get up. Good night."

"I'm sure you'll find me in my office," Dana said with excitement. "G'night."

***

Sammy was looking out the airplane window, trying to count all the lakes scattered across the land below. The turbulence made her stomach do flips, which was already flipping with excitement at seeing Jake in less than an hour.

She loved to fly. She thought of a line in Marc Reisner's *Cadillac Desert* that was something like, if you don't have a window seat on an airplane, you're not getting your money's worth. She read that book more than a decade ago and agreed with that thought so much that it has always stuck with her.

But the bumpy flight made her a little nervous today. She thought of her sister, Cass, and her fear of flying, or rather her fear of crashing. It's a normal fear. Sammy wondered if Cass was ever able to relax and enjoy the view.

Her mind drifted back to the whirlwind adventure her life had become over the past six weeks. She had no idea the last time she landed in Minnesota that she'd drive across the country only to have missed Maxie's birth by less than an hour or that she would drive to her aunt's in California.

She laughed out loud as she recalled their excursions to Bigfoot country. Thoughts of the seaside inn at Shelter Cove filled her with peace.

It was only six weeks ago when Jake called asking Sammy for help. Never intending to whisk Dana to California, Sammy sure hoped that she had done the right thing for Dana. All the pieces seemed to be falling in place.

She wondered what adventures might be in store over the next six weeks. She couldn't imagine, but figured they *had* to be quieter than the last six.

The pilot announced they were landing soon. Sammy was so nervous and excited; she worried that if it was a bumpy landing she might throw up. Lucky for her, the landing was smooth and uneventful.

Sammy saw Jake standing with his back to her in front of the luggage carrousel. Her heart skipped a beat.

As though he felt her there, he turned and looked directly at her.

She was mesmerized. California was a blur. *Dana who*?

She was suddenly consumed with her desire and love for Jake. Somehow, someway, she knew she truly loved this man. And his "welcome home" kiss let her, and everyone else around her, know that he felt the same way.

"Hiya," Sammy said breathlessly.

"Hiya," he said back. "I missed you." He gave her another small, gentle kiss.

"I missed you too."

He collected her bags and said, "Let's get you home."

An excited, girlish smile was her only reply.

On the way back to the lake, Jake stopped at a pizzeria for takeout. It was the same pizzeria he stopped at on their first date last summer, when they went to a drive-in movie.

Her desire for him intensified. She was taken aback by how strong it was. It was almost primal.

When they arrived at the resort, it was already early evening. The resort was quiet, with only a few cabins in use. Sammy was surprised to learn that Vince was staying in one cabin for a few days.

By the time they parked the car, the sexual tension between Sammy and Jake was unbearable. Within minutes they found themselves back in Jake's bed getting reacquainted.

***

"Is it just me, or was that the best ever?" Sammy asked dreamily.

"It wasn't just you. That was amazing. You're amazing. I really missed *you*, not just *this*," he said as though he thought she might assume otherwise.

She smiled at him lovingly. "I missed both too."

"I'm starved. How 'bout you?" he asked.

"I am too." She started to get up.

"No, no. You stay put. I'll be back in a flash. Our special tonight is pizza in bed," he said.

"Sounds perfect." She stayed in bed and watched him go.

With closed eyes, she heard the distant call of a loon. She thought about how happy she was to be back here, with Jake, where she belonged.

Moments later, Jake was back with a warm pizza and cold beers.

"So, what's new around here? How long is Vince sticking around?" They hadn't talked much on the drive back to the lake. They were both too excited.

"He's only here through the weekend. He wants to get back to his mom on Monday. I saw him last week when I went back to visit my folks and Aunt Jeannie. He looked like hell. I convinced him to come here for a few days to refill his soul, so to speak."

"Refill his soul," she repeated. "I *love* that." She loved *him*.

"I think he'll enjoy visiting with you too," Jake added.

"Yes, I look forward to seeing him. I don't know what to say. I'm not very good at condolences," Sammy said.

"His mom's not gone yet," Jake said, almost shocked.

"Yes, but he's been suffering through her whole illness already. I've seen cancer before. It's almost awkward to give condolences after the person passes away. The real pain is in the dying part, watching them go…" Sammy's mind wandered.

"Who did you know that died from cancer?" Jake asked.

"My next door neighbor. She was a wonderful woman and friend. It was five years ago. I only knew her for a few years, but we were good friends. It was hard to watch her *go*," Sammy said, searching for the proper word. "Anyway, I feel for Vince."

There was silence for a moment. Sammy quickly changed the subject. "Anything else new?"

"Not around here, but I talked to Dana this afternoon. Apparently, Kathy got Dana some company?" Jake said mysteriously.

"Company?" Sammy asked.

"Yeah, she got Dana a guard dog, a three-year-old golden lab. Kathy was worried about Dana staying in the guesthouse alone, which Dana said she was too."

"I was worried about her too," Sammy interjected.

"Kathy figured the dog was old enough to not need much attention and would be a good companion for Dana. Her name's Judy."

"The dog's name is Judy?" Sammy asked with a grin. "Judy and Ginger sound like bridge partners rather than dogs. I love it. Was Dana okay with it or happy? Is she even a dog person?"

"Yes, she was very happy with it. She loves dogs. She said Judy's a sweet, quiet dog. Dana asked Kathy what would happen to the dog when she leaves. Kathy told her not to worry, she would always be an Escondido dog unless Dana wanted to take her with her."

"Leave it to Aunt Kathy to think of every little detail. I'm relieved. Last night when I went to sleep, I was slightly concerned about leaving Dana there in that house alone. I feel better knowing she won't be alone tonight. How else did she sound? Dana, that is?"

"She sounded good. Apparently, there was a staff meeting this morning and she met every winery employee. She can't stop talking about how wonderful Kathy and Hank are. She's excited to be there and to help Kathy do something successful with the place."

Jake looked lovingly at Sammy. "Thanks again for doing all that you did for her. You're amazing." He kissed her sweetly.

"It was my pleasure," she said.

"Speaking of pleasure…"

CHAPTER 11

Sammy woke the next morning to the smell of bacon and the sound of laughter coming from Jake's kitchen. She lay there awhile listening to the two cousins reminisce about a time they crashed a boat into the swim dock. Sammy quietly laughed at the story too.

She hated to get out of bed, as she relished eavesdropping on them. But she wanted to join in on their fun.

Shuffling into the kitchen, wrapped in a cozy robe and wearing fuzzy slippers, she said with a grin, "Good morning, fellas."

"Hey, there she is. It's so great to see you, Sammy. And even better to hear you're with this guy," Vince said as he gave Sammy a hug.

Sammy noticed right away that Vince did look different. His twinkle was gone. He was as handsome as ever—maybe even more handsome, looking rugged and worn. But that light that Dana mentioned was gone.

Sammy gave Vince a tight, loving hug back. "Vince, I'm so sorry to hear about your mom. How are you holding up? I know it's an awkward question. How do you answer? 'Not well. I'm sad. It's all miserable.' I'm so sorry." Sammy rambled on as they released their hug.

Vince grinned at her sadly. "You get it. All of the above. I am sad and have been for months now. It is miserable, that's for sure. But I'm spending as much time with my mom as I can and trying to enjoy the everyday stuff. My perspective on a lot of things has changed. I'm maturing, darlin'," he said with a wink.

There he was: the old Vince. Sammy smiled and knew that deep down he would be okay. And she knew he was maturing and growing wise. She could see it all in his eyes. The twinkle may be gone, but it was replaced with something different.

"What's new with you, Sammy? Hear you're working for the witness relocation program. That's cool. What can you do for me?"

Jake chuckled.

Sammy laughed too. "Depends. What do you want to do?"

"I'll let you know when I figure it out."

"Sounds good. I'm sure I can find something for you. Aunt Kathy was shopping for a little property. She'll likely need a caretaker or two if she buys one of those gems," she said.

Sammy told the men all about the *little* properties Kathy was looking at. She continued to dazzle them with stories of Bigfoot country and Napa adventures as they enjoyed their breakfast and coffee.

"So, I hate to do this to you two," Jake said, "but I have to go to town for a meeting. One of my neighbors has a civil suit going and asked me to be a character witness. Vince, would you mind entertaining Sammy a bit this morning? Maybe take her on a boat ride? It's gonna be a nice warm day."

"You trust me with your gorgeous gal?" Vince asked with his boyish charm.

"No, but I trust Sammy won't fall for your bull," Jake said as he gave Sammy a tender smile.

"Touché," Vince said, "I'd love to entertain her. Whatcha say Sam, wanna go for a ride?"

"Yeah, that'd be fun. We never made it out on the lake last month," Sammy said with a funny little look on her face.

Jake smiled back.

Vince caught this silent conversation. "Yeah, I heard all about it. Hubba, hubba," he teased.

"But seriously, I'm gonna go call my mom and we can head out in about an hour. Sound good?" He rinsed his breakfast dishes and put them in the dishwasher.

Sammy silently watched in awe as Vince did this. She was impressed that he didn't leave the dirty dishes in the sink. "Yup, I'll be ready."

"See ya soon," Vince said as he headed out the door.

"I'm sorry I have to leave you two. I know Vince is only here for a few days. But my friend's really counting on me," Jake said.

"No worries." Sammy gave Jake a proper "good morning" kiss. "I'm here for as long as you'll have me this summer, or until I get bored, whichever comes first.

"Plus, it'll be nice to have some one-on-one time with Vince. I was worried that it would be uncomfortable between us because of Alex. It isn't, but I still want to talk about some things with him."

"Good. I'm sure he needs to talk about some of this stuff that's happening with his mom, and needs a good listener, which you're great at. I shouldn't be gone too long. Do you need anything before I go?" Jake cleared the remaining breakfast dishes.

"Nope," Sammy said as she watched Jake clean up the kitchen. She loved watching these grown men clean up after themselves. She could distinctly remember specific meals where her sisters' husbands, especially Gabby's husband, never helped with a thing.

Jake let Ginger in and gave Sammy a lingering good-bye kiss.

Sammy sat and watched his truck drive away from the resort. She was sad to see him leave. The fear of not seeing him again suddenly squeezed the air out of her. *What if he never came back*? She shook her head. She was crazy.

Taking a deep breath and looking out over the lake, she was reminded that it was a beautiful day in late May—the start of summer. She still had months with Jake.

The sky was clear and bright blue. The lake was calm and inviting. It was the perfect combination for a boat ride.

Sammy and Vince headed out on the lake. Sammy sat back happily, with the wind blowing in her face. The memories of past boat rides filled her mind.

She pictured her dad driving the boat while she and her sisters, all quite young, sat in a row, wearing those awful bulky orange life preservers around their little necks.

The memory of running out of gas last summer with Gabby made her laugh out loud.

Vince drove the boat to the end of the lake, where he stopped and tossed the anchor near the bank by a lily pad field. "This is the perfect place to get some sun. Is that okay with you?" Vince handed Sammy a bottle of water and beach towel.

"Thank you. Yes, this is perfect," she said as she stretched out in her seat.

"This is also the spot where a mink family lives," Vince explained. "It'll be fun to watch for the mamas and babies. I've spotted them here the last few years; hopefully, we can see some today."

"Ooh, that would be cool," Sammy said. "Speaking of mama and babies, did Jake tell you about Kelly?"

"Yeah, he mentioned she had a baby girl," Vince said.

"Here's a photo of the two of them." Sammy showed Vince a picture on her phone. She took the photo right before she left Arizona.

"She's adorable. And the baby's pretty cute too," Vince said with his charming drawl.

Sammy laughed. She enjoyed seeing the old Vince sneak out every now and again. "They are both pretty adorable."

"I'm happy for Kelly. Did you know that last summer when I brought her to the lake I picked her up in Minneapolis?" Vince asked.

With raised eyebrows, Sammy answered, "Really? You drove with her for three hours up here? I never knew that. I bet *that* was a fun car ride. What did you think? Isn't she fun?" Her voice revealed her genuine love for her friend.

"She was fun. I liked her a lot. I dunno, it was unusual for me. I felt like we made a real connection. I knew she was married so I had a different angle than I usually do. It was easy to talk to her without the pressure of trying to woo her."

Sammy laughed. "I doubt you feel much pressure to woo a woman. Doesn't that just come naturally to you?"

He laughed. "I try to make it look that way. But it's not always the case," he said honestly. "But I really liked Kelly. She told me about her brothers and a summer camp she went to as a kid." He seemed to drift off into his thoughts.

"She's so open and honest—so easy to talk to," said Sammy. "I still remember the first night I met her at a fundraiser. We talked the night away and became fast friends. But she's enjoying domestic bliss right now. Her baby is so sweet. What about you? You want kids someday?" Sammy figured what the heck, *let's talk*.

He laughed. "You sound like all the women I've dated and my mother. If you would've asked me that last summer, I would have said, 'Probably, someday.' But now, the answer is a definite 'yes.' And soon, I think, which is tricky, seeing as though I've hit a bit of a dry patch." He chuckled again with a hint of embarrassment.

"I assume that's because of your mom—the soon part, not the dry patch," Sammy said with a shy smile. "If you don't want to talk about it, that's okay," she added.

"No, I'm fine talking about it. In fact, I probably need to talk to someone who's removed from the situation. It is because of my mom. Or, at least, my mom's condition." He added that last part awkwardly.

"Over the last few months, I've really reflected on my childhood and growing up. I grew up with Jake and Dana. Even though we're only cousins, we're as close as siblings, even closer than some siblings I know.

"I recently found out from my mom that she miscarried twice before I was born and once after. I was her miracle. She never told me this before. I think learning that information as a youth would have changed my young mind somehow. Isn't that crazy that she never mentioned it before?"

Sammy nodded silently. She felt as though he was really asking himself that question.

"She's told me a lot of things these last few months that I never knew. I guess I always thought we had time *later* to talk about these things," he said sadly.

Sammy's heart was breaking for him as he continued, "But there is no later. We've been talking about the past and future, what was and what will be, all at the same time. It's been gut-wrenching."

"I'm sorry Vince. It must be so painful," she said. "For both of you."

"It is. Anyway, she has me thinking about my future: a wife, kids, maybe a dog someday. I never really pictured it before, because I never met a girl I could settle down with. But now I know I want that. I want that life. I just don't know who the woman is."

Sammy suddenly felt the elephant in the boat. She knew she had to bring it up, she didn't exactly know how. "So, is there anything I need to say about my sister, Alex, or anything you want to say?"

Vince smiled fondly. "There it is. You've been wondering how to bring up Alex, haven't you?"

Sammy nodded.

"There really isn't anything to address, Sammy. Your sister was very mature about the situation. I think, honestly, I was attracted to her recklessness and passion. I knew she was an angry little pistol, and somehow I liked that last summer. She was different from any other woman I had met. Most women I meet try to impress me with fake stuff. It was pretty clear from the beginning that Alex didn't care what people thought of her. I liked that."

"Yeah, that's Alex all right." Sammy agreed with a shake of her head.

"You know, we tried to stay in touch and keep the fires hot, so to speak. But your sister was completely honest with me from the get-go, telling me she had other fires to feed. She was excited about her new job and a new city. I know the allure of Chicago and its fun nightlife. I've been there, done that. I was ready for something different. So we said our good-byes."

Looking off into the distance, he continued. "Shortly after, I found out about my mom and haven't really given your sister much thought—other than I was sort of thankful myself that I wasn't in a new relationship. I needed to give my mom my full attention."

"Okay, then. So what have you been doing with your mom?"

"Watching *General Hospital*," he said with a charming smile on his face.

Sammy laughed; she was genuinely surprised by his answer.

"Is that still on?" she asked, smiling.

"Yup. Rumor is it might be canceled soon, which is causing my mom great despair. I swear she's hanging on just to see the next episode," he said with a wide grin.

Sammy was trying to picture him watching this soap opera with his mom. She absolutely loved the image. "So, do you enjoy watching it?"

"To my surprise, yes, I do. I used to watch it in college; it helped me get the ladies," he said with a wink. "It was always important to know who the hot couple was."

"How Vince of you," Sammy teased.

"Wasn't it?" He smiled guiltily.

"Anyway, my mom's been watching it for, like, forty years. Can you imagine? And they're bringing back lots of old characters. She's really enjoying it. We watch it and talk about it every day. It's fun to escape our 'day in the life of cancer' and just be normal.

"We've also been looking at old photos and going through her stuff. It's been a real bonding experience. It's painful, but nice to be able to experience it with her. She's sad about dying. She actually never talks about it or says the words."

He paused. Sammy didn't know if he was done or if she should say something.

After a moment, he continued. "We never talk about the dying part. I know you never got the chance to say good-bye to your mom. I sometimes wonder if it would have been better if my mom died suddenly of something else and I never got the chance to say good-bye instead of this painful, sad time with her. When I left my mom yesterday, I wondered if it was the last time I would see her."

"Vince, there is no 'better' scenario here. Losing a parent or loved one—regardless of whether you say good-bye or not—is the worst pain ever. I always tell myself, 'At least I never saw my mom or dad suffer.' I've given up that 'what if' scenario a long time ago. It hurts so much no matter how it happens. They aren't with you the next day. Period."

Suddenly, as though Mother Nature wanted to change the subject, a large splash happened about a foot from the boat.

There in the water, close enough to touch, was a mama mink with her baby. The mama appeared to be helping the baby float. They both looked up and blinked at Sammy and Vince as though they were asking "What kind of animals are you two?" Then, with flips of their little tails, they disappeared into the dark water.

"Wow, that was so cool," Sammy whispered with delight.

"I'm happy they're still here," Vince said. "I was hoping you'd see them."

The two sat silently in the boat for a few more minutes, watching and waiting for some sign of the little creatures. The minks never returned.

Sammy didn't know what else to say to Vince. She figured she would give him one last chance to spill his guts. "So Vince, is there anything else you want to tell a stranger before we head back?"

"Sammy, you're no stranger," he said in his charming drawl. "And no, I've said plenty for now. There really isn't anything more to say. But thanks for listening. We should head back and see if Jake's home yet. He said something about a poker game tonight. You interested?"

"Poker? You bet," Sammy said.

"You know how to play?" Vince asked, sounding surprised.

"Of course. Kathy thought that was something any self-respecting woman should know how to play. And surprisingly, it's come in handy a time or two."

"I fall more and more in love with that Aunt Kathy of yours. I need to find myself a Kathy." Vince winked and started the motor. He hoisted the anchor and they headed back to the resort.

***

The night ended with cards and beer. Jake's neighbor Dave came down to make it a foursome. Sammy enjoyed being one of the boys. She silently watched the interaction between Jake and Vince. Jake seemed to look after Vince, engaging him in conversation whenever Vince seemed to drift off. It was as though Jake could read Vince's mind. Jake was always there to help bring Vince back.

***

The next morning Sammy heard Jake get up before sunrise. He and Vince headed out on an early-morning fishing trip. The boys were still gone by the time Sammy out of bed.

She thought that she must be like her Aunt Kathy, referring to these grown men as *boys*. But she couldn't help herself. Each had a boyish charm about him, youthful and fun loving.

The morning was clear and cold. The sun was shining, and the sky was littered with big, white, marshmallow clouds.

Sammy was happy to have some time alone to enjoy her surroundings. Dressed in jeans, her cowgirl boots, and a fuzzy, knee-length sweater—the kind of outfit she could only wear in the Arizona winter—she poured herself a cup of coffee and headed out the door. The cold air greeted her as she stepped outside, reminding her she was up north on a late May morning. It was still early on a Saturday morning. The few guests that had stayed there were clearing out their things and packing up their cars.

Sammy found the old wooden two-person swing that had been standing guard in front of the lodge for as long as she could remember. She sat and gently swung, enjoying her coffee and her thoughts.

She looked out at the lake, out at the dock she'd spent many hours on as a kid and teenager. She wondered how many novels she read on that dock while lying in the sun. She discovered Judy Blume on that dock. Her Danielle Steel phase occurred on that dock.

She thought of all the guests and their novels that dock must have seen over the years. Tens of thousands of books have been read on that dock, she figured. It was here that her own novel was born. She wondered if a second might be born this summer.

As she sat there in silence, a dragonfly landed on the tip of her boot. It was a large one with blue wings. She thought of the article she had written a few months before.

"How many days do you have left to live, little guy?" she asked him in wonder. The question echoed in her mind and she caught her breath. It was the same thing she wondered about Vince's mom. Her eyes and throat stung as she held back tears as she thought of Vince and his sorrow.

She thought of Dana, off on a new exciting adventure. Dana was filled with hope and dreams, and with less despair. "I think Dana's like you too, little guy. She's newly transformed and is living in the moment. She doesn't know what her future has in store. But she's likely going to be experiencing quite a bit these next few months, just like you."

She reached down and tried to touch its delicate wing with her finger. The dragonfly zipped away.

She was so engrossed in her thoughts that she didn't see Jake's boat come in. By the time she looked up, the boys were climbing onto the dock.

She finished her coffee in one big swallow and headed their way.

"Hey there, how was the fishing?" Sammy asked as she reached the dock.

"Lots of fun, and successful," Vince said with a grin.

"For some more than others," Jake added with a crooked smile.

Vince held up three large bass on a stringer. "All mine," he said proudly, as he dropped the stringer in the water.

"Nice," Sammy said, looking at Jake, who shrugged his shoulders and smiled.

"Whatcha been up to this morning?" Jake asked Sammy as the three walked up to the lodge. "It was cold out on the water."

"Just swinging on that wooden swing. Is that the old one Pat used to have?" Sammy was thinking of the old owner who planted his rear end on that swing practically every evening.

"Yup. It's been mended and varnished a million times over, I'm sure. But it's the same one."

"Can you imagine how many asses have sat in that thing?" Vince asked in his unique way.

Jake laughed and put his arm around Vince's neck. "So classy this one."

Sammy shook her head, holding back a smile. "You talk like that in front of your students?"

"Nope, but they do. That must be where I get it." The two men lightly shoved one another away, acting like brothers.

Sammy finally had to laugh.

Since it was Saturday, the rest of the morning and day were going to be busy for Jake. The old guests were setting to leave, and new ones would arrive. All the cabins needed housekeeping and laundry service, while the lawn needed mowing and the common areas needed cleaning. Jake's hired help did most of the work, but there always seemed to be something in need of last minute repair, and Jake had to collect payments from the guests.

The three tried to prepare breakfast before Jake had to get to work. But since the kitchen couldn't quite fit all three, Jake insisted Sammy stay out of the way.

Happy to oblige, she checked her e-mail while the men made breakfast.

"Holy moly, she did it," Sammy said in awe as she read an e-mail and followed an Internet link.

"Who did what?" the cousins asked at the same time.

"Your sister, Dana, started her blog this week. Wow, this is awesome," Sammy said as she read the blog to herself.

"It's called *New Life in Napa* and her first blog post is titled 'From Bigfoot to Big Boobs.'" Sammy laughed wholeheartedly.

"Really?" Jake asked as he set breakfast on the table. "I knew she was pretty jazzed up about sharing her experiences. How cool. Please read it."

"What about big boobs?" Vince asked, again in his unique Vince way, as he refilled their coffees.

Sammy laughed as she thought, *How can Vince pull off saying these things? When he says it, it's charming or funny, whereas, if someone else said it, it wouldn't be so cute.*

She read Dana's blog post to the boys as they all enjoyed their meal. They listened, laughed, and agreed it was a great start to her blog. Sammy marveled at Dana's writing skills—she was genuinely funny. They were all very happy for Dana.

Breakfast was over in a flash, and Sammy shoved Jake out the door, insisting she'd clean up the kitchen. Vince tried to help, but Sammy told him he needed to go clean his fish, which he promised was for their evening meal.

Finding herself alone again, Sammy read Dana's post one more time before clearing the table and cleaning the kitchen. It *was* good and funny. She was so proud of Dana. She could tell Dana was passionate about her project with Aunt Kathy. Sammy looked forward to reading about Dana's adventures.

Sammy quickly cleaned the kitchen. She was dying to call Dana and to catch up with Kelly.

***

Sammy and the men didn't sit down together until later that evening. Vince built a bonfire on the beach and got the grill going. The day never warmed up, and the bonfire was the perfect ending to the cold day. The three sat around the flames, enjoying some beers and talking about their day. Sammy had the most interesting news.

"So, I called Dana this morning to tell her how much I loved her blog and how we all thought it was funny and great. Aunt Kathy has given her free reign of Escondido, and Dana sounded over the moon. But the most interesting thing she told me was about Kathy's property hunt. Remember how I told you about those two properties she loved and couldn't decide between?"

Both men nodded. "Yeah, which one did she pick?" Jake asked.

"She's buying *both*," Sammy said, incredulously.

"Both?" Jake asked. "Isn't that like over eight million dollars? She has that kind of dough?"

Vince whistled. "Like I said yesterday, I fall more and more in love with that Aunt Kathy of yours. I need to find myself a Kathy."

"I know. I was as shocked as you guys. I knew she had cash, but I never imagined cash of this magnitude. I don't know—maybe she's financing most of it or borrowing some from Cass. But regardless, she's scooping up acreage like a foreigner," Sammy said.

The men laughed. "What's she going to do with both places?" Vince asked.

"I have no idea. I didn't know what she was going to do with *one* place," Sammy answered, the confusion showing on her grinning face.

"I guess we need to keep reading Dana's blog to find out," Jake added.

"Maybe," Sammy said.

Vince chimed in next. "Speaking of property, Jake, I went down to Old Man Brink's cabin today. Asked him if he was interested in selling."

Jake seemed genuinely shocked. "Really? Was he there? What'd he say?"

"He was there. Said he wants to move back to St. Paul, be closer to kids and grandkids. We talked about my mom. Told him how I wanted to own his cabin ever since I was a young kid coming here. He said to make him an offer he can't refuse."

Sammy watched this conversation as if she were watching two dogs speaking English. How in the world do these people casually decide to buy property?

Her eccentric Aunt Kathy was one thing, and Jake, he had a pretty good plan in place. But Sammy couldn't figure out what Vince was thinking. *What would a young, single guy who lived several states away want with a rundown fishing cabin in the woods? Granted, Loon Lake was beautiful and serene, but it seemed pretty extreme.*

"And? Are you?" Jake asked impatiently.

Vince stretched out his long legs and finished his beer. "I think I might."

"What would you do with the place? It needs a lot of work." Jake sounded worried.

"I've been thinking about it for a few months. I would fix it up a bit—okay, *a lot.* But I got time," Vince said distantly.

There it was. Sammy knew what Vince wasn't saying. He had time; his mom didn't. He was facing his own mortality. She knew how that felt. He was faced with the rest of his life and wanted to act on it. She got it. Jake wasn't quite privy to those feelings.

"Which cabin is it?" Sammy asked, looking down the beach at some.

"You can't see the cabin from here. But you can see the

beach and property. Look around the corner there." Vince pointed toward the bend of the shore.

"You can see the beach there and it has an old, unstable fishing dock. It needs to be replaced in order to dock a boat or two. You can only see the cabin from the water, or if we walked down the road. I'll take ya down there tomorrow if you want, Sammy." Vince had a twinkle in his eye.

"Oh yes, I want to see it. I can't remember what cabins are down that way. Why did you want that cabin since you were a kid?"

"Honestly, it was because of one morning in particular. It was an early morning, I was probably about eight years old. My dad and I canoed all over this end of the lake. We quietly followed the shoreline there and just as we rounded the group of trees to the open beach…" He paused for effect and reached for a new beer.

Cracking open his beer, he continued. "We saw a mama deer and two fawns climbing out of the water. We were only about ten yards from them. There was a reed bed that hid them from view until we were that close. They walked straight from the lake to the front door of the cabin.

"They looked at us in the canoe, twitching their ears and blinking their big brown eyes. It was by far the coolest thing I'd ever seen. From then on, I thought that would be the *coolest* place to live, in a cabin like that, with deer at your beach and front door. It was awesome." Vince finished his story with a grin.

"Wow, Vince. That's a great story. I thought you were going to say something like you had your first kiss on that dock." Sammy teased him.

"Yeah, well, that happened too. She was a sucker for the deer story also," Vince said victoriously.

Jake burst out laughing. Sammy smiled and shook her head. She loved these men.

Vince proceeded to grill the fish and some veggies. They all ate around the bonfire while discussing what kind of an offer Old Man Brink couldn't refuse.

***

Later that evening, Sammy and Jake were finally alone on his screened-in deck.

"I'm not sure what Vince is thinking about buying this cabin up here. I'm worried he's acting on emotion," Jake confided.

"I'm worried too. I know he must be struggling with his own mortality. It happens in his situation, you know. Maybe he sees how happy you are up here and he wants to be happy here with you," Sammy said.

She quickly reasoned, "He's a teacher with the summers off. He would have time in the summers to spend up here. He could make it work.

"Does he have money to buy a second home? They must pay teachers much better in Ohio than Arizona. I thought Alex mentioned he owned a condo in Cincinnati. Is that right?"

"Yes, he has a condo there. And he can afford to buy that cabin. He used to model and often works construction in the summers. He saves all his money. So he should have plenty of cash."

"He used to model? Like, clothes?" Sammy was surprised.

Jake laughed. "Yes, like, clothes. What'd you think? Underwear? Aunt Jeannie wouldn't let him." Jake laughed again.

"No, I didn't know what to think. He's never said anything or acts like it. And that's hilarious about his mom. How cute," Sammy said.

"Yeah, he'd probably kill me if he knew I told you. He never ever tells anyone. He would always tell his friends he had to go to the mall instead of a 'shoot.' He was approached by a modeling agency when he was, like, fourteen, and he thought it was a joke.

"But his mom called the contact on the business card, and it was legit. Once he found out he could buy his own car and pay his way through college, he kept doing it and modeled until he graduated college. Anyway, don't tell him you know, please?"

Sammy smiled. "I won't say anything. I think it's cool you or Dana never mentioned it either."

"Don't think I didn't tease him endlessly as teenagers and into our twenties. But when I discovered how much money he was making, it wasn't funny anymore. He got the last laugh," Jake said fondly.

Returning to the cabin conversation, Jake said, "But what really worries me was something he said this afternoon. When Vince was helping me clean the fish house, he casually said he might quit teaching and run a fishing shack."

"That does sound pretty extreme. What did you say?" Sammy asked.

"I didn't know what to say. I think I said, 'Oh, that'd be cool.' I wanted to show support. I didn't really think he was serious. I thought maybe he was just sort of day dreaming. But after tonight by the bonfire, I think he really wants to do it."

"I think he wants to do it too. What's a 'fishing shack?' What does that mean?" Sammy wondered if this was a common practice on lakes.

"I'm not sure what he means by that either. He's right about one thing, that place is a shack. It would need a ton of work. Maybe tomorrow, when he takes you to see it, you can find out more information?"

"Yeah, I can try. You don't want to see it?"

"I know what it looks like. I think it would be good for you two to talk freely without me around. I think he'll open up more to you on your own."

"Okay, I'll investigate for you," she said.

He kissed her gently. It was a less passionate evening for the lovebirds. They cuddled quietly on the deck and simply said what came to mind.

"It's so weird how last summer, you and your family were all so happy-go-lucky. I thought you, Dana, and Vince hadn't a care in the world. And here I was with my freaky family with our drama and secrets. And now this summer, my family is easy-breezy, happy and no drama, while your family is a mess of emotions. Isn't that ironic?"

"It is. It just shows you that everyone has troubles, no matter how big or small, and we all have our ups and downs. You can't judge people until you know what hard time they're going through or went through, you know?

"One thing I've learned running a resort is to never assume anything about anyone. The guests are on vacation here, from work maybe, but they all tend to bring their worries with them. Anyway, I wish both our families were happy this summer. Maybe next summer…" Jake said.

"Maybe," Sammy said. She liked the idea of having a next summer with him.

***

The next morning, Vince came by to take Sammy to his potential cabin. He'd made arrangements with Old Man Brink to have another look around inside. Sammy was excited to see the place.

"Now, remember," Vince said, "it's a fixer-upper. It's not going to be as pretty as Dana made Jake's cabins. But the potential is there. The property is pie shaped too. The lakefront beach is the tip of the pie and the property flares out as you go deeper into the forest. It's about fourteen acres total, I think."

Sammy could hear the excitement in Vince's voice. She knew he needed to be excited about something. He needed something to hold on to.

Vince walked Sammy down to the beach. From there they had a good view of Jake's resort. The beach was nice: it had clean sand and the lakefront there was a wide, shallow bank. It was a lovely spot, and Sammy said as much.

She was a little wary of stepping onto the old dock. But it seemed to be sturdy enough for the two to walk on.

From the dock, the cabin didn't look too bad. But as they approached it, Sammy could see how worn everything was, from the mossy roof to the torn screens. Jake was right: it was going to need a lot of work.

Mr. Brink met them at the door and let them in. It was a small open cabin. The main room was the sitting room and dining room with an open kitchen in the back. It had a beautiful old stone fireplace. There were two bedrooms and a bathroom in the back. That was it.

Two outer buildings, a large storage shed and a garage, were included with the property. There was also a screened-in gazebo where Mr. Brink left the two to talk in private.

"Well, what do you think?" Vince asked excitedly.

"I like it. As Aunt Kathy says, it's a diamond in the rough," Sammy said.

"Yeah, it needs a lot of work," Vince admitted.

"So if you get this place, Jake said you mentioned something about giving up teaching to run a fishing shack, is that what you called it? Are you sure about this?" Sammy prodded gently in a concerned tone. She didn't want to sound unsupportive.

"Yes, I need to give up teaching for now. Something inside me has changed. I'm not excited about that anymore, and believe me: a teacher needs to be excited for these kids in order to survive the school year. And more importantly, the kids *deserve* teachers who are excited. I can't do it anymore." Vince sounded tired and frustrated.

"Okay, I get that. But what's this plan of a fishing shack?" Sammy asked hesitantly. She didn't want to hurt his feelings, but she didn't understand his thinking, at least not yet.

"Okay, fishing shack is a bit rustic of a term. But I had an idea as I've been watching my mom slip away. She's spent the last few months literally stuck in her own home, mostly in her own bedroom. She's content there, but I know she's wanted to be out and about.

"I know she would give anything to be here at Loon Lake one last time or on her favorite street in Paris. She loves Paris and went several times in her life…

"Anyway, her condition got me thinking. I would like to

run this cabin as a sort of summer camp for old folks. That's not a very glamorous term either, but I can think of another name for it later.

"I'm sure I can find some residents in retirement homes that would love to spend a few summer months up here on the lake, fishing, relaxing, thinking about past loves, playing cards, and in general just shooting the breeze. I want to try at least.

"It would be different from Jake's resort, obviously, as I plan to renovate the cabin to have four guest suites with small attached bathrooms and sitting areas. It will be a big construction job, but not too difficult. I want to expand the kitchen and great room and add two master suites upstairs."

"Sounds like you have it all figured out," Sammy said cautiously. "And it sounds pretty fantastic for the guests that will stay here. But how in the world do you plan to meet the woman of your dreams? You think you'll meet her here?" Sammy worried about Vince and his future happiness.

"Jake met you here, didn't he?"

Whoa. That got her attention. She never thought of herself as the woman of anyone's dreams. But she liked it.

"Good point," she conceded. "We did meet here, and chances are good you'll meet someone here too, I suppose. Any single granddaughters or daughters of the old geezers who stay here will likely fall for you hook, line, and sinker. Okay, you have my blessing here, Vince, not that you need it, but I see your vision. It sounds possible, and I hope you can make it work."

"Thanks for looking out for me. I'll be the first to admit I may be in way over my head here. But it's something I feel strongly about—in my bones. I've thought about it a million times these last few months. I've even talked to my mom about it a couple of times. She thinks it sounds like a good idea.

"There are plenty of logistics for me to figure out and a lot of work ahead of me. But I'm ready to reinvent myself and put myself to the test. This is a shaky time for the world: lots of folks have to reinvent themselves, start new careers. It's a good time for me to be brave and go for it." He smiled and winked.

There it was again: a flash of the old Vince. Sammy sure liked seeing him surface. "So what's the next step?" She wondered out loud.

"I'm heading back to my parents' tomorrow morning. A pal of Jake's is running some comps for sales in the area. I'll likely have my realtor give him an offer by the end of the week." Vince said this all matter-of-factly.

"Okay, then," Sammy said with a smile, "easy as that." She admired these guys, who acted on their hunches.

As Sammy watched Vince say good-bye to Mr. Brink, she couldn't help think that in a way, Vince's story was beginning to sound somewhat similar to Hank's. They both fell in love with their land at young ages and felt it in their bones. Heartbreak led them both to new lives. *One of these days, Vince might just get his own Kathy after all*, Sammy thought.

***

Sammy and Jake enjoyed Vince's company one last day before he headed home. Sammy thought that Jake was right: Vince did refill his soul.

Somehow Sammy felt like she was refilling hers a little too. Being with Jake and watching him take care of his cousin, made her know Jake more and love him more. He was a good man.

Vince left the following morning, Memorial Day, the unofficial kick-off to summer. As Sammy and Jake waved good-bye to Vince while he drove off, Sammy thought of all the happy school kids out for summer vacation, if not today then within a week or two. She thought of all the swimming pools opening for the summer; of all the friends that who were saying, "Good-bye, see you next fall."

She was sad for Vince, for what was in store for him this summer.

But, she was excited for her and Jake, excited to be alone and in love. She deserved this summer; she wanted to make the most of it.

CHAPTER 12

The next several weeks flew by. The weekly change of guests made life more interesting than Sammy expected.

Last summer Sammy and her sisters mostly kept to themselves, only interacting with Jake and his family.

This summer, with much free time on her hands, she enjoyed talking to all the guests and learning their histories with the lake and the resort. Many families had been coming for decades.

She spent time with the fishermen talking about what kind of fish they caught, where, and with what kind of bait. She took photos of the fishermen and women with their prize catches and created a new photo collage in the lodge.

She was also fascinated with what kinds of books the guests were reading. None of the cabins had a television, so the guests, at least the older ones, still read for entertainment. Most of the young kids were plugged into their numerous games and gadgets.

She secretly started a scrapbook for Jake, by taking photos of everyone, pasting them in the book, and having folks sign it or write Jake a message. It was going to be a surprise for him at the end of summer.

Down-the-Road Dave, as Sammy jokingly called him (since that's what Jake said every time he mentioned Dave's name), and his teenage sons took Jake and Sammy water-skiing several times. Sammy hadn't water-skied since the last summer she was at Loon Lake with her parents. To say she was a bit rusty was quite an understatement. But it was a skill she still had and enjoyed. She didn't even mind the pain she felt in every muscle of her body following the first several days of skiing.

Sammy and Jake enjoyed a "hotter than usual June." Sammy playfully reminded Jake that he'd said the same thing last year. They swam and fished, and skinny-dipped at night. It was a wonderfully self-indulgent few weeks. The guests arrived and the guests departed. There were problems that popped up, but nothing Jake couldn't handle. It was a fairly smooth month. It allowed the two to fall more and more deeply in love.

***

They were soaking in Jake's hot tub on a Sunday night, four weeks after Vince left. Both were lost in thought.

"I'm afraid Aunt Jeannie won't make it much longer. I'm actually surprised she's held on this long," Jake said.

"I'm amazed too," Sammy admitted. "I'm thankful that Vince has had this time with her, though. I've actually been surprised that it's been so calm around here these last few weeks. Everyone's been great, your sister is happy, nothing's gone wrong. It makes me worry that we're in for something big."

"I wish I could tell you, 'you're nuts,' but I feel the same way, like it's the calm before the storm," he said as he checked her fingertips for pruning. "We still have some more time to soak, I see."

"Yes, I don't want to leave this hot tub…ever," she said, closing her eyes and sinking a little deeper. "It's so relaxing. I feel it in my bones even."

"I know. It feels great. Hey, I have a favor I want to ask you. I thought of it today when I was rummaging through the old desk in the lodge. I know you've been keeping yourself busy with things around here. But I wondered if you wouldn't mind working on a book for me."

"What kind of book?" Sammy was instantly curious, worried that he knew about her secret scrapbook.

"A book about the resort. I know it was started as a logging camp in the early 1900s, and I have several photos of it through the years. But I don't have anything that captures the whole history. It would only be for me, of course—nothing for the public or advertising. There's just stuff I don't know about the place and thought you, being the reporter and writer that you are, could probably find out for me."

"Of course. I would love to," Sammy said with a laugh.

"Why are you laughing?"

"Your sister said you'd have a project for me, to keep me busy."

"I'm sorry—I didn't think of it as busy work. I only thought about it today. Actually, there have been many times that I wished I had more info on the place. But this *project* wasn't intentional. I simply thought you might enjoy it."

"No, no"—she kissed him gently on his blushed cheek—"I would love to do this project for you. I've been getting a little antsy. There's a new novel I want to work on, but the timing's not right. This little project would be perfect."

"A new novel? About what? Can you tell me?" Jake asked.

"I'd rather not. It's still brewing," she said. She noticed he looked disappointed. "I'll tell you about it as soon as it comes together."

"Good. Let's get out of here before we shrivel up. Do you want to see some of the photos I have on the place?" he asked excitedly.

"Yeah, I do." She was suddenly very interested in her new project. She never knew the resort started out as a logging camp. Her curiosity was piqued.

Once they were dressed and back in the lodge, Jake brought them some wine and dragged out a box of old photos, letters, and newspaper clipping, mostly copies of the previous owners' originals.

Sammy and Jake poured over the items, reading bits and pieces out loud to each other, handing each other photos to look at.

Sammy was suddenly struck by a photo of her parents in the box. Her parents' happy faces stared at her. Her dad was proudly holding up a large fish. Her mom was pregnant.

There was no year on the photo. Sammy wondered who was in that belly. She couldn't hold back the tears.

Jake leaned over to see what she was looking at. "You okay?" he asked.

"Yes, I'm just surprised to see them here. But it's cool to see that they're still a part of the resort's history," she said as she wiped the tears from her eyes.

He looked at her lovingly and smiled.

"What?" she asked.

"I'm surprised to see *you* here too. But it's cool to see you'll be a part of the resort's *future*," he said.

"Oh, really, how's that?" she asked.

"I'm not sure yet," he answered with a smile.

They continued to sift through Jake's treasure box, finding all kinds of goodies about the resort and Loon Lake.

They stayed up late talking about their own histories with the resort and laughed about the more recent events. It was a special place, indeed.

Sammy enjoyed learning the histories that all the other guests had with the place. She wondered if she could capture all this information and nostalgia in one book.

Sammy went to sleep that night thinking that with each passing day, her connection to Jake was getting deeper. It was the kind of relationship she never imagined would happen to her. She was happy. Something was certainly going to go wrong.

***

The next day was another scorcher. Sammy had spent the majority of the day floating on a raft on the lake with Jake and most of the other guests.

Heat records broke across the country, and Loon Lake was no exception.

The thermometer hanging outside the lodge read ninety-five degrees at 5 p.m. Sammy lightly tapped the plastic cover, as though she could magically make the temperature drop ten degrees.

Having just gotten off the phone with Jake, who was in town looking for more fans for the cabins, Sammy sat on the wooden swing, gently swinging and fanning herself with a magazine. It was hotter inside the lodge and cabins than it was outside.

She closed her eyes and wondered what Dana was working on this Monday afternoon.

She heard a car pull up and opened her eyes. It was a dirty maroon minivan that looked oddly familiar. Sammy didn't think it belonged to any of the guests.

It stopped in front of the lodge. Jake hadn't mentioned someone was coming, so she hadn't been expecting anyone.

She watched as a woman appeared from the other side of the van. She knew the moment she saw the woman that is was her younger sister, Gabby. Sammy was on her feet in a second, and she greeted Gabby with a hug.

"Gabby, what in the world are you doing here? What a wonderful surprise," she exclaimed as she hugged her sister tightly.

"Oh, Sammy," was all that Gabby could whisper. She erupted in tears while still in Sammy's embrace.

"What is *wrong*?" Sammy asked and felt a horrible tightness in her throat. She heard it in Gabby's voice: something terrible had happened.

Gabby limply let go of Sammy and took off her sunglasses.

It was then that Sammy noticed Gabby's eyes were glazed over, swollen, and red.

"What is it? What's wrong?" Sammy asked as she led Gabby to the swing.

Sammy thought the worst—something has happened to Cass or her babies or Alex. But then it dawned on Sammy that the minivan was Gabby's. Gabby had driven from Denver, *more than twenty hours*, to see her.

"What is it? Eddie? The boys? Gabby, you're scaring the hell out of me. What's happened? Where are the boys?" Sammy was shaking Gabby gently by the shoulders.

Gabby sobbed. The dam broke and the floodwaters gushed. Sammy couldn't stop Gabby from crying. She helped Gabby stumble into her bedroom in Jake's lodge.

Gabby collapsed on the bed, sobbing.

Sammy had no idea what was wrong, but knew it was bad, very bad. She went to get Gabby a glass of water. When she came back in, Gabby had finally stopped crying.

Gabby sat up, looked at Sammy, and attempted a smile. "I'm sorry. I'm so exhausted right now. I'm sorry I'm intruding on your time with Jake, but I didn't know where to go. I got in my car and just drove and found myself driving here.

"I've been driving for twenty hours straight. I haven't slept since yesterday morning. That's probably why I'm crying so hard. I somehow can't stop." She began crying again.

"Here, drink this," Sammy said as she handed Gabby the water. "Can you please tell me what happened?" Sammy pleaded, but she somehow already knew. It was Eddie.

"Saturday morning Eddie and I took the boys to summer camp for the next three weeks. It was especially exciting because it's the first time all three boys were going for overnight camp—and for three weeks. They were so excited to be there for the ghost stories on Friday the thirteenth." She took a long swallow of water.

"After dropping them off, Eddie and I spent the day in the mountains. Colorado this time of year is so beautiful. We had a lovely, romantic night together Saturday night, with the boys all out of the house. We even had sex for the first time in ages." Gabby sounded sad and angry at the same time.

"Eddie left yesterday morning. He went to Seattle for a business trip. Or at least that's what he told me." Gabby was sounding angrier now.

She continued. "There's this new restaurant that recently opened in town that I wanted to try. I was going to do takeout and relax with a bubble bath and good book—ya know, take advantage of having the house all to myself. That *never* happens.

"So last night I went to the restaurant, sat at the bar. I was feeling good and happy. I ordered a drink and placed my food order. As I sat there enjoying my drink, I saw Eddie at a table with another woman.

"At first, I thought that it wasn't Eddie, only a dead ringer. Then it sunk in that it was Eddie. As my mind was processing it all—that he lied to me and was with this woman—she leaned over and kissed him right there at the table. Not just a little kiss either; she stuck her frickin' tongue down his throat." She spat the words out.

"I practically threw up right there at the bar. The bar started to spin; I couldn't breathe. I left some cash on the bar and stumbled out of the restaurant. I somehow got to my car and couldn't stop crying." She took a deep breath, trying not to break out in fresh tears.

"Not Eddie," Sammy whispered, shaking her head as she held Gabby's hand and rubbed her shoulder.

"I got in the car and started driving. I never stopped, except for gas and coffee," Gabby said with a pause.

She gave Sammy a pained look. "I didn't know where to go. My only thought was 'Sammy can make this better.' I don't know how, but I already feel better being here with you."

"Oh, Gabby, I'm so glad you're here. Although I wish you didn't drive straight through the night. That's so dangerous," Sammy said, counting her blessings. "You must be exhausted. Do you want to sleep? Are you hungry?"

"I don't know what I need." Gabby sounding defeated.

"Well, I do. I'll be right back."

Sammy walked out the bedroom door.

Moments later she came back with a bowl of cold, crisp pasta salad. She'd made it earlier in the heat of the day to be a nice cool dinner for her and Jake. She'd also brought Gabby another tall ice water and a short glass of Chardonnay.

She sat in silence and watched Gabby force down the food and drinks. When Gabby was finished, Sammy gave her a new toothbrush that Sammy kept as an emergency backup and told her to take a shower. Gabby quietly did as commanded. She was in a trance, both from a broken heart and exhaustion.

While Gabby showered, Sammy moved the minivan. Looking around inside the van, Sammy saw there was nothing to bring in except a tiny little handbag. Gabby had no clothes, makeup, or toiletries. It was obvious she didn't plan to leave home. After moving the minivan to the parking lot, Sammy hurried back to the lodge to find Gabby still in the shower.

Sammy dug out some of her clothes that she knew would fit Gabby. Gabby was slightly shorter and thinner than Sammy, but in lightweight summer clothes it hardly mattered. She placed them in the bathroom while Gabby continued to shower.

Sammy suddenly worried that Gabby passed out.

"You okay in there?" she asked.

"Yeah. Be out in a minute," Gabby answered.

Sammy waited on her bed as she heard the shower stop and Gabby shuffle around in the bathroom. Sammy was not expecting this—not Gabby. As the reality of Gabby's situation sunk in, Sammy suddenly wanted to strangle Eddie.

"I feel much better," Gabby said as she tottered out of the bathroom. "Thanks Sammy."

"I want you to sleep now. Okay? Sleep as long as you need to. We'll talk when you wake up. The boys are still at camp, right? No one's expecting you?" Sammy wondered if anyone knew where Gabby was.

"Yes, they're fine," Gabby said as she climbed into Sammy's bed. The bedroom was still hot, but Gabby snuggled under the cool sheets. As Gabby began to drowse off, she mumbled, "Everything's fine." She was asleep almost instantly.

"Everything's fine," Sammy quietly repeated as she shut her bedroom door. "You always say that, Gabby."

Gabby always kept things together. She took care of her boys and Eddie and rarely complained. Sammy remembered Gabby complaining a bit last summer, but not really *complaining*, rather longing for something new for herself. And apparently, Eddie wanted something or *someone* new for himself. Sammy's anger grew again.

She didn't know what to do. She didn't know the details, so wasn't about to call her sisters or Aunt Kathy. She needed to wait until Gabby woke up and could tell her the whole story. She wished Jake would get home soon.

It seemed like forever that Sammy paced around the lodge waiting for Jake to get back. Then she heard his truck. Moments later he came in the door carrying two large boxes.

"Whose minivan's in the parking lot?" Jake asked as he noticed Sammy's ashen face. He put down the boxes and went to her. "What's wrong?" he asked with growing concern.

"It's Gabby's van. She's sleeping in my room," Sammy whispered.

"Why is she here?" Jake asked, unable to hide his surprise. "Is everything okay?"

"No. Apparently, Eddie took a lesson out of George's book and is having an affair," Sammy said accusingly.

Shaking her head, she continued, "At least that's what it sounds like. I don't know the details yet. She saw him kiss another woman last night at a restaurant and got in her car and drove straight here, *through the night.*"

As the words sunk in, Jake grew upset. "That shit. What's with these guys? They got a great thing and mess it all up. I'm sorry. You okay?"

"Yeah, I'm just confused and worried. I don't know what to do for Gabby. She'll probably sleep until tomorrow." Sammy felt a heavy weight on her shoulders.

"I would think she needs to. I'm sorry, but I have to get these fans out and set up in all the cabins. And since there isn't anything you can do for Gabby while she sleeps, you want to help me? Get your mind off Gabby for a few minutes?"

"Yes, I do. Let me leave Gabby a note in case she wakes up and then I'll unpack those two fans. You have more?"

"Yeah, they're right outside. I'll bring them in." He gently kissed her forehead and headed back out.

Sammy and Jake unpacked and delivered fans to every cabin. Sammy felt like Santa delivering toys to all the happy little campers. It was a good distraction, but she couldn't help worrying about Gabby the whole time.

Sammy checked back in on her before heading to the waste transfer station to drop off the fan boxes in the recycling center.

"She's still out," Sammy said as she climbed in Jake's truck.

They sat in silence for the first few minutes of the drive. Then Sammy broke the silence.

"So when did they quit calling it the 'dump'?" she asked. She wanted to talk about something frivolous and silly, to keep from worrying about Gabby.

Jake laughed. "Well, I still call it that. But it was cleaned up and changed years ago, probably right after your family stopped coming. Did you guys ever come here to see the bears?"

"Of course. Didn't everyone?"

She was suddenly blasted with an old memory and let out a laugh. "One time when we were really young, my parents took us to the dump. We all were given a Twinkie as a special treat to eat as we watched the bears. Alex decided to roll down the window—I remember everyone was so surprised because it was one of those old, crank-down windows and we had no idea she was strong enough to do that.

"Anyway, she rolled it down and threw part of her Twinkie out the car window to feed the bear that was there. Well the cream filling of the Twinkie made it stick to the side of the car door and this bear saw it and started running for the Twinkie *and the door.* Alex couldn't crank up the window fast enough, so Cass of course had to shove her way across the seat to do it. All of us girls were screaming as the bear was charging toward us." Sammy started laughing.

"My mom was freaking out, and my dad was yelling at all of us to be quiet. Cassy finally got the window up, right as the bear pounced on the car door. Oh, that was so exciting." Sammy was smiling from ear to ear. "It gets funnier and funnier each time I think of it," she said with a twinkle in her eye.

Jake laughed. "What I wouldn't give to have seen that. Look at you now, telling that story." He looked lovingly at her. "You look so happy—and twenty years younger. I swear you do," he said as he touched her cheek.

"That memory makes me feel happy and younger," she said as tears welled up in her eyes.

"Hey, hey, no tears, not even happy ones, okay?" He quickly tried to distract her. "An occasional bear still shows up at the dump once in awhile looking for food."

"Really? That would be fun to see. Too bad we don't have any Twinkies. I remember a three-legged bear there. Do you?"

"I do remember it. The locals called him Trey," Jake said with a smile.

"Listen to you, passing on the local folk lore. I love it," she said. "I didn't know it had a name. That's cool. Remind me to tell Gabby." Just saying Gabby's name made Sammy worry about her sister again.

Jake tried to reassure Sammy. "She's going to be okay, you know. Look at Dana. She's on her way to healing and a new future."

"Yeah, but Gabby and Eddie have three kids. If they separate, it's going to be terrible for them all," Sammy said sadly.

Jake pulled into the station. "You be on the lookout for bears, will ya?" he said as he hopped out of his truck.

"You bet," Sammy said enthusiastically. She knew they wouldn't see any bears, but the possibility of seeing one still filled her with excitement.

Jake quickly tossed the boxes into the recycling container and got back in the truck. The sun was setting as they headed back to the resort. They drove in silence, enjoying the ride.

Sammy knew Gabby would still be asleep, but she also knew that when Gabby woke up, the real drama would begin.

Jake reached over and took hold of Sammy's hand as if he could read her mind. "Everything's going to be okay," he said.

"This is all my fault, isn't it? What did I say a few weeks ago about how great everything was with my family?" Sammy asked.

"I think the words you used were easy-breezy and drama free," he reminded her with a wink.

"There you go. What the hell do I know?" she said as she looked out the window.

CHAPTER 13

Jake and Ginger snuck out of the house early the next morning to give the sisters plenty of private time. Jake had several errands to run and planned on returning in the early afternoon.

Sammy kept busy in the kitchen while she waited for Gabby to wake up. She made an egg casserole for breakfast, prepared a garden salad for lunch, and fixed some other goodies. She tried to occupy her mind, because every time she thought of Gabby, she got upset.

Sammy wasn't sure she could be another cheerleader. By the time Sammy arrived at the lake to help Dana, Dana had dealt with all the hard parts of her breakup. This was fresh for Gabby, and Sammy figured it would be hell. Sammy wanted to help Gabby and was thankful Gabby came there to see her, but she wasn't sure *how* to help her yet.

By the time Gabby woke up, Sammy had all her speeches and pep talks ready.

"Good morning," Gabby said groggily as she walked into the kitchen.

"Try 'good afternoon.' It's almost one o'clock."

"Lordy, I was tired," Gabby said. "I didn't realize how late it was. Sorry about crashing in on your and Jake's special time. Where is Jake?"

"Running some errands. He'll be back later. I baked an egg dish for breakfast but also have a salad for lunch if you prefer. Does either sound good to you?"

"Yeah, the eggs sound yummy," Gabby said as she checked her cell phone for messages. "That jerk hasn't even called yet. He doesn't even know that I saw him."

"Really? You never called him on it?" Sammy was shocked.

"No. I was too angry and I didn't want to call him while I was driving. I needed some time before I talked to him." Gabby poured herself some coffee.

"So he hasn't called you since he supposedly left for Seattle?" Sammy was surprised that Eddie didn't even call to cover his tracks or check in with Gabby.

"No, I talked to him Sunday afternoon after he supposedly landed. The last we spoke he was going for dinner and calling it an early night since he had meetings all day yesterday. It's not unusual for him not to call much when he travels. I guess now I know why."

"And now?" Sammy asked cautiously "How do you feel?" She handed Gabby her plate of food.

"Angry. But mostly hurt. But I'm ready. I woke up in the middle of the night last night and thought about all of this with a clear mind. I'm divorcing Eddie. I want the house. We just paid it off last year. Fifteen years we've been in that house. Then, I want to sell the house.

"I want a nice SUV; it doesn't have to be new or fancy, just something else. I want to get rid of that hunk of metal minivan that Eddie wanted me to drive. He even picked out that ugly maroon color. I wouldn't have minded the van if it were gray or silver, but he had to choose that hideous color. I've always hated that color. It was like a control thing with him." Gabby paused and took a breath to calm down.

"Matty starts high school in a year, so I have this coming school year to get my act together," Gabby said calmly.

Sammy was surprised by Gabby's state of mind. She was expecting her to be a mess. "That's it? A divorce?" she asked.

"You want me to stay with him?" Gabby asked, sounding appalled.

"No, I don't know. I guess I thought you would try to work it out or something," Sammy replied, mostly to herself.

Gabby played with the eggs on her plate and sipped her coffee. She looked out at the lake and sighed. "Wow, I've missed this place. I have such wonderful memories of Mom and Dad here."

Sammy could tell Gabby was beating around the bush. There was something Gabby wasn't telling her.

Gabby's cell phone rang. She looked at it and said, "Well, look who it is."

Closing her eyes and taking a deep breath, she answered, "Hello? Yeah, how's Seattle?"

Sammy sat and watched in awe.

Gabby continued, "No, I'm not home. I had the wild idea to drive to Loon Lake and spend some time with Sammy. I figured you were going to be working so much, and with the boys at camp for so long, I didn't want to get lonely."

Sammy couldn't imagine what Gabby was thinking.

"Well, that's fine. If there's a problem you'll have to deal with it. The boys are fine. I checked with the camp yesterday afternoon. They know to call you if they need anything. Yes. Okay. I'm not sure how long I'll stay. You're getting back early now? Oh, I see. Okay, well I'll keep you informed of my plans. You too." Gabby hung up.

"What in the world are you doing? Letting him get away with that?" Sammy was shocked.

"Heavens, no. I just need time to get the upper hand," Gabby said distantly as she looked out at the lake.

"Gabby, what's going on? Talk to me," Sammy pleaded.

"Well, I'm assuming you're under the misguided notion that this is the first time Eddie has cheated on me. And well, why would you think differently, since I've never told anyone otherwise? But unfortunately, that's not true. I have an attorney who has all the information." Gabby spoke matter-of-factly.

"What are you saying? He's cheated on you before?" Sammy couldn't believe her ears. *How could Gabby have not said anything?*

"Twice," Gabby whispered as she took another sip of coffee.

She finally looked Sammy in the eyes. "The first time was eleven years ago. Matty was just a toddler, two years old. I was devastated. Eddie promised to end it and that it would never happen again. We went to couples therapy for a few months. I got pregnant again. I wanted to be with him. We were going to have a new baby, a new life. I forgave him. I had to." Gabby looked sad now.

"The second time was five years ago, when Bobby was two. See a trend here? Hell, who knows? Maybe he had one eight years ago too when Tommy was two," Gabby was mumbling to herself.

Speaking up, she continued. "Anyway, the last time was so much harder to forgive him. We had three kids together. I didn't have any money or a job or skills for that matter. I had worked so hard making our money stretch. I was a savvy little shopper, always using coupons, buying everything on sale. I mended the boys' clothes so that they lasted longer and could be handed down from one to the next. I never bought anything nice or new for myself. I felt trapped." The way Gabby explained it, Sammy understood her despair.

"I did tell him, though, if it ever happened again that I was leaving him and taking the boys, the house, and the money with me. He said, okay, it would never happen again," Gabby recounted without emotion.

Sammy was stunned. "Why didn't you ever say anything?" She felt horrible that her sister endured such pain alone.

"I almost told you last summer, but Eddie and I were okay last summer. At least I thought so. I wanted to tell you each time it happened, but I kept thinking that if I told you, Eddie and I would be over for sure. I was never ready to leave him I guess. I forgave him, but never forgot. Apparently he did. But I got smart after the last time." She gave Sammy a knowing look.

"Five years ago I opened my own savings account and started putting money in there every month. This past year, since Bobby was in first grade, I started babysitting some toddlers in the neighborhood during the day. Eddie never knew. I stashed that money away too.

"I also started to help friends sell their shoes, clothes, and handbags on the Internet for a cut. Last summer, you told me I'd be a great business woman someday. Do you remember that?" Gabby asked.

"I do and apparently you are. I'm impressed that you've been so entrepreneurial," Sammy said with a smile.

Gabby laughed. "*Entrepreneurial*," she repeated. "I was thinking *sneaky*, but I like your word better."

"Well, it was sneaky of you not to tell Eddie. Why didn't you? Did you suspect something?" Sammy asked.

"No, I didn't suspect anything. I only knew he wouldn't be supportive of me working. He would only give me resistance. Again, it's a total control issue. He's not crazy about my independence."

"That's what I remember you saying last summer. Dang! You did it. You said you were going to work on your independence this year and you sure did."

"You're right. I did say that and took it to heart. I left here last summer thinking I needed to get my life back on track. All the boys were off to school finally; I needed to find something for me.

"The truth is too, that I met with an attorney right after Eddie's second bout of infidelity. He advised me to set up a bank account and start saving my own money and not to let Eddie know. He said that most second offenders become third offenders and I should be prepared. He documented all the info from the first two incidents. I'll call him this week and give him the new info. He should be able to file my divorce papers fairly quickly."

"Will Eddie fight it? Want to work it out?" Sammy couldn't imagine that the two would end it so easily. They were Gabby and Eddie. But Sammy never knew it was Gabby and

Eddie and mistresses.

"I doubt it. He looked pretty happy with Bachelorette Number Three. I can't get the image of them kissing out of my mind," Gabby said as she closed her eyes.

"I know I'm acting calm, and this is the third time, so it shouldn't be a big deal, but it hurts so much—more than anything. But I have to end it. I stuck with him for the boys' sake the first two times. I can't be responsible for raising three men that think it's acceptable to cheat on their wives. Right?" Gabby was asking for reassurance. Her confidence was shaken. Sammy could tell she needed to hear that she was doing the right thing.

"Yes, you're absolutely right! You have to leave him. It has nothing to do with raising your boys, though. You deserve love and respect from a partner and from yourself. By staying with Eddie, allowing him the opportunity to do this again, you deny yourself the respect you deserve." Sammy didn't think she needed to say much more. She felt that Gabby was finally ready to accept her fate. She may have fought it the last two times, but not this time.

"What's next?" Sammy asked.

"I don't know," Gabby said somberly. "I need to relax and think about these things with a clear mind. I guess I need to make a list of things to do and start doing them."

Sammy was so surprised by Gabby's inner strength. She was taking action and doing something about her situation. Sammy was relieved that Gabby didn't need help the way Dana did. Gabby was taking matters into her own hands and Sammy was happy to support her one hundred percent. She could see that Gabby was different from last summer: stronger, more independent.

"Well, you're welcome to stay here as long as you need to," Sammy said.

"Don't you think you better check with Jake before you make that offer?" Gabby asked.

"It was his offer. He told me that this morning before he left," Sammy said.

"He's a good guy, Sammy. I'm happy for you," Gabby said.

"I'm happy for me too. Why don't you finish your food and we can go for a boat ride. Sound good? That should cheer you up a bit and get you thinking clearly."

"That sounds perfect," Gabby answered as she finally started to eat her breakfast. "I'll get changed and we can go. Crap, I don't have any clothes to change into. I really didn't think this through, did I?"

"How could you possibly plan for what happened? You followed your instincts, and I'm happy you're here with me. I have an extra swimsuit you can borrow. We can drive into town later and get you some clothes. No problem. I'll get that extra swimsuit."

***

The boat ride over the cool, blue lake did both women some good on that hot afternoon. After about two hours on the lake, Sammy noticed thunderheads building to the north and hoped it might finally rain. Since it hadn't rained in weeks, everything needed a good soaking. The air was so thick with humidity that Sammy felt like she could use a good cleanse too.

"Looks like it might rain soon," Gabby shouted over the boat motor.

"Yeah, I hope it does," Sammy shouted back. "But I hope it waits until we get back," she added as she noticed the clouds were building faster than she thought.

Both women sat in the boat as they watched the storm approach. The clouds were turning black before their eyes. The lightning began off in the distance. They were getting close to the resort, but the storm looked like it might beat them there.

Sammy couldn't make the boat go any faster. They had to ride it out to see who would win the race.

The boat reached the end of the lake. Sammy could finally see Vince's dream cabin and thought it looked even welcoming in this storm.

Right when the boat was docked, the rain started. It wasn't a light, refreshing sprinkling of rain; it was the hard, large drops that seemed to forewarn of hail.

The women struggled to tie up the boat. The rain began coming down in sheets. The temperature dropped over ten degrees. Once the boat was finally secured, the women ran for the lodge.

Jake greeted them at the doorway with towels in hand.

The women laughed hysterically as they dripped from head to toe. Wiping her face with a towel, Sammy said, "Now *that* was exciting. I didn't think we'd make it."

"Whoa!" all three exclaimed as a crack of thunder shook the lodge. The lights flickered, but the power stayed on.

"Jake it's so great to see you again," Gabby said. "I'd hug you but I don't want to get you all wet."

"That doesn't matter. Come here," he said as he gave her a light hug. "It's so nice to see you too. I'm so sorry for the circumstances that bring you here. You feeling okay now?" he asked.

"I wish I were here under better circumstances too. But I'm okay. That rain cleansed my soul I think," Gabby said with a smile as she continued to dry off.

"I was thinking the same thing!" Sammy exclaimed. "I felt like I needed that as much as all the plants and animals."

"Yeah, we all needed it," Jake agreed. "It should help lower the humidity too. It was getting unbearable. This storm is moving pretty fast and there's another behind it expected later tonight. But after that it should be clear and cooler for a few days."

After drying off, the women changed into Sammy's jeans and sweatshirts. Sammy hadn't worn a pair of jeans in weeks; it had been so hot and muggy.

The first storm passed along with daylight, leaving behind a rainy evening. Jake baked a few pizzas that he picked up in town, tossed the salad Sammy made earlier, and put together a bucket of beer.

The threesome along with Ginger, food, and beer bucket

got comfortable on the screened-in deck, where they could listen to the rain. Jake turned on the twinkling holiday lights. Gabby exclaimed how she loved the deck.

The three talked about the lake, the resort, and the changes Dana made to the cabins. Jake mentioned that Vince was closing on his new property this week. They all talked about light, happy topics. They didn't talk about Gabby's troubles and she seemed good with that.

Sammy noticed Gabby drifting off in her thoughts, but she was easily drawn back into the conversation. It was a nice evening among friends and family. Sammy figured Gabby would talk about her situation if she wanted to. But they were enjoying the moment, free from discussing Eddie. Sammy knew that when Gabby returned home, her situation would consume her; right now Gabby needed some light conversation.

Calling it an early night, Gabby left Sammy and Jake on the porch in the cold rain.

Sammy looked at Jake in the twinkling lights. She thought he was so handsome and so sweet to her sister. Considering how horrible Eddie was, Sammy felt blessed to be with Jake. Her love and affection for Jake took over. Climbing into Jake's lap, she gave him a passionate kiss that overcame both of them. She had to force herself away from his embrace.

"Hey, I liked where that was going," he said happily.

"Me too. But, seriously, it can't go anywhere with Gabby here. My heart couldn't do that to her," Sammy said.

"My heart couldn't either, but other parts of my body could," he said temptingly.

Sammy laughed in answer to his invitation. "I'm sorry to get your hopes up. I was just suddenly consumed with the need to show you how much I"—she paused slightly as she caught herself—"like you."

"You can show me that anytime. Now, what the hell's going on with Gabby and Eddie? I've been dying to find out, but neither of you said squat. What's up?" Jake asked anxiously.

"Sorry, I wanted to tell you too. This is the third time Eddie's cheated on her. She seems to be handling it well. She said she's going to divorce him, get the house, sell the house, get the boys, and has one year until Matt starts high school to figure out what she's going to do. It's all very calculated and planned out. It's almost like she's been planning it for a while. The reality, I suppose, is that she has been planning for it for the last five years. That's when he had his last affair."

"Seriously? Three times? What a bastard. Good, I'm glad she's divorcing his ass. He doesn't deserve her. Colorado is a no-fault divorce state, so hopefully they can amicably figure it out and not make it too tough on the boys. Does she have an attorney?" Jake asked with concern.

Sammy was caught off guard by Jake's Attorney-at-Law Superhero attitude. "She does. She met with him five years ago. That was when he told her to open a savings account in her name and start saving money. Apparently, he saw this coming and she's kept in touch with him."

"Yeah, he probably knows better than her how these things turn out. She seems really calm about everything right now. Are you sure she's okay and not in denial?" Jake asked.

"She didn't deny a thing. She said she's angry and hurt, but ready to take action. She seems much stronger than she used to be. I hate to say this, but I think this divorce will be good for her. I know the boys will really be hurt the most. But, she can't stay with Eddie for the boys' sakes. I only hope they can figure this out without too much trouble for the kids," Sammy said sadly as she finally slid off Jake's lap.

"They will," he said putting his arm around Sammy's shoulder and pulling her close. They sat there together quietly, listening to the rain. They could hear the next thunderstorm rumbling its way to Loon Lake. "Let's get to bed before the next storm hits."

CHAPTER 14

The days went by quickly. Gabby arrived Monday night and by Friday afternoon, the last Friday in June, Sammy and Jake were able to help her take control of her situation. Gabby had plenty of setbacks and moments of despair and sadness. But those moments were brief and Sammy was amazed by Gabby's sheer determination to be strong and in control.

The women had many heartfelt conversations about marriage and fidelity. Sammy mostly listened and let Gabby have her say. She wanted to support Gabby and help her through her ordeal.

Over the course of those few days, Jake gave Gabby advice and information on what to expect next. He knew plenty about the divorce proceedings, both legally and personally, from Dana's recent experience.

Gabby talked to her attorney several times, and he had all the papers and details of the separation completed. The only thing left was for Gabby to confront Eddie. It was the part she dreaded the most.

Sammy kept Gabby preoccupied throughout the week by dragging her into town to look at different real estate and county records in search of historical information about Jake's resort. Sammy hit the jackpot at a small local forestry museum, where she unearthed extensive details about the lumber company that logged around Loon Lake at the turn of the twentieth century.

Gabby was of great help to Sammy, as she took copious notes on everything Sammy read out loud. The sisters agreed that they made a good team. Gabby even joked about becoming a private investigator since she was learning so much from Sammy.

The women also enjoyed buying Gabby all new clothing, makeup, toiletries, and "unmentionables," as Gabby called them. Gabby said she felt like a completely different person. Everything was new from head to toe. She couldn't remember the last time she had treated herself that way.

The boys outgrew their clothes and shoes so fast; she was always buying things they needed. She remained last on her priority list. However, that week, she was the only one on her priority list. She even soaked in Jake's hot tub the last two nights, either alone or accompanied by Sammy and a glass of wine.

Friday afternoon Sammy and Gabby went back into town to get digital scans of all the photos they'd collected on the resort and Loon Lake. It was going to be a time-consuming task, but the photos were too precious for Sammy to drop off for someone else to scan.

Sammy noticed Gabby eyeing a hair salon across the street from the copy shop.

"Go for it," Sammy said and nodded toward the hair salon. "I can scan these while you see if you can get your hair done."

"But it'll take you forever if you do all those by yourself," Gabby said.

Shrugging her shoulders, Sammy replied, "What else do we have to do? It'll likely take you a while too. What kind of cut do you have in mind?" Sammy wondered what Gabby would look like in anything but her blonde shoulder-length blunt cut. Gabby had worn her hair like that for as long as Sammy could remember.

Gabby gave Sammy a devilish smile. "I was thinking of cutting it all off—go super short and color it."

"That sounds perfect for you. That cut would be beautiful with your big, round eyes. What color?" Sammy asked excitedly.

"You'll have to wait and see. I'll be back if they can't squeeze me in or if it looks like they can't handle such a dramatic change," Gabby said as she walked across the street.

Gabby never came back, at least not before Sammy finished scanning the photos.

Sammy was about to cross the street to find Gabby when she saw her emerge from the salon—with short auburn hair. Even from across the street, Sammy could tell Gabby was enchanted by her new look. Sammy thought Gabby looked stunning, a bit older, and downright sexy. Gabby had a bounce in her step too.

Sammy whistled and said, "Dang, you look amazing, stunning, and sexy."

"Thanks, Sammy. I'm *so* pleased with it. I was a little worried about it when I saw all my hair fall to the floor. But it feels great. That took forever. I'm sorry I couldn't help you."

"No worries. You look great. It was worth it. Do you feel like a different woman? Because you look like a different woman."

"I do feel different. I like it. I like it a lot. Let's get home. I'm hungry." They climbed in her minivan. "Now, if I could just get rid of this hunk of junk, I'd be set."

Sammy feared that Gabby was moving too fast. She worried that Gabby might get to a place where she wouldn't recognize herself and regret it. But in the moment she could not deny that Gabby looked happy.

As they drove back to the resort, Gabby slowly became distant. Sammy knew something was weighing on her mind.

"What's up, Gabby? Whatcha thinking about?"

"Would Mom and Dad be disappointed in me and the failure of my marriage?" Gabby asked somberly.

"Never," Sammy said adamantly and without hesitation. "They would never judge you like that. Look at Aunt Kathy. Mom absolutely loved and respected her sister. And you remember last summer when Aunt Kathy basically said it was her fault she and Stan got divorced. Mom never blamed her. No, absolutely not. Mom and Dad would support you one hundred percent through this. Eddie is completely to blame. You cannot think of it as…" Sammy caught herself.

She was going to say *your failure*, but was instantly reminded by how Dana felt like a failure. "Do you feel like a failure?" Sammy asked gently, not wanting to upset more.

Gabby didn't answer right away, but seemed to roll the question over in her mind.

"No, I don't. I did after his first affair. I felt somehow that it was my fault—that I caused his infidelity. But with therapy, I accepted it as part of our evolution as a couple. We married right out of college, and I understood he still had some wild oats to sow." She let out a strange laugh. "I was ridiculous, making excuses for him."

Sammy interrupted Gabby, to stop her from retreating into the past. "I only asked, because Dana said she felt like a failure, and I wondered if you did too."

"I can see that with Dana. They weren't even married two years, were they?" Gabby asked.

Before Sammy could answer, Gabby continued, "No, I don't feel like a failure. I feel more like I'm…grieving. I feel like someone died. The reality is something did die. Our marriage died. Eddie just doesn't know it yet. But I can see where Dana would feel that way." Gabby was distant again.

"You should visit Dana sometime this fall at Kathy's. I think you two would be able to help each other out a lot," Sammy said.

"That actually sounds like a fun idea. Anyway, back to Mom and Dad…Thanks for the reassurance. I sometimes worry about what Mom and Dad would think about how my life turned out." Gabby sounded so sad.

"They would be so proud of you. You're a selfless and loving mom. And they would love your children immensely," Sammy said thoughtfully.

"Gabby, you still remind me so much of Mom. The way you love your kids…even the quiet strength you're showing through this ordeal with Eddie. You can be proud of yourself. You have nothing to be ashamed of. And now, with your new hairstyle, you even look like Mom."

"Really, ya think? Thanks, Sammy. That's so cool to hear. I just need to get some cat-eyed sunglasses to really look the part, huh?"

"Or some Jackie O's," Sammy added with a smile as she pictured their fashionable mom.

They drove the rest of the way in silence. Sammy could sense that she was able to reassure Gabby, for now.

When they were back at the resort, Gabby had declared that her new hair had given her superpowers and she was ready to face the music. She excused herself from visiting with Jake and Sammy to call and confront Eddie while she still had the guts.

However, she also proclaimed that she was scared to death as she shut herself in Sammy's bedroom. Sammy and Jake went down to the dock to wait, to give Gabby the freedom to yell and scream profanities if she needed to.

***

About an hour later, Sammy and Jake heard the screen door to his lodge snap shut. They both looked toward the lodge to see Gabby walking their way carrying Jake's bucket of beer.

"Hmm, now that's something you don't see often," Sammy said.

"What?" Jake asked.

"Gabby instigating happy hour," Sammy replied with a half-smile.

Gabby walked out on the dock and sat down next to Sammy. She passed out beers, opened hers, and then passed the opener on. Sammy and Jake waited for Gabby to say something.

"Well, looks like we're getting a divorce," Gabby said as she took a sip of beer. Tears welled up in her eyes, but she kept her composure.

"So it seems that he wants to be with this one. He'll move his stuff out of the house next week, while I'm here. Is it okay if I stay another week?" Gabby looked blankly out at the water.

"You can stay as long as you want, Gabby," Jake answered.

"He's going to pick the boys up from camp in two weeks and tell them about our situation on the drive home. I'll get the boys full-time. He'll get the boys every other weekend. That should work out nicely for his new dating life." This hint of sarcasm was something new for Gabby.

"I'll get the house and he'll work with my attorney to figure out child and spousal support. It's all very civilized," Gabby said calmly. "But he did say he was sorry for not telling me sooner." Her tears spilled at that last part.

Hugging her sister, Sammy whispered, "I'm so sorry, Gabby. I wish I could do more for you. Make the pain go away."

"I know. I wish you could too."

The three sat in silence sipping their drinks. They sat on the dock for hours, taking turns making beer and snack runs. They watched as bats hunted insects over the water.

After the sun set, Jake brought out some blankets for the women. He left them under the starry sky. The two sisters cuddled under blankets. They didn't talk. Gabby cried a bit. Sammy hugged her. They sat under the stars and mourned the loss of Gabby's marriage and her family unit.

They both knew Gabby was in for more suffering once her children learned the news. But tonight was Gabby's time to be sad and reflective. She announced to Sammy that tomorrow she would be strong.

***

The next morning was a typical Saturday morning for Jake. The guests were packing up and clearing out. He had bills to collect, cabins to check, and people to manage. It was a pretty smooth morning, with no real issues anywhere.

It was a nice cool day. The storms from earlier in the week had cleared the heat out. But it hadn't rained since those storms, and things were drying out again. The forecast was for more heat over the next several days, right in time for July's arrival.

Sammy was sitting at Jake's kitchen table catching up on Dana's blog. Gabby was still sleeping, which was unusual for Gabby, whose typical night consisted of about six hours of sleep. Sammy began to worry, as it was nearing nine in the morning.

Jake finally came in to wish Sammy a good morning. He'd barely sat down when his phone rang.

"It's my dad," Jake said as he looked at his phone. "This can't be good. He never calls." Jake stepped out onto the screened-in deck.

Sammy sat still, trying to eavesdrop. She could only make out one word: Vince.

A moment later, Jake came back in and sat at the table. "Aunt Jeannie passed away this morning, about an hour ago," he said, wiping tears from his eyes. "I feel so bad for Vince…Shit. I knew this was coming, but it still hurts so much."

"I know," Sammy said and hugged him.

He cried softly in her embrace. "I'm sorry. I'm trying to be cool here, but I can't do it."

"It's okay to cry," she said gently. She was moved by his vulnerability. It made her love him more. "I'm so sorry for you, your parents, and Vince," she whispered.

Wiping his eyes with the back of his hand, he looked up at her. "Thanks. I know you are. I told my dad I'd call Dana and let her know. I'll be back in a few minutes. She should be up this early on the West Coast, don't ya think?"

"I would think so," Sammy said. She watched him go back out to the deck.

As the door to the deck closed, Gabby walked into the kitchen.

"Hey," Sammy said as she saw Gabby.

"Hey, I heard. I'm sorry. I didn't mean to eavesdrop. I was walking in and heard you two talking. I stopped myself in the hallway. I didn't want to intrude. Did she pass away this morning?" Gabby looked concerned.

"About an hour ago. He just went to call Dana," Sammy said.

"I feel so bad. What can I do?" Gabby asked.

"I'm not sure yet," Sammy answered. She really didn't know what she could do either.

About an hour later, Jake came back in and was in lost in thought. The scent of something baking in the over was the first thing he noticed. "It smells wonderful in here." Then he noticed Gabby helping Sammy clean up the kitchen. "Good morning, Gabby. How are you?"

"I'm fine, thanks for asking. It's you we're worried about. I'm so sorry to hear about your aunt. Is there anything I can do for you?"

"Yes, actually there is. I just made several phone calls. Aunt Jeannie's funeral will be on Friday. I would like to go spend a few days with my folks and Vince. Dana should be flying in for it too. I talked to Dave, down the road, and asked if he wouldn't mind stopping by a few times a day and send his boys down to help you. But I was hoping I could leave the resort with you two in charge. I know it's a lot to ask, but it would mean so much to me if I could be with my family without worrying about this place."

"Of course," the women said in unison.

"We're completely capable of handing the day-to-day stuff, and we're more than happy to help," Sammy said.

"Yes, and I was planning on staying another week, so at least I can earn my keep," Gabby said with a crooked smile.

"Dave knows how to fix practically anything, and if he can't do it, he'll find a person who can. His boys can help with anything that might come up too. He said one of them should always be home."

"When did you want to leave?" Sammy asked.

"Tomorrow morning. If that's okay with you two," he said.

"Yes, of course," Sammy answered. "Gabby whipped up a three-cheese quiche with spinach and artichokes for breakfast. It should be ready in a few minutes."

"Is that what smells so good? That sounds delicious. Sorry I'm making you eat so late." Jake looked at the clock. It was already after ten. All the guests were finally gone.

"It's fine. I figured you had calls to make, and since we got the fixings for it in town yesterday, she decided to make it quickly." Sammy realized she was babbling on about nonsense when his aunt just passed away. But the sisters had wanted to do something to help, and well, people bake when they're trying to help.

"The guests have all left. I need to check on two of the boats after breakfast. The cabins are being cleaned, laundry service already arrived, and the boys should be down soon to do the trash pick up and mowing. These are the things that you might have to worry about next Saturday. I don't think I'll be back until Saturday night. Can you handle it?" Jake looked worried.

"I think we can handle it. I've seen you do this the last several Saturdays. I know the drill. And I'm quite capable of doing manual labor, even though I've shown you otherwise," Sammy said with a grin.

Gabby had set the table, and she now announced that breakfast was ready. The three sat down to eat while continuing to discuss their plans.

"When is Dana flying in?" Sammy asked.

"She didn't know yet. She might try to get out in the next day or two. She said Kathy already told her when the time came she could take as much time away as she needed." Jake took another bite of breakfast. "This quiche is good."

"It's Gabby's own recipe," Sammy said proudly.

"Thanks, Jake. I'm glad you like it," Gabby said with a smile.

"I have tons of airline miles. I'll check if I can get Dana a free flight," Sammy said, still thinking about Dana.

"That would be helpful. I know she's worried about money right now so I offered to loan her some cash. But if you have miles to spare, I know she would appreciate it."

"I'll check right after breakfast," Sammy said.

"There is one thing that needs to be done on a daily basis that I've never really mentioned to you, Sammy," Jake said mysteriously.

"Really? What's that?" Sammy was intrigued.

"It's kind of gross. I'll need one of you to check the fish house a few times a day. It can get really disgusting if it's not kept clean. Dave's boys know what to do. All you have to do is check to see that it's clean. And when the buckets get full, call Dave and ask that the boys come down and clean it."

"When the buckets are full of what exactly?" Sammy asked.

"Fish heads and guts," Jake said dryly.

"Gross. I can't do that." Sammy feigned gagging. "Gabby, that'll be your daily job."

"Okay," Gabby said agreeably.

"Really? You're not going to fight me on this one?" Sammy asked, surprised.

"Please. I have three boys. I've dealt with all kinds of gross bodily fluids and dead things from outside. What are a few fish guts?"

Jake laughed. Sammy was proud of her confident sister. "Okay, then, Jake, sounds like we'll have everything under control."

"Sounds like it," he said with a small chuckle.

After breakfast Gabby cleaned up the kitchen and started a shopping list for the next several days.

Sammy ducked away to check about flights for Dana.

Jake set out to inspect the boats that needed work.

Later that afternoon, the women hung out with Jake in the lodge to meet the next round of guests as they checked in. With each new introduction, Jake explained he'd be away for the week and that Sammy and Gabby were in charge. The women recognized a few faces from last summer.

Sammy talked to Dana a few times and was able to get her a free flight for Monday. Sammy thought Dana sounded great in spite of the reason for their calls.

By Saturday night the women were schooled in all operations of the resort. They felt confident in their ability to run the place. After making another grocery run, Gabby cooked and baked up a storm. She made dinner for the threesome and packed Jake a cooler full of lasagna, pasta salads, cookies, brownies, and another dessert for him to take for his family—all comfort foods.

After dinner, Gabby called it an early night.

Sammy and Jake took a quick soak in the hot tub. There were a million things Sammy was feeling toward Jake that night. But she didn't know what to say.

As they sat and soaked, however, one thing came to mind.

"Jake, you know that I care about you very much, right?" she asked.

"Yes, I kind of figured that out. And you know I care about you very much, right?" he asked openly.

"Yes, I figured that too," she said.

She didn't smile, making sure he didn't question her sincerity. "Anyway, in my heart I wish I could go with you to your parents' house and be there for you and Vince this week. I know I can't go and shouldn't go. But if I could go, I would want to be there with you, for you," she said.

He looked at her lovingly. He slid over closer to her. He held her chin and looked into her eyes. "I love you, Samantha McGreggor," he said with a smile and gave her that "first kiss" kind of kiss. She felt it everywhere. It took her breath away. It hurt when he stopped.

Before she could say anything else, he continued, "I wish you could be there with me too. I want you by my side forever. But I know you need to be here with Gabby, and the fact that Gabby's here is a wild coincidence. I would never leave you here by yourself or expect you to be in charge. I only asked because I know you and Gabby can handle it together, and you two might have some fun with it. You will be with me in my heart, and I'll call you all the time, and…"

Sammy put her finger to his lips, shutting him up.

"I love you too, Jake Hunter," she said.

He kissed her again—took her breath away again. She loved everything about this man, especially his kisses.

They quickly climbed out of the tub and retreated to his bedroom. It had been days since they'd been together physically. They were hungry for each other. They had just proclaimed their love for each other, and now they ached to make love.

This time it was different: like the first time, but more intense. Sammy knew he loved her. She loved him. He was suffering a loss of family and experiencing great sadness for his dearest friend and cousin—feelings she'd known most of her life.

She was aware how precious their time together was, especially with the demise of her sister's marriage, of both of their sisters' marriages. She knew this life, this love, could be brief. These thoughts and feelings heightened her presence and awareness and made their night together extraordinary.

CHAPTER 15

The next morning, Sammy was up early to give Jake and Ginger a proper send off. She had a heavy heart as she waved good-bye to him from the window.

It was a quiet Sunday morning on the lake. She went out to the wooden swing with her coffee and was suddenly overwhelmed with grief. She didn't know why. It consumed her.

As she was about to cry, a hummingbird flew right up to her, merely a few feet from her face. It zipped away to the nearest tree and sat on a branch as though it was watching her.

She instantly felt better. During the editing phase of her novel, she'd read so much about angels and the presence of deceased love ones. She'd read somewhere that loved ones who have passed often make themselves known by the presence of hummingbirds.

She couldn't remember the details or how in the world that worked. But she wanted to believe it. She wanted to believe it was her mom with her at that moment.

As if the bird understood her, it flew right back to the same spot in the air a few feet from her face and then zipped off.

Sammy felt a sense of relief. Her grief disappeared. She knew she was sad for Vince and the Hunter family. But her grief in that moment was for herself and her sisters and for the loss that they've carried with them for decades.

She looked around. It was this place—the lake, the resort—and being outside immersed in nature that made her remember life's poignant moments. Her everyday life was always so hurried and so removed from these emotions.

She loved feeling these deep emotions most days. The grief, she could do without. But these powerful feelings—they made her feel alive.

"Where in the world are you?" Gabby asked as she sat down next to Sammy on the swing. "I just asked you three questions and you didn't hear me."

"Sorry, I was thinking about heavy stuff. This lake makes my mind conjure up crazy ideas."

"I know what you mean," Gabby said. "It makes things so clear, doesn't it? Last summer I experienced so many flashbacks of our family vacations here. This time around, unfortunately, I've been consumed with my own ordeal. But watching Jake talk about his aunt—it makes me think about when Mom and Dad died.

"Sometimes, I still feel like I'm that sixteen-year-old kid when they died. And then I wonder how do I have this husband and these children? I know *how*, but I mean *when*? And now my husband will be past tense. So, I'll feel like a *divorced* sixteen-year-old with three kids."

"That's quite an image," Sammy said with a chuckle. "But I know what you mean. I always feel like that teenager who lost her parents. It must be psychological, some sort of survival mechanism our brains create to help us cope. I have no idea. Maybe Alex's therapist might give her some insight to share with us."

"I could use some insight," Gabby said. "So, enough of this sad stuff, okay? Let's focus on having a fun few days; because when I go home, my life will be torture. I choke up when I think about what our divorce is going to do to our kids—my boys, my babies. Are they going to hate me? Or will they hate him? Or both of us? I just don't know." Gabby threw her hands up in the air.

"Will they love his new girlfriend? Will Eddie be stupid enough to introduce the boys to his new girlfriend right away? My mind goes 'round and 'round with these questions—questions that have no answers. So I might as well stop asking them. Now, what can we do around here to have fun and take advantage of being in charge?" Gabby wore a devious grin.

Sammy laughed. "I haven't a clue. Any suggestions?" she asked as she quietly thought of some answers herself.

"Well, Wednesday's the Fourth of July, we should do something fun that day, right? And it's supposed to start getting hotter again this week too," Gabby added.

"That's right. I forgot about the Fourth. You were okay with the boys going to camp over the Fourth?" That fact just dawned on Sammy.

"No, I wasn't. But the boys had friends going these weeks and that was the most important thing for them, especially Matty, or Matt. He hates it when I call him Matty now. I forget he's a teenager. I figured since this would be his last summer at camp that I'd let him go when he wanted. So, we should have a pitch-in cookout, don't ya think?" Gabby started to perk up again.

"Yes, that would be good. I wonder if they can do fireworks here. Hmm, I'll have to ask Dave. Maybe tonight we should have a bonfire. That would give us the chance to chat with all the guests and see if they want to join us for the Fourth." Sammy was inspired.

"You want to go into town with me and go to church? I think we can make the early service and be back before anyone needs us." Sammy wanted to pray for comfort for Vince and his family, and Aunt Jeannie in her new home.

"Yes, that's a great idea," Gabby said as both women got off the swing to start their day.

***

The sisters made it back to the resort in time to enjoy the hottest part of the day. They took to the water with all the guests. They floated on rafts, swam, relaxed, and talked to the guests, who were all in agreement that a pitch-in on the Fourth would be perfect.

The night turned out to be too hot for a bonfire. So the women stayed in and worked on Jake's book.

Gabby helped with the layout of the photos, labeling each and putting them in order. On several occasions, Gabby mentioned how nice it would be to have copies of her own. Sammy thought that most repeat visitors would. So, she set out to create a second book, as a surprise for Jake. She loved the idea of making a small printable full-color book, available for guests, which contained the history and photos of their beloved resort and lake.

After hunching over their projects for a few hours, both women agreed a soak in the hot tub would do their aching backs some good.

About twenty minutes into their soak and discussions about their projects, Gabby whispered, "Quiet!" She put a shaky finger to her lips. "Do you hear that?" she said barely audible.

"Hear wha—" Sammy didn't finish her question. She did hear it. The hairs on the back of her sweaty neck and wet arms pricked and tingled. Her heart raced as she turned to look out the nearest screened window. Gabby's eyes followed hers.

At first they couldn't see a thing, only darkness. But they heard it: the heavy, close, and *loud* breathing and snorting of something. And it was getting closer.

There! Mere inches from the window a huge bear face appeared with a gaping mouth.

The women screamed like three-year-olds as they jumped out of the water and ran, slipping and sliding, across the wet floor. They were bumping into each other, fighting for the door. Once inside with the door safely slammed shut, the reality of the situation hit them.

"Holy crap!" Gabby said. "My heart is pounding outside of my chest. I've never been so scared in my life."

Sammy scrambled for the light switches. She turned on some flood lights that lit up the entire area behind Jake's lodge. They both watched out a side window in awe as a large brown bear galloped off into the darkness.

Sammy collapsed into the nearest chair. "Holy crap is right. That was the scariest thing ever. I'm still shaking. I'm not sure I'll ever get the image of that face out of my mind."

The women looked at each other and began laughing hysterically. It was the kind of laughter born from nervousness and fright. And they couldn't stop for some time.

"It reminds me of the Twinkie incident at the dump," Gabby said once she finally stopped laughing. "Do you remember that? How the bear charged at us?"

Sammy laughed. "I do. I just told Jake that story the other night. We went to the dump that first night you arrived and I remembered it out of the blue. Do you remember the three-legged bear? Its name was Trey. I've been meaning to tell you that." Sammy started to calm down and breathe normally.

"I do remember the three-legged bear," Gabby said and nodded toward the window. "Do you think our screams scared that one off?"

"I hope so. We were pretty loud. How embarrassing. Do you think the guests heard us?" Sammy worried only mildly about the guests; her bigger worry was that the bear would be back.

"I'm sure of it. Tomorrow, we'll be the talk of the lake," Gabby said as she covered her mouth with her hands and laughed again.

"Let's go to bed. Can I sleep with you tonight?" Sammy felt like a kid again.

"I was hoping you would," Gabby answered.

***

Sammy dreamed of bears that night—*all night*. When she woke she wondered if, like the hummingbird, a bear's presence was symbolic of something. Lately, she was trying to find symbolism and meaning in every little encounter with nature.

When Gabby woke she found Sammy sitting at the kitchen table, drinking coffee, and reading something on her laptop. "Whatcha reading about?" Gabby asked as she shuffled over to the coffee pot.

"The symbolism of bears. I dreamt about bears all night long, I swear. Did you have any bears in your dreams last night?" Sammy asked.

"No. It took me a long time to fall asleep. But when I finally did, I slept hard. That's how all my nights have been here. I toss and turn for hours and then sleep like a rock late into the mornings."

That explains Gabby's new sleeping habits, Sammy thought.

"What kind of symbolism are you talking about? It was just a bear looking for food, wasn't it?" Gabby said.

"Maybe, maybe not," Sammy answered. "I did a series of articles last spring about insects, and in my research I learned that dragonflies symbolize change and living in the moment, and even some cultures believe that a dragonfly's presence has meaning to those whom it visits.

"Anyway, a hummingbird visited me yesterday morning and I remembered something I read once about them bringing messages from loved ones who've passed. So, it dawned on me to look up the symbolism of an encounter with a bear.

"I know it sounds silly, but every so often these little things make some sort of cosmic sense, like God's sending messages and we need to be alert enough to pay attention."

Gabby sat down next to Sammy with her coffee. "Scootch over. It doesn't sound silly. It sounds interesting. So what did you find out about the bear encounter?" Gabby leaned over to look at Sammy's laptop.

"There are a few things that could apply to both of our situations," said Sammy. "It's crazy.

"Like one source says a bear can represent patience and

that we should hibernate with our idea or project until the time is right to act. Another source says a bear represents confidence and that we can be larger than life if we lift ourselves up to our highest potential, like a bear physically does when it stands on its hind legs.

"A bear also symbolizes our nurturing and protective instincts, like the way a bear is a fierce and loving mother to her cubs." Sammy raised one eyebrow and looked at her sister.

"Whoa, that's so weird. All three of those things apply to me in a way, don't they?" Gabby asked, dumbfounded. "And here I thought the bear was only looking for food."

Sammy laughed. "It probably was looking for food. But you know me, I crave hidden messages."

"I know you do and that's one of the many things I love about you. You're always looking for insight and answers to our natural and heavenly questions. You're an odd mix of science and fiction, magic and realism, spiritual and physical. Is there anything that pertains to you with the bear symbolism?"

"Yes, actually there is. It has to do with encountering a bear, which can symbolize the need for fun, relaxation, and play. It says here"—Sammy scrolled down the page—"Yes, here it is. 'The more we allow ourselves to relax and enjoy life, the more our lives begin to take on a light and lively perspective.' That's exactly what I need to do."

"Really, *you* need to lighten up? I think you're tons of fun," Gabby said.

"Thanks," Sammy said with a smile. "But I take life too seriously sometimes. I know it stems from losing Mom and Dad so young. But I need to take some lessons from Aunt Kathy and live in the moment and enjoy life."

"Yes, that woman sure knows how to have a good time," Gabby said.

"Speaking of Aunt Kathy, have you talked to her recently? Did she mention anything to you about New Year's Eve?" Sammy asked.

"I did!" Gabby exclaimed. "I knew I forgot to talk to you about something important. That was it. Yes, she asked me if we would come to their 'Second Wedding.' That's what she called it. I talked to her a few weeks ago and told her of course we wouldn't miss it for the world.

"Obviously my situation will be a bit different than what I expected then. But the boys and I will definitely be there. And what's up with her buying those properties? I think she has a problem. She's addicted to real estate."

"Oh good, I'm glad you talked to her. Seriously, I know what you mean about the properties. I haven't a clue what she plans to do with either one. But they both were lovely in their own way. The big one is a major fixer-upper and the little one is like a wonderland. When are you going to tell her about Eddie?"

Gabby sighed. "I guess I need to take some time to call her, Cass, and Alex, huh?"

"Yes, you should. They would all want to know what you're going through. Remember what happened last summer with our great lack of communication?" Sammy asked.

Gabby laughed in response. "I sure do. It was like teenage years all over again. Last summer was fun, Sammy. I don't know what you're talking about needing to have more fun in your life. You're a blast. But that bear symbolism sure is pretty cool."

Gabby gazed out at the blue water. "Thanks for helping me see things differently sometimes. I think you do that for your readers too. You have a gift."

Sammy was touched by Gabby's words. "Thanks, Gab. Sometimes I worry that I'm too daydreamy or whimsical for the general public."

"The general public needs daydreamy and whimsical," Gabby said.

"Okay." Sammy wanted to quit talking. "So what were we saying? We need to have more fun? Let's go fishing this morning. You up for it?"

"Definitely, that's a great idea." Gabby practically squeaked with excitement.

"Good. Go get dressed. I'm gonna walk around and see if that bear bothered anyone else last night. I'll take everything we need out to the boat. Can you pack a few snacks and drinks in the cooler?"

"You bet," Gabby answered as she headed to her room to change.

Within twenty minutes, the women were in the boat and on their way.

Sammy drove them to Vince's property and slowed the boat down, quieting the motor.

"That's the place Vince is buying," Sammy said, pointing to the cabin up the bank.

"Did he buy it yet?" Gabby asked.

"It was supposed to close last week. By the looks of that moving truck, I assume something's happening," Sammy said as she steered the boat away from shore and sped up.

It was another hot day and the air stood still. There was no wind, and the sky was cloudless.

As the boat flew over the calm lake water, it splashed up some refreshing mist on their smiling faces. Sammy watched as the strain on Gabby's face softened. Both women found themselves relaxing during the ride.

Sammy, spotting something moving along the shore, slowed the boat down to take a closer look. Gabby looked quizzically at Sammy, who answered by pointing toward the shore. A deer was knee-deep in the water, likely cooling off on that hot morning. Gabby grinned from ear to ear.

The women cruised around the lake, looking for a shady spot to fish. Finally, Sammy found a spot that looked like it would stay shady for a while. She cut the motor and sailed the boat into the perfect spot. Gabby dropped the anchor.

The women fished and chatted about nonsense. Sammy mentioned that none of the other guests she checked with that morning had seen the bear. It was only them. This seemed to reinforce the bear encounter symbolism for them.

Gabby asked, "Okay, then, was that deer we saw symbolic too?"

Sammy laughed. "Okay, I get your point, but no, I don't think it was. It didn't approach us like the hummingbird or bear did, right? We were just lucky enough to observe it."

"All right, I see the difference. I'm glad you do too. Honestly, I would worry about you if you started to glean messages from every little wild critter we see," Gabby confessed.

"Well, I would worry too. Let me know when I start doing that. That bear was just too intense. It was so big and powerful. Do you remember the size of his mouth and those teeth?" Sammy shuddered.

"I do," Gabby said. "That's when my instincts told me to run."

Both women started to giggle as they imagined what they must've looked like.

"Have you talked to Jake yet?" Gabby asked. "Did you tell him about the bear?"

"I talked to him briefly yesterday when he was still on the road. He said he'd call tonight and check in. I think he was planning on seeing lots of friends and family," Sammy reported.

"Do you think he'll see Heather?" Gabby asked.

Sammy was shocked. She'd never even thought of that. "I'm not sure. I would doubt it." Sammy's mind drifted off to the image of Jake and Heather kissing last summer before she really knew Jake or who that spiderwoman was. "That's a weird question to ask me, Gabby. What made you think of that?"

"I just thought of it. I guess I'm going to have a tough time trusting men," Gabby said.

"Okay, fair enough. I don't think she'd contact him, but I can't say with any certainty. I don't really know much about his pals from back home either," Sammy said.

"I didn't mean to worry you," Gabby said reassuringly.

"I'm not worried. I trust Jake. If he wants out of this relationship, he's free to choose that. All he has to do is let me know," Sammy said.

Suddenly a splash directed the women's attention overboard.

"Hey, I got a big bite," Gabby announced as she started to crank in her fishing pole.

"It looks like it's a big one," Sammy said with excitement. She got the net ready as Gabby continued to struggle.

As the fish neared the boat, Sammy slipped the net under its belly and helped Gabby pull it out of the water.

"Wow, look at that baby. She's a keeper all right," Sammy said.

Gabby beamed with pride and joy. "This is my first fish in ages. That was fun."

After the fish was safely on the stringer and overboard, the women decided to put the poles away and enjoy their snacks. They silently sat in the boat soaking up the sounds of nature. Sammy noticed the lack of man-made noise. She suddenly felt complete bliss and present in her body. It was a rare moment.

"Can I tell you a secret?" Gabby asked, breaking the silence and Sammy's meditative state.

"Yes, please do," Sammy said with curiosity.

"I miss my boys, but mostly I'm relieved to not be with them right now. Does that make me a bad mother?" Gabby asked timidly.

"No, you're human. It's actually kind of serendipitous that this is happening to you and Eddie while they're away. It has given you this unique opportunity for self-reflection and to take care of yourself. You're going to need your energy to focus on their feelings when you get home and begin the real separation. It's important for you to rest while you're here," Sammy said.

"Dang!" Sammy slapped her knee.

"What?" Gabby jumped.

"That was totally another meaning for the bear I read this morning too," Sammy said as she pointed to her forearm. "Look at my arms. It's giving me goose bumps."

"What was the meaning?" Gabby asked.

"I can't remember the exact words, but it had to do with hibernation as a time for self-reflection and self-observation and about being reborn after a temporary period of silence or solitude," Sammy said as she tried to recall some of the information she read.

"That's wild. You're a trippy woman, sister," Gabby said, shaking her head. "I'm trying to wrap my brain around all of this and it literally blows my mind. It's all so fitting. Maybe that dang bear was sent to bring us messages."

"I think so," Sammy said. "Ready to head back and see what's up at the resort?"

"Sure," Gabby said. "We can't forget my fish." She leaned over and pulled her fish out of the water.

Sammy started the motor and off they went. Sammy was thinking about that darn bear and the hidden messages he left behind. She looked at Gabby and wondered if she was thinking the same thing.

Gabby looked back at Sammy. "Damn bear. Can't get these ideas out of my head."

Sammy laughed. "Me neither."

CHAPTER 16

The next few days dragged on. The heat slowed everyone and everything down. Sammy missed Jake. The resort wasn't the same without him. She talked to him every day and appreciated the updates on Vince and Dana.

Gabby took the bear's messages to heart and slept—*a lot.* The hot afternoons were the perfect time to nap, Gabby concluded. She finally talked to Aunt Kathy, Cassy, and Alex. Each conversation sucked more energy out of her, but they needed to be had.

By the time the Fourth rolled around, few people at the resort felt festive. It was uncomfortably hot and humid.

But Sammy and Gabby rallied to the occasion. Sammy made posters with old Fourth of July photos from Jake's collection. She also put together a nostalgic collage of photos from a lunar landing party that the old owners threw in July 1969, just because the photos were so fun.

As the sun set and the air dropped a mere four degrees, the guests started coming to the beach with their dishes to share. Down-the-Road Dave and his wife showed up, as Dave promised to be the grill master. Dave's boys built a bonfire in spite of the heat.

Everyone enjoyed the evening and looking at all the old photographs. Seeing everyone's excitement over the old photos made Sammy want to complete her projects sooner than later.

After dinner, marshmallows were roasted, s'mores made, and sparklers lit. The stars came out by the dozens as darkness fell.

Dave's teenage boys wrapped up the evening with fireworks. Sammy worried about the guests' safety. The boys didn't take many precautions, and Sammy couldn't help reminding herself that these were the same boys who crashed logs and a homemade crane into Dave's wall of windows.

"These guys are making me nervous," Sammy whispered to Gabby.

"They're fine," Gabby reassured her.

"To you maybe—you have loads of experience with boyish high jinks," Sammy said nervously.

The crowd enjoyed the fireworks, which the boys shot off the dock out over the lake. The reflections on the lake were dazzling.

The boys announced that the grand finale was set to go. As they were lighting the fuses, one of the rockets fell over and blasted off prematurely. It whizzed past the crowd into the trees behind the resort.

Dave and his sons took off running after it.

"Holy…" Sammy said as she started after them. Gabby ran with her.

"See? Told ya," Sammy said breathlessly.

"This sort of thing happens all the time. No big deal." Gabby panted as she tried to keep up with Sammy.

Sammy and Gabby found the men behind Jake's workshop dragging out Jake's hose.

The forest was already ablaze. Sammy froze with fear.

"Find some buckets!" Dave shouted to her.

Sammy shook herself out of her trance. "Come on!" she told Gabby.

They dashed into Jake's workshop. The darkness made it difficult to see. But light from the flames suddenly came in through the windows and lit up parts of the workshop. Sammy could see some boats, motors, and plenty of other junk. She continued tossing things aside looking for buckets.

"Here!" Gabby yelled as she uncovered a stack of buckets.

The women ran out with the stack. By then several guests had arrived to help. Sammy and Gabby passed around the buckets, which were quickly filled from the nearest cabins' faucets. Some people ran down to the lake for water.

The boys were hosing down as much as they could. Dave found Jake's backhoe and proceeded to scrape up earth, dumping it on the fire. The group worked together this way for about a half hour until every last ember was put out.

When it was finally over, everyone was accounted for, no one was hurt, and Jake's workshop was intact. Dave turned off the backhoe and said, "Yep, those are my boys. I'm so proud."

The group erupted with laughter, mostly out of relief. Sammy felt like she held her breath the whole half hour. She was so worried someone or something would be lost. She had reacted automatically and watched Gabby rise to the occasion as well. Sammy saw Gabby's supermom skills in action.

When everyone knew the fire was out, they trickled back to the bonfire and cleaned up their messes. Most folks called it a night.

Dave told Sammy that he and the boys—mostly the boys—would as their punishment take turns throughout the night, watching the forest to make sure no fires started up again. Sammy was thankful for that, as she knew she wouldn't sleep a wink if she had to worry about the fire.

Sammy and Gabby were too worked up to go in for the night. Instead they went down to the dock to stargaze.

"Well, that sure was an exciting way to end the Fourth," Gabby said.

"That's one way of looking at it," Sammy said. Then she began to laugh. "Holy cow, I can't believe that happened. I was afraid I was going to have to tell Jake his resort burned down on my watch. Can you imagine?"

"I was sure Jake's workshop was gonna go up in flames. The fire got so close. I'm not entirely sure that the back side of his workshop isn't scorched," Gabby said.

"If that's all that comes out of this, I'll be happy with that."

"Hey!" both women exclaimed as they simultaneously saw a shooting star.

"That was cool," whispered Gabby.

"It was," Sammy said. "I think we should make some wishes."

"Out loud?" Gabby asked.

"Sure, why not? Got any good wishes?"

"I wish my boys strength and courage to handle our separation well and that they forgive me and Eddie. Oh, and that they still love me when it's all over."

"Wow, that one was really good. I like how your wish was for their courage and strength. See? You're such a good mom," Sammy said in awe.

"Thanks Sammy. What's your wish?"

"I wish that Jake and I live happily ever after," Sammy said dreamily.

"That's a really good one too. I'm gonna wish that one on the next shooting star I see," Gabby added.

The women spent the next hour watching the night sky and listening to Dave instruct the boys on their night watch. They chatted a bit between stargazing sessions, but in general, just took in the vastness of outer space. It was so dark now that the stars were bright and numbered in the thousands.

"It's just so pretty isn't it?" Sammy said as tears snuck out of her eyes.

"It is. It makes me and my problems feel so insignificant," Gabby said.

"I'm so happy you're here with me, Gabby," Sammy whispered.

"Me too," Gabby whispered back.

A few hours later Sammy woke up on the dock. Her aching back had forced her awake, as well as her cold body parts. In a state of confusion, she sat up abruptly, not realizing where she was. With relief, she looked over to see Gabby sleeping too. They had fallen asleep stargazing.

She gently woke Gabby and they headed toward the lodge after a brief check in with Dave's boys. The boys were vigilantly keeping watch and were surprised to see the women up at 3:00 a.m.

The sisters fell quickly back to sleep once safe and sound in their own beds.

***

The next morning, Sammy found Gabby already up and cooking.

"This is a surprise," Sammy said.

"Yes, a nice turn of events. I'm feeling really energized this morning. I don't know why. But I'm filled with hope and excitement," Gabby said happily.

"Wow, okay, you're way too peppy for me this morning. I need some coffee," Sammy said groggily.

Gabby made a cup of coffee quickly appear in front of Sammy. "Just the way you like it."

"Thanks," Sammy said. "What are you cooking?"

"Ham and cheese croissants."

"What? We have the ingredients for that?" Sammy asked.

"Yes, I bought it all the other day."

"Okay," Sammy said, taking a gulp of coffee.

"What should we do today?" Gabby asked.

"What do you want to do today?" Sammy asked in return.

"Host an art class," Gabby announced.

"Host a what?" Sammy asked. *Who is this person and what happened to my sister?* Sammy was quite amused by this conversation.

"An art class. Jennifer in cabin three is an artist. I caught her painting with watercolors the other day and she made it look so easy. There are eleven women and girls here this week. The other day, when Jennifer was heading into town for art supplies, I asked her to get supplies for fifteen and I would pay her back so we could have a class here in the lodge." Gabby took the croissants out of the oven.

"Were you going to tell me about this class? And how many croissants do you think the two of us need?" Sammy asked as Gabby pulled two trays out of the oven.

"These are for the class. I forgot to tell you, just like I forgot to tell you that I talked to Aunt Kathy. My mind is jumbled with all kinds of thoughts right now and I forget what I've told you and what I haven't. Is it okay if we host an art class here today?" Gabby asked with a grin.

"Sure," Sammy said in amusement. "What can I do to help you?"

"Nothing. I found Jake's stash of folding chairs down in storage and I figured we could put them around all the tables downstairs in the game room. I have these croissants and I've cut up some veggies and made some dip. I'll make some cookies next and then check with Jennifer about what time she wants to do this. Then I'll go around and invite people." Gabby had it all figured out.

"Okay, then. I'll plan on attending. It'll be fun. Thanks for setting it up," Sammy said with a shrug of her shoulders.

After downing a few cups of coffee and stealing one of Gabby's croissants for breakfast, Sammy got dressed and headed out to assess the extent of the fire.

When Sammy arrived at the spot of the forest fire, she found Dave there surveying the damage.

"Jake's gonna kill me," Dave said. "I can't believe I let my boys set off those fireworks. I had a bad feeling about it, but my wife assured me that they'd be fine."

Sammy laughed. "That's what Gabby said too. How bad is the damage? It doesn't look too bad. The workshop was spared."

"It's not too bad. But a few trees were really burned and need to be removed before they fall over. They could fall over onto the cars in the parking lot; or if they fell in that direction, one could hit that cabin." Dave pointed to the nearest cabin.

"Oh dear, I didn't even think about that. Well, Dave, it made for an exciting evening," Sammy added.

"Yes, it did that. I'm gonna call Jake in a bit and see if he wants us to cut these down today. Have you talked to him yet today? Does he know about the fire?" Dave asked.

"No, I wanted to see what the damage was before I called him. Ask him to call me after you talk to him, will ya?" Sammy asked.

"Sure," Dave said. "I'll be back later."

"Hey, tell your wife that my sister is hosting an art class in the lodge this afternoon. If she's interested in coming, have her call me and I'll let her know what time," Sammy said.

"Will do. I bet she'll like that," Dave said and he started off for home.

***

The art class was a huge success. Jennifer made it look so effortless. Every student was able to paint a lake and pine trees easily with the watercolors. The finer details were slightly more challenging, but everyone who participated was happy with their masterpieces.

They all enjoyed the lesson, the food, and the friendly conversation. Sammy couldn't help but notice that Gabby was in her element. She was a natural hostess, engaging each participant, commenting on everyone's work, and making sure they all enjoyed themselves—the things moms do.

Sammy noticed how everyone responded to Gabby with joy and enthusiasm. It was the quickest four hours of the entire week. The women all commented that they should do this sort of thing every day.

After Jennifer and the class participants left, Sammy and Gabby cleaned up.

"Gabby, you are so good at this. This could be something that people would pay to participate in. You could actually make some money doing this," Sammy said. "I'm serious. This was so much fun. The food was fantastic and the art lesson was great. You should've at least asked the women to pay for their supplies."

"Well, now that you mention it, I've thought about pursuing something like this at home. I have an artist friend, and I've often told her we should do this. But our schedules are always so out of sync. So I did this today sort of as an experiment to see if I could make it work—how much it would cost."

Gabby continued. "I didn't want to charge anyone since I invited them. It didn't cost much really, especially since the watercolors we used were so cheap. I mostly wanted to see the logistics of it—what worked, what didn't—and get some feedback."

"It seemed like it all worked to me. Gabby, this was fantastic and so much fun." Sammy beamed. "You're really surprising me, kiddo. I think you're going to be just fine on your own. You know that?"

Gabby stood a little straighter, pushing her shoulders back with confidence. She took a deep breath and smiled. "I think you're right."

After the art lesson, the women spent the rest of the day relaxing on the beach and splashing in the water.

***

The hot weather continued the following day and forced the women back out on the water.

As they floated around on rafts, sunning their bellies like cats, Sammy had another thought.

"Gabby, your art work yesterday was really good. I think you have a knack for that too. Have you ever taken art classes?"

"You think so? Thanks, Sammy. No, I haven't taken any classes. I always wanted to take some evening classes at the community college near our house, but Eddie never liked the idea. I guess now would be a good time, huh? Except the boys are always so busy at night."

"Well, there are all kinds of online classes you can take. I've seen some really cool ones. I looked into it once, when I was interested in writing children's books. I wanted to try to do my own illustrations. But I'm not very artistic. Maybe you could be my artist." Sammy spoke as the idea suddenly came to her.

"Interesting idea. I've never looked online. I'll have to check it out sometime," Gabby said.

"Or maybe you can find an art retreat for one of the weekends Eddie will have the boys. You go and take lots of classes in just a few days. That would be cool too. I bet there are some great ones in the mountains around Denver," Sammy added.

"That sounds fantastic too. I would like to help host one of those sometime. It would be wonderful to do what we did yesterday but on a much bigger scale," Gabby said dreamily.

"You should do that—find an art retreat to go to." Sammy sat up on her raft, almost tipping it over. "I bet you could convince Dana to join you on something like that. I know Kelly has always mentioned wanting to attend an art retreat, but I doubt that will happen for a while now with Maxie around."

"Speaking of Kelly, is she going to keep working for you now that she's had the baby?" Gabby asked.

"Honestly, I have no idea what to expect." Sammy flipped her body over on the raft. "We haven't talked about it. But the truth is, I basically pay her to keep me company and motivate me. She doesn't really need the money. Greg makes plenty as an architect. She's like one of those lucky ladies who only work at clothing stores for the discount."

Gabby laughed. "She was an architect too, though, wasn't she? Why can't I remember how you two met?" Gabby asked as they happily floated around on the rafts.

"Yeah she was. She and Greg were business partners and already married when I met her. But before that, they were both young successful architects working at two separate firms that teamed up together on a lot of projects, so they worked with each other a few times. Greg wanted to start his own firm and asked her to be his partner. She accepted and they were associates for a few years and then ended up getting married. Later she felt it was too much, working together as a married couple. It was also about the same time that she started to hate the politics involved in the bigger projects.

"That's when I met her at a fundraiser for a science center. We had a few cocktails together that night. I mentioned what I did and how I was looking for an assistant to help with the business side of things and that I wanted to stay a small two-women crew doing what I love." Sammy smiled as she thought back to that first night with Kelly.

"I remember that night clearly. She was so smart and funny. I remembered laughing all night with her. She was great. She also told me all about her family and her brothers. We even shared a heavy, heartfelt talk about her brother's young-adult challenges as a gay man. We really connected on many levels," Sammy said.

"And then what happened?" Gabby asked as she splashed her arms and legs with the cool water.

"I remember we exchanged business cards earlier in the night, but I never thought about it except that I should call her sometime to go out drinking with her. She called me the following week and asked if we could meet for coffee to discuss her becoming my assistant. I automatically told her she was far too overqualified and that I knew I couldn't pay her what she was worth. She said that didn't matter. She didn't need the money or benefits; she only needed a job that she enjoyed showing up to every day or less." Sammy laughed.

"It was the 'less' part that made me laugh. She was always free to come and go as she pleased and it actually turned out to be a perfect balance. I don't know if she'll want to stay home with Maxie every day. We never talked about it. It was sort of taboo to talk about the baby until we knew it was born happy and healthy and we both just assumed we'd have this summer to figure it out."

"Well, what if she doesn't want to go back to work?" Gabby asked. "And as another part of this dilemma, what's up with you and Jake? What happens after this summer? Or when do you decide it's time to go home? When the temperature back home drops under one hundred?"

Sammy laughed. "That's not a bad idea. I hate the summer heat there. I don't know what to expect with Jake and me. It could work: spend the summers here and the winters in Arizona. That would be perfect for me. And if we got married and had babies," Sammy said quietly, "we could still live that way for several years until school was an issue."

Gabby blinked at Sammy. "What? Have you been thinking about *that*? Did you guys talk about *that*?"

"No, no, no, heavens, no. We did tell each other that we loved each other, though." Sammy blushed.

"Aw, you did? I'm so happy for you."

"Yeah, it was a really moving moment. But that's it. No mention of marriage or even what we'll do after this month is over. It's sort of this weird unspoken thing."

"And of course it doesn't help that I come barging in with my issues. Well, I'll be leaving in a few days and you can figure it all out then," Gabby said.

"Okay, but first of all, you didn't barge in. And secondly, you seem to be handling your issues well. Do you mind me asking how you're doing that? I saw Dana practically six months after her marriage hit the skids and she was a mess. You snapped out of it in days. What's up?"

Gabby sighed and flipped over so that her stomach was on the raft now too. She turned her head to face Sammy. "I don't know, Sammy. At night while I lay awake for hours, I cry because I loved him, love him still, and somehow hate him. When we met in college…I still remember the day I met him, the handsome cowboy from Colorado. I remember thinking he was adorable and sweet, but he came on so strong it scared me. I liked him, but I was always hesitant to love him. It's hard to explain. But something was off.

"Over the years, I forgot about that 'off feeling' I had, so to speak. But I remembered it with each of his affairs. I was crushed the first time he cheated on me. If I had been braver then, I would've left," Gabby said sadly. "Bottom line, I've mourned the loss of our marriage too many times over the past eleven years. I'm done. I'm only thirty-seven years old. I have plenty of time to heal, find myself again, and maybe even be lucky like Aunt Kathy and find love again."

"You will," Sammy said, "do all three. It's so strange that both you and Dana are thirty-seven and transitioning into a similar phase in life. Her marriage was short-lived and yours was more mature. But you're both starting to face life's challenges again as individuals."

"That is a wild coincidence. I wonder if she's developing her sense of personal purpose too," Dana said.

"Her what?" Sammy asked.

"I don't know. I feel like I'm starting to sense the empty places in my life and it's important to fill them intentionally with purpose," Gabby said. "I think you're rubbing off on me this week. I'm getting all existential on you."

"I think you're right. I love it," Sammy said with a wide grin. "You make me proud."

The women floated in silence for a few minutes.

"If Kelly doesn't come back to work, I'll miss seeing her every day. I've missed her this summer. You said you were leaving in a few days. Do you know when you're leaving?" Sammy asked.

"Yeah, I think I'll leave Monday morning, stay overnight somewhere. That should get me home Tuesday afternoon. I'll have a few days at home to get used to things and see what mess Eddie left behind. The boys will be home on Saturday and we'll have about four weeks before school starts to figure out this separation."

"It all sounds so civilized," Sammy said.

"I hope so," Gabby answered. "When's Jake coming home? The funeral's today, isn't it?"

"Yes," Sammy said somberly, "it's this morning. I

somehow can't stop thinking about Vince's pain. I miss Jake and look forward to seeing him tomorrow. But this morning my heart aches for Vince and his loss."

"Amen to that," Gabby said.

The women spent the rest of that Friday lost in their own thoughts and projects.

Sammy had given Gabby her laptop that afternoon to investigate online art classes. Sammy was happy to see Gabby eagerly embrace the idea. The more classes Gabby found, the more enthusiastic she became about things.

While Gabby sleuthed online, Sammy worked on Jake's two scrapbooks. Later that evening when Gabby was done using Sammy's computer, Sammy finished the surprise booklet and ordered one-hundred copies from an online printer. She would receive the copies by next weekend. She was excited to give Jake her finished projects.

The women went to sleep early that night, as they expected a busy Saturday morning. Sammy tossed and turned as she thought about Jake coming home.

CHAPTER 17

The Saturday morning checkout went off without a hitch. The guests left, the cabins were cleaned, and everything was fine.

The afternoon arrived and new guests settled in without incident.

Sammy anxiously waited for Jake to come home. She had talked to him briefly in the morning. He would be there by dinnertime and promised to bring dinner with him.

Sammy and Gabby were swinging on the wooden swing, watching some children play on the beach. One child caught a frog, which got the women's attention.

"My boys would love that. I wish I could bring them here some summer," Gabby said longingly.

"What's stopping you? You should. This is such a magical place for kids," Sammy said.

"Well, Eddie always thought it was too far to bring the boys for a vacation. But apparently he won't be an issue now, huh? Maybe we can come up next summer," Gabby said.

"That would be great. I hope I'm here next summer," Sammy said.

"Yeah, about that…You and Jake really need to have a talk, don't you? Do it soon," Gabby commanded. "I need to know."

"I need to know too. But I'm scared to ask," Sammy said.

As they continued to gently swing, Sammy said, "You know Gabby, I know these next few months are going to be some of the most painful, sad days of your life. I know how much you're going to miss Mom during all of this. She was the one that told us it would all be okay, and just by her saying that, we felt better. She was our loudest cheerleader and biggest supporter." As if on cue, the sisters watched the mother of frog-boy gush over his catch.

"Please don't go it alone. I know you have friends in Denver, and many of them are your and Eddie's friends, so that will complicate things," Sammy said cautiously.

"But, please if you need me, call me, come see me, or tell me to come to you. And talk to Cassy and Aunt Kathy. Heck, even Alex will help in her own weird way." Gabby chuckled at the truth of that last statement.

Sammy continued, worried she was sounding preachy. "And if you want to come see me in Arizona with one, all, or none of the boys, you're all welcome anytime. And if you want to see Aunt Kathy or Cass, go. Make Eddie take the boys a little longer and go. And if you can't afford it, borrow money from Aunt Kathy or Cass; they have plenty and would love to help you out. Or at least Aunt Kathy did before she went property shopping." Both women laughed, easing the tension.

"Anyway"—Sammy perked up a bit—"life's too precious to suffer needlessly. You will hurt plenty—let us help ease your pain."

"Thanks Sammy. You do know how I feel. I do miss that comfort Mom gave us. I would like to go see Aunt Kathy too. But I don't want to intrude on Dana's time there."

"Intrude? Are you serious? They would love to have you. In fact, you should go for sure and hang out with Dana. I think you two would have a blast. Heck, you might even consider a business opportunity together. Wait 'til you see the guesthouse, Escondido. You and Dana could host some seriously groovy art retreats there," Sammy said excitedly.

"That would be cool. I never thought about that idea. I will definitely pursue it," Gabby said. "And thanks for bringing the word 'groovy' back, Sammy." Gabby jabbed Sammy with her elbow and they both laughed.

Just then, Jake's truck pulled up and stopped in front of the women. Ginger hopped out and ran to them, jumping around, happy to be home and to see them.

As Sammy stood to greet Jake, Ginger jumped up on her first. Sammy gave Ginger a hug and even accepted her doggie kiss of a lick on the cheek.

"Oh, I've missed you too, Ginger," Sammy said. She was surprised by how happy she was to see Jake's dog.

"What about me?" Jake asked as he came around the back of his truck.

Sammy greeted him with a tame kiss, not wanting to make her sister uncomfortable. "I missed you more," Sammy said with a smile.

"I missed you too, gorgeous," Jake said.

"Hi, Jake. How's the family?" Gabby asked.

"As good as can be expected. Thanks for asking. How 'bout you? Heard you almost burnt the place down," he teased Gabby.

"I totally had help with that," Gabby said with a guilty smile.

The women carried in bags of Chinese takeout as Jake carried in his travel bags. Ginger took off down the road likely in search of her mate.

The three stuffed themselves with the delicious takeout until they all claimed they could not eat another bite. The women retold the story of their encounter with the bear. Gabby delighted in telling Jake about Sammy's bear encounter theories. They talked about the fireworks gone bad and falling asleep under the stars.

Jake told them all about Vince and the family. He enjoyed talking about Dana's change in attitude and life. The women talked about the art class. Gabby told of her dreams of taking an art class or two and helping to host more classes.

It was a jovial night of conversation and catching up among friends. They were each filled with hopes of better tomorrows.

Since Gabby was leaving Monday morning, this was their last late night together and they took advantage of it. They stayed up talking, drinking, swimming, and simply enjoying their time together.

***

Gabby's last day went by in a blink. Jake had plenty of work to catch up on, leaving Sammy and Gabby free to spend the day on the boat. The women relaxed in the sun and kept all discussions light and lively and filled with hopes and dreams for brighter days ahead.

They fished. They swam. They drove the boat around looking for wildlife. Gabby said she desperately wanted another encounter with wildlife, so Sammy, the Bear Whisperer, could interpret it for her.

Sammy noticed that Gabby looked different—and not only because of her new haircut and color and glowing gorgeous tan. Her eyes sparkled when she talked about art classes, and she smiled more when she told Sammy silly stories about her boys.

Sammy knew Gabby's reality would change dramatically over the next few months, but today was Gabby's last day of freedom and the sisters simply enjoyed it.

When the women returned to the resort, Jake had finished work for the day and had a lavish spread of appetizers ready for them. He waited on them the remainder of the day and on into the evening.

By nightfall, Gabby had her bags packed—her *new* bags that was. As an early birthday gift, Sammy gave her two adorable Hawaiian-print, high-tech, lightweight travel bags that she found online. Sammy thought Gabby needed some fun new luggage to encourage her to travel more this fall and the coming year.

The threesome ended the day with a soak in the hot tub, where the women once more discussed Sammy's bear encounter symbolism. Gabby announced she would live up to her end of the deal—exuding patience and confidence and reaching her highest potential, while being nurturing and protective—as long as Sammy lived up to hers to have more fun. They both agreed and Jake added he would do his best to help.

***

Gabby left early the next morning. Sammy was sad to see her go and worried about what Gabby was returning home to. But she was proud of the strength she saw in her sister.

She knew Gabby would be fine in the end. Gabby was transforming into a new woman and her old self at the same time. Sammy was suddenly excited for Gabby's second chance.

"Hello in there," Jake said as he lightly tapped Sammy on her head.

Sammy laughed and stopped staring at the sunny blue lake. "Sorry, did you say something?"

"I wondered where your mind was," Jake answered as he sat down next to her on the couch.

"With Gabby. I'm excited for her new beginning. I know she's got a lot to go through first. But I see her getting there," Sammy said.

"And rather quickly I think. How do you do it? You're like a sorcerer," Jake teased.

"Do what?" Sammy asked, shaking her head in confusion.

"Fix everyone's problems," Jake said.

"How do I do that?"

"Well, first you whisked Dana away from her misery into 'heaven'—that's the word she used. Then, you fill your sister's head so full of hopes and dreams about art lessons and classes that she'll be sporting rose-colored glasses for the next three months, straight through her whole divorce process. That's how."

Sammy flashed a small devilish smile. "I did pack Gabby's pipe pretty full, didn't I?"

"I should say so. And I like that metaphor, by the way." He smiled fondly at her. "But I'm not sure she can smoke that much."

"I think she can. She's going to surprise us all, especially Eddie. He'll rue the day he ever hurt that girl," Sammy said.

"Listen to you, 'rue the day,'" Jake teased her.

She laughed in spite of herself. "Well, it's true. He will."

Jake kept laughing as he put his arm around Sammy and squeezed. "Oh, how I missed you."

She smiled at him. "I missed you too."

That's all it took for the two to race one another back to Jake's bedroom. They had restrained their new love while Gabby was there the last few days. But now that Gabby was gone, nothing could keep them apart. They got reacquainted all morning.

***

"Did I tell you Vince is coming up this week?" Jake asked as he set about making dinner that evening.

"No, you didn't. When's he coming?" Sammy asked as she chopped lettuce for a salad.

"Wednesday," Jake said.

"For a visit, for good, for what?"

"I'm not sure. I didn't tell you the heavy shit when Gabby was here, because I wanted to stay positive around her. But he's in a bad place. He sold his condo in Cincinnati already and resigned from his job."

"When did he do all that? Just this past week?" Sammy asked, shocked.

"No. I guess when he put the offer on Brink's place, he put his up for sale and it sold within a week. It even closed quickly too. I guess cash buyers can do that," Jake said.

"Who has all this cash?" Sammy shrugged her shoulders with the knife in one hand and a cucumber in the other.

Jake gave her a knowing look.

"Okay, okay, besides my Aunt Kathy or Cassy. But seriously, who does this?"

"Anyway," Jake said with a roll of his eyes, "that was about the same time he told his school he wasn't coming back in the fall. He resigned as teacher and coach and is officially unemployed and his only home is the dump down the road."

"It's not a dump," Sammy said defensively. "It just needs a little love—okay a lot of love and *construction*—to make it what he wants. But the potential is there and if Vince has the passion, then his life as he envisions it has potential too."

"See? How do you do that? Glass half-full, huh?" Jake asked.

"I wasn't always like that. I think it's you. Remember last summer? I wasn't so hopeful. This summer, getting to know you better, it's changed me," Sammy said.

"Well, it sounds like you have everything figured out now," Jake said as he handed Sammy a glass of wine and took her by the hand. He led her to the couch. They sat down.

"Not everything," she said as she sipped the wine. "What the heck are we doing with our lives? There, I said it. Where do we go from here? What happens after this summer? After Wednesday when Vince gets here? After July? What happens?" Sammy's frustration was clear.

"And there it is. I don't know. We're there, aren't we? At that make it or break it point," Jake said.

"Sort of. We aren't in our twenties anymore where we can just wing it and see where this goes," Sammy said.

"Can't we wing it just a little bit longer?" Jake asked.

Sammy smiled. "Yes, we can. But I'm no spring chicken. I can't wait around for you forever."

"Okay, summer chicken, I won't make you wait around forever," Jake said.

CHAPTER 18

Wednesday afternoon Vince arrived at the resort in a shiny new pick-up truck. As Sammy waved from the dock, she noticed how handsome he looked sitting in the silver truck and thought he could always go back to modeling if the fishing shack didn't work out.

Vince waved back as he headed into Jake's lodge.

A few minutes later Vince strutted down to see her.

She met him halfway, greeting him with a hug.

"I'm so sorry about your mom, Vince. I'm thankful you had some time with her though. It's good to see you," Sammy said.

"Thanks, Sammy. You look good. The Minnesota sun is doing wonders for you," he said with a wink.

"I think it's your cousin, not the sun. Got plenty of that in Arizona," Sammy replied.

"Lucky bastard," Vince said. "Want to come down and see my cabin again? I can't believe I own that place now. I have this scary sort of excitement thing going on."

"Yeah, I would love to see it again. What's Jake up to?" Sammy asked.

"Looking for motor parts online," Vince said. "Let's walk down. I've been in that truck all day."

"Yeah, nice truck. So starting out with new everything, huh?" Sammy asked.

"Might as well," Vince said quietly as the two headed down the road toward his new cabin.

"Yup, might as well," Sammy agreed. "If you want to talk about anything, I'm a good listener. I know the pain and sadness from losing your mommy," Sammy said as she lightly tapped his arm.

"Then you know the strange feeling of not having to be accountable anymore?" Vince asked cautiously.

"Yes," Sammy confirmed. "I do know the feeling exactly. It's strange, isn't it? Losing that connection to the world, that one person that grounded you the most your whole life. When my mom, my parents, died, I became this balloon of a person, no longer grounded to the world. I remember feeling like a free-floating shell. Thank goodness my Aunt Kathy was there to help keep all us free-floating balloons from drifting away for good."

"You explain it well. I did and still do feel like my connection to the world has been broken. Of course my dad's still here, but I still feel that disconnect. Does it go away?" Vince asked shyly as he shuffled his feet in the dirt.

"It changes intensity, but never goes away—at least for me it hasn't. Maybe it'll be different for you. I look forward to finding out."

"Yeah? How long you sticking around? What's up with you two? You should stay through the fall. September and early October are absolutely gorgeous around here. But you'll want to be the hell out of here come November," Vince said. "It can be unbelievably cold."

"Hard to imagine," Sammy said distantly. "And I'm not sure what our deal is. We're sort of on the fence about it right now."

"You don't have to tell me about fences. I've sat on 'em my whole life. But no more," he said as they arrived at his cabin.

He reached in his pocket, pulled out the keys to the cabin, and jingled them in the air. "Hear that? That's the sound of me getting my ass off that fence."

He dramatically unlocked the door and had to knock it open with his hip.

"First thing I'll fix," he said with a grin as he fiddled with the sticky door.

Sammy laughed and said, "The first of many things, huh? But I'm excited to see what you'll make of this place. You did a great job on Jake's deck. I imagine this will be a beautiful place for your guests to stay."

"Sammy, thanks for…everything. You're a good friend," Vince said.

"I haven't done anything," Sammy insisted.

"You've been extremely supportive of this idea of mine and I think you're the reason Jake's so supportive too. He invited me to stay at his place during construction as long as I need to, and he even offered to help with the job as long as he's not in Arizona," Vince said with a grin.

"He said that?" Sammy asked, trying to hide her shock.

"Yeah, apparently he's planning on wintering in Arizona," Vince said.

"Wow, that's pretty exciting to hear. He hasn't mentioned that to me," Sammy said.

"Well, apparently you haven't invited him to go with you to the 'Second Wedding of the Century.' Dana told us all about it, and since Jake didn't know a thing about it, he assumed you weren't interested in taking him. I swear, you two are worse than the students in my classes, texting love notes back and forth."

"They can text during class?"

Vince shook his head. "That's not my point. But yes, sometimes I have them use their phones for good and not always evil."

"Are you going to miss the students and teaching?" Sammy asked.

"Yeah I will. But if this place turns out anything like I envision it, it'll be like high school for old people. I'll be teaching a new group of old kids stuff and learning as much from them too," Vince said.

"I like that analogy," Sammy said.

"There's not much to see here, huh? Ready to head back?" Vince asked.

"Sure," Sammy said.

As they walked back to the resort, Sammy said, "There was something else I wanted to tell you."

"Yeah, what's that?" Vince asked, kicking a rock off the middle of the dirt road.

Sammy thought walking with Vince was like walking with a twelve-year-old boy. She fully expected him to stop walking and start throwing rocks in the lake.

"Your mom passed away on June thirtieth right?" Sammy asked gently.

"Yeah, why?" Vince asked.

"That's Meteor Day or Meteor Watch Day. It seemed like a significant day to go to heaven," Sammy said.

"What does Meteor Day mean?" Vince asked.

"It's a day to remind everyone to look to the sky, to the stars, and observe. It's just kind of symbolic that everyone will be reminded to look to the heavens that night, ya know?" Sammy asked.

"You sure have a unique way of looking at things, Sammy. I like it. Alex said that about you. Jake did too. They're right," Vince said with a small smile.

After another quiet moment, he continued, "I was there when my mom passed away. I swear I could literally feel her spirit leave her body and be in the room after she stopped breathing. Do you believe me?"

"Yes, I do. It sounds wonderful, like an affirmation of life after death. What did you think about the most that day?"

"I was pissed that she would never get to see what happened on *General Hospital* on Monday," he said with a chuckle. "I'm serious. That's what I thought about that day."

Sammy smiled and thought maybe Jake didn't look deep enough at his cousin. She was happy to see Vince smile and laugh. It made her think that Vince might be okay.

"It's strange how the mind processes grief, huh?" she asked.

"I guess," Vince said.

"What's your next step?" Sammy asked.

"I'm not sure. I have a lot to do if I want this fishing shack up and running next summer. I need to start right away: it's almost mid-July and construction season will be over by November. I need to figure out the overall design of the compound and what buildings I need and their designs and then figure out permitting. Permits will be my big holdup, but I got guys on the inside, so I know how to expedite things." He laughed.

"I'm sure you do," Sammy said with a smile.

Back at the resort, they found Jake finishing up his work.

"You done for the day, Cuz?" Vince asked.

"Yeah pretty much. I just ordered all the parts I need and everything's been running smooth around here, knock on wood. Why? Got something in mind?"

"Yeah. I wondered if you two want to ride with me over to a lake about an hour away. I found a guy who has some log cabins for sale. They're like prefab cabins that he can take apart there and put back together here," Vince said.

"Wow. That sounds cool. I'd like to see that," Sammy said excitedly.

"Sure, we'll go. When do you want to leave?" Jake asked.

"We should leave soon if we want to be back by dark. I'll drive," Vince said.

"Okay, give us a few minutes to get ready. We'll meet ya at your truck," Jake said.

Ten minutes later, they were on the road. Sammy was sitting in the middle of the two handsome cousins in a shiny new silver truck. She didn't recognize herself or her life.

***

Later that night, back at the resort, when the three were sitting on the couch eating pizza and drinking beer, Sammy felt like a happy, carefree teen.

"So, what did you think about the cabins?" Jake asked Vince. They had looked at four log cabins in a range of sizes and layouts.

Sammy loved all of them.

"Well, I liked them all. Didn't you guys?" Vince said.

"Yeah, I did. I loved the little A-frame the most, though," Sammy said. "But what are you looking to do exactly? I didn't think any of them would be good for your fishing shack concept."

"Yeah, I'm not following ya either, Vince. Whatcha thinking?" Jake asked.

"Well, here's the deal. I think permitting is going to be a big issue for me and could hold up construction, especially the septic systems, ya know? Sorry Sammy, glamorous talk here…"

Sammy replied, "Actually, I know quite a bit about septic systems and treatment wetlands. I might be of some help." Feeling embarrassed, she followed up with a nervous giggle.

"You know *what*?" both men asked at the same time. They laughed. Jake shook his head and lovingly said, "You never fail to surprise me, gorgeous."

"Anyway…" Vince began to explain his construction and renovation ideas. After several minutes, Jake and Sammy were still confused.

"Do you have some paper?" Vince asked.

Jake got up and found some oversized paper, pens, and colored markers. He placed them on the coffee table in front of Vince.

Vince looked up at his cousin with a dropped jaw. "You have this stuff just lying around?"

Jake laughed. "Dana had all this when she redid the cabins. I kept it, thinking it might come in handy sometime."

Sammy smiled at the adorable exchange between these grown men.

Vince quickly began making sketches using the different colored markers. Sammy could make out the current layout in blue. Vince drew over that layer with new buildings in red.

"There," Vince said as he sat back. "The current cabin will be replaced with the new two-bedroom A-frame with the loft. I'll use the loft as my office. This will be home base for me and also allow me to have personal guests. And later when things expand and I have another office, I can always stay in the fishing shack and save this cabin for any families that might want to visit 'Grandpa' while he's a guest at the fishing shack," Vince explained.

"Ah, I like that idea, Vince," Sammy said.

"I'll keep the shed and garage for now, until I know what improvements and future needs will be. Here's the new fishing cabin, and it'll need its own larger septic system also. Those are the two pieces that will require the most permitting." Vince excitedly pointed out each piece on his sketch.

"So if I move on this quickly, I might be able to have the new A-frame cabin up and operational by this September. I'll be able to stay there through the winter while working on the other buildings. It'll be a lot of work, but I think I can have it running by next June, July at the latest," Vince said.

"Okay, sounds good. I'm behind you one hundred percent. Just let me know what I can do to help," Jake said.

"I can't wait to see it come true," Sammy added with a smile. "I think it'll be beautiful."

"Thanks, Sammy," Vince said. "Thanks to both of you, especially for letting me crash here for a few days, Jake. I can always get a cot and sleeping bag and sleep in my own cabin down there."

"That's not necessary. You're always welcome here. You know that," Jake said.

"Okay, well I'm gonna call it a night. I've got a lot to do tomorrow." Vince went off to his room.

"G'night," Sammy and Jake said together as he left.

"Well, what do you think?" Jake asked as he eyed Vince's drawings.

"Looks like a lot of work and money," she whispered back. "But I think he's got the passion for it and that's the most important part."

"I couldn't agree more. Speaking of passion…" Jake leaned in for a kiss.

She happily accepted it.

CHAPTER 19

The next three weeks flew by. Sammy was busy playing house and helping the men with anything they needed. She worked on her tan and read novels. She truly enjoyed every moment and treated each day like a vacation.

Her secret box of printed books arrived that first week. Luckily, Jake was down at Vince's cabin when the delivery arrived, so Sammy accepted the package and stashed it away for the right time.

Vince's old cabin and septic system were removed and the new ones had already arrived for installation. It was an exciting time for Vince. Sammy was happy to be there to see it.

Jake helped Vince nearly every afternoon and the two men were physically exhausted most nights. In spite of the warm weather, the three soaked in the hot tub nightly, soothing sore muscles and sharing the events of the day.

Sammy enjoyed her lazy days talking to the "women folk" as the men loving called Sammy's family and friends, including Dana. The men enjoyed hearing the latest gossip each night in the hot tub. They teased Sammy, calling her "Anchorwoman Sammy." She got a kick out of their joke and hammed it up with her "Nightly News Reports."

Sammy talked to Dana every few days. Dana told Sammy all about her shopping excursions, fancy dinner parties, and the everyday joy she felt working for Aunt Kathy. Sammy continued to read Dana's blog and loved looking at all the pictures of Escondido's transformation. Dana was doing a beautiful job.

Aunt Kathy had been a frequent caller the past few weeks as well. Kathy called Gabby daily and relayed the Denver news back to Sammy, most of which Sammy already knew from her daily chats with Gabby.

Aunt Kathy also gave rave reviews of Dana's work and still struggled over what to do with her new properties. Aunt Kathy was "pleased as punch" with Vince's land purchase. Sammy told Vince as much, endearing her to him further.

Kelly was thrilled with mommyhood. Sammy couldn't believe Maxie turned three months old without her. But Kelly reassured Sammy that she was in the right place. Kelly's mom was staying with her for a few weeks as Greg's work schedule picked up with out-of-town trips.

Cass, the happy mom of healthy six-month-olds, called often to tell Sammy about their latest skills.

Alex was a little harder to get a hold of. But she had returned a call or two over the past three weeks. She was busy and good—loved her job still. Not too much information from Alex, but Sammy felt that no news was good news regarding Alex.

These were the things Sammy was thinking about as she sat on the old wooden swing. It was the first day of August, and summer was almost over. The weather had taken an abrupt turn and cooled about twenty degrees. Sammy enjoyed the jeans and sweatshirt weather and longed for some rain. July had been a hot, dry month.

A dragonfly appeared again on her boot. Sammy looked at it wondering if it could possibly be the same one that landed on her weeks ago. It could be. She thought about where she was in her life a few months before.

She couldn't imagine what her summer would've been like if Jake had never called. She came to help Dana. And she did. Their whirlwind trip across the country to Arizona and California was so fun. She knew California changed Dana's life forever even if she only stayed there a few more months. At this point, Sammy didn't know what Dana's future plans were.

She thought of Vince and knew that losing his mom had changed his life forever. But she was so impressed by how *he* was changing his lifestyle now.

Then there was Gabby. She was changed too, and was continuing her change. About a week after Gabby returned to Denver, she called to tell Sammy that the boys were handling the separation quite well. Since then, there were tough days, but overall, the boys were taking it all in stride. Apparently, many of the boys friends' parents were already divorced, which lessened the blow. Gabby was pursuing her dreams. Sammy was thankful she was part of Gabby's transformation.

"I guess it was a summer of dragonfly changes, little guy. But what about me? How did I change?" she whispered.

She looked up in time to see Jake and Vince walking back from Vince's. Jake, with his shirt off, was tanned and sweaty. Sammy loved him completely. She wanted to be with him always. "That's how, huh?" she said quietly. The dragonfly zipped off.

She waved to Jake. He waved back. Her heart filled with painful love for him. She didn't know where they were going or what the hell they were doing. She suddenly needed to know.

"Hiya," Jake said as he met her by the swing. Vince waved a quiet hello and headed straight into the lodge.

"Hiya," she said back with a smile.

"What's up?" he asked as he plopped down on the swing beside her.

"Nothing," she said.

"Nothing? Sorry, do I stink?" he asked as he wiped dirt and sweat off his arms.

"No. You're good. What were you two doing?" she asked.

"You don't want to know," he said with a smile.

"You hungry? I made lasagna," she said as she wore a permanent smile.

"I'm starved and that sounds delicious. Are you sure nothing's up? You have a funny look on your face," he said.

"Sorry," she said, trying but failing to control her smile. "I'm just very attracted to you right now, if you know what I mean. What does Vince say? 'Hubba, hubba'?" She moved her eyebrows up and down suggestively.

Jake burst out laughing. "So damn cute," he said as he kissed her—lovingly at first and then more passionately. She felt it deep inside. She almost cried as she realized how much she loved him.

He pulled away and stood up. "Okay, I'm sure this is quite inappropriate in public." He took her hand, pulled her up, and led her to the lodge.

"Yes, quite inappropriate, indeed," she said with a smile, as she quickly followed him inside.

Vince was standing in the doorway as they entered.

"Better get lost, buddy," Jake said.

"Say no more." Vince chuckled as he walked out the door, cold beer in hand.

Jake and Sammy quickly found themselves in Jake's bedroom finishing that kiss.

Jake pulled away again. "What about that lasagna?"

"We have about forty minutes, so quit talking," she said with a giggle.

***

After dinner, Vince made himself scarce again, taking Ginger for a walk. Jake built a fire in the stone fireplace for he and Sammy to enjoy.

"How do you like sharing Ginger with Vince?" she asked.

"Don't mind. Rather share her than you. I think Vince feels he's intruding on us," Jake said.

"I don't think he is. Do you? I've liked having him here, keeping an eye on him. I know he's a grown man, but losing a parent can catapult a person out of their known world. I'm glad we can be here for him."

Jake looked at her fondly. "You really have a way with words. But I guess you know firsthand about losing parents. I'm glad we're all here together too. I've loved having you here this summer. Thanks for coming. You've changed Dana's life forever."

"I was thinking the same thing earlier on the swing. Except, I actually thought California will change her life forever, not me."

"Well, you're the reason she's in California," Jake said. "You've changed my life forever too, I think."

"Ya think?" she teased.

"Yeah, I think," he said as he gently kissed her.

"I have something for you. I'll be right back," she said as she got up and headed to her room.

She came back with a few wrapped packages and a large brown box. "For you," she said as she put them down in front of him.

"What in the world?" he asked as he surveyed the pile of packages.

"Here, this one first," Sammy said and gave him a large package wrapped in brown shipping paper with pinecones attached to it with twine.

Jake opened the wrapping paper to find a large worn leather journal. As he turned the pages, the life of his resort and Loon Lake unfolded before his eyes. She had handwritten all the text, notes, and information. All the photos were digitally restored, but printed in their original black-and-white color schemes until the 1960s. As Jake turned each page, Sammy could read his emotions in every facial expression.

"This is truly more than I ever expected," he said, putting the book down and pulling her close. "Thank you," he whispered in her ear.

"You're welcome," she said as she watched him wipe his eyes. "Here, now this one." She handed him a second similarly wrapped package the same size and shape of the first.

He again carefully untied and opened the package, not knowing what to expect. It was the same kind of worn leather scrapbook, but the content was much different. As he turned the pages, he couldn't help but laugh out loud. "This is wonderful," he said as he looked at the photos of all the guests from that summer, as well as their heartfelt and funny notes. "You are so full of surprises—"

"Wait there's more," she interrupted him. She pushed the large shipping box toward him.

"I can't even imagine," he said. As he opened the folding lid to the box, he peeked in and was taken aback. "Sammy! What is this?" He pulled out a handful of booklets the size of his fancy tablet.

It then dawned on him that he was holding several copies of the same thing and the box was filled with them. "What are these?" he asked as he began to flip through the pages.

"Booklets for you to sell to guests if they want them. You had such awesome old photos of this place that we all love so much, I wanted to share them with everyone. I made them so you could sell them for the cost of printing, no big deal. When you run out of these, I can have more printed up. I took some of the best stories and photos of the lake and this resort and put them in here. You like it?"

"I love it. The guests will love it too," he said as he smothered her with a hug. "My, you've been busy, haven't you? Saving my family and yours all the while putting these wonderful books together. And here I thought you were just reading books and tanning that gorgeous body."

"Yes, that's what us women like you to think. We're actually quite diabolical in our laziness," she teased.

He laughed as he snuggled in close and the two leafed through the pages of all three books. About an hour later, Vince came in and joined them. He loved the books too and asked Sammy to think about capturing his resort like this someday, suggesting that she start now with its infancy. She happily agreed and said that she'd already photographed the transformation of the past three weeks.

The three stayed up late that night, enjoying the rich history of the resort. By the time they called it a night, an unexpected rainstorm had moved in. As Sammy drifted off to sleep, she thought about how it was a blissful night—one that made her thankful for everything in her life.

CHAPTER 20

The rain continued through the night and on into the morning.

Sammy stayed in bed until late morning, cuddled up with the latest novel she was reading and listening to the rain on the roof. It was a perfectly lazy morning, something to savor.

The men's chatter in the kitchen finally lured her out of bed around ten.

She found Jake and Vince taking the rainy day off from working on Vince's cabin. Ginger was stretched out in front of the fireplace warming her belly near the flames. The men were sitting on the couch, drinking coffee, and reading the news on their tablets.

Sammy, wrapped in her long fuzzy sweater, poured a cup of coffee and quietly snuggled in tight next to Jake.

"Good morning, sleepyhead," Jake said, placing a gentle kiss on her cheek.

"Mmm, morning." She smiled back as she put her head on his shoulder. "Nice rain and cold weather. I love it. What's new in the world?" Sammy asked happily.

"Look here," Jake said and showed her a photo on his tablet. "There's a fire burning in the mountains in Northern Arizona. Started this morning after a small private plane crashed."

"Oh that's terrible. Who was in the plane?" Sammy asked.

"Doesn't say. It just happened a few hours ago, about sunup in Arizona. Authorities are still notifying family. But this says they have the fire contained and should be out by tomorrow. Apparently, they've had some good rains there the last week, so the forest wasn't too dry," Jake reported.

"Well, that's good news for a change. Usually those darn fires burn for weeks in the dry forests. We've lost hundreds of thousands of acres these past several years. Entire ecosystems were destroyed, and because we're experiencing such a dramatic climate change, these ecosystems will be lost forever. More drought-tolerant species are replacing the forest trees."

"There she is, Miss Doom and Gloom. I knew she was still there somewhere," Vince teased.

"I know. I've really been working on that," Sammy said with a smile.

Vince continued ribbing her. "You've been doing really well. Keep up the good work."

He stood and went to put on his rain gear. "Well, I need to head down and see what all this rain is doing to my lot. I can't imagine what kind of muddy mess it is. I'll need a week of sun to dry it out before I can start the heavy work back up."

He snapped his fingers for Ginger to join him. She barely lifted her head and gently put it back on her front paws. "Yeah, I don't blame ya, Girl," he said as he went out into the cold rain without her.

After a few minutes of quiet, Sammy asked, "What are we doing?"

"Reading the news? Drinking coffee? Enjoying the rain and the fire?" Jake asked. "What do you mean?"

Sammy released a flurry of words. "I mean us. What are we *doing*? This. You and me. Sunny days, rainy days, we're here together. But what about after Labor Day when the resort is closed? What do we do then? Aren't you worried about us? Gabby and Eddie ended up in Splitsville right next to Dana and George. Why do we bother if we're just going to end up there too? But I guess we actually have to be married first to get there. And technically we've known each other for over a year, but have only *really known* each other a few months. It's so confusing."

"Okay, first of all, someone needs to be drinking decaf this morning," Jake said as he took her coffee cup from her. "And secondly"—he kissed her reassuringly—"but most importantly, those guys had their shot and it didn't work out. This is our turn. I want to take it. There are no guarantees in life. We know that. You McGreggor girls have known that most of your lives. But if we don't risk it and try, we'll never know.

"I had so many regrets about last summer," Jake said, then paused. "After you left last summer, I regretted not telling you how I felt about you. About waiting to kiss you until the day you left. What was *that*?" He asked himself rather than her.

"And then last fall," he continued, "I regretted not flying out to see you, or visiting you sometime last winter. I kept thinking that some man scooped you up while I was dropping the ball and that I had missed my chance. Even when I finally got the guts to leave you that voice mail in April, I wasn't sure you'd call me back."

Sammy sat, blinking at him, listening to him pour out thoughts she never knew he had.

He stopped rambling. "My point is, I do not know what to expect tomorrow, but I know I want to be with you today."

"Okay," Sammy said calmly.

They sat looking at each other for about thirty seconds.

"Is that it?" Jake asked impatiently.

Sammy laughed. "Sorry, I was just processing everything you said. I didn't think men had regrets. You never talk about them. You men plug away no matter what stupid thing you do. You do it like it never happened. Women, we regret everything and gladly report these regrets, from relationships to bad lipstick colors. So, to hear this from you is sort of taking me by surprise."

"Well, yeah. Men typically don't admit regret, it's like admitting defeat. If you don't mention it, it didn't happen that way," Jake said.

"I had regrets too, Jake. And I don't want to leave here this summer with anything else left unsaid. I guess that's why I needed to ask about where we stand. I want to know what to expect from us," Sammy said.

"I can't give you that answer," Jake said. "But it's not the same as saying I don't want to be with you. I do. But I'm confused about Vince moving here and Dana going to California, and I feel like one of us has to stay in a holding pattern and see where everyone lands. That doesn't mean I won't live my own life. I just need some more time."

"I need more time too. I'm confused by Gabby's and Dana's marriages ending in infidelity. It makes me wonder if we stand a chance. But I don't want to be with anyone else. So, here we are. Reading the news. Drinking coffee. Enjoying the rain and the fire," she said.

"Are you okay with that?" Jake asked.

"For now," she said as she snuggled in tighter. "Can I have my coffee back?" she asked.

Jake laughed as he handed it to her. "Can I get you a refill?" he asked as he stood up to refill his own cup.

His phone rang.

"Hold that thought," he said, answering his phone in the other room.

Sammy could hear him talking, but couldn't make sense of anything. He was on the phone for a few minutes. It didn't sound good. Sammy worried that something else happened to someone Jake knew.

Jake came back and sat next to her on the couch and held her hands. "Sammy, I have some very sad news. That phone call was for you. It was Kelly's brother, Tim. He tried your cell phone several times this morning," he said calmly.

"What's wrong? What happened? Not Kelly? What aren't you telling me, Jake?" Sammy asked as her heart sank and panic squeezed the air from her chest.

"Kelly's fine. Maxie's fine. It's Greg. He was in that plane crash this morning," he said tenderly as the words sunk in for Sammy. "The one we saw in the news."

Sammy shook her head. "No," she said as tears erupted and her heart broke. "Not Greg. Oh, poor Kelly. And the baby!"

Sammy sobbed and Jake held her as she cried. It was several minutes until Sammy could come up for air.

"What happened?" she asked as new tears welled up in her eyes.

"Greg, two other designers, a client, and the pilot were in the clients' private plane. They were flying over a spot in the mountains where the client wanted to build a new golf community. It was a typical morning. Nothing was out of the ordinary weather-wise or mechanically. The authorities don't know what went wrong. There were no survivors," he said quietly.

Sammy cried again. She was heartbroken for her friend and the baby who would never know her daddy. She cried for the friend *she* lost. She'd known Greg for as long as she'd known Kelly.

Jake held her, trying to comfort her.

"I have to go to her," Sammy said, abruptly sitting up and wiping away her tears. "Who's with her now?"

"Tim said their mom's been staying with her, which is a blessing. He's flying down there this afternoon. I'll check out flights for you this afternoon. We'll get you there. Do you still have miles for a free flight?" he asked.

"Yeah, I should. But if not, money doesn't matter," she answered.

"I wasn't thinking about the money. I just thought maybe it might help us get you out on the next available flight," he said.

She gave him her airline info. He got on his tablet and started checking out flights.

Within the hour, Jake had lined up flights for her that afternoon. She was taking a puddle-jumper from Saw Mill to Minneapolis and a commercial flight on to Phoenix. She would be in Phoenix by sundown.

He quickly helped her pack her two bags and they were on the road to the local airport. She never even said good-bye to Vince.

They drove to the airport in silence. Her tears quietly came and went, in regular intervals. She grieved but tried to be brave and strong and stifle her sadness.

Jake held her hand as they drove. "You want me to come out next week, whenever the funeral might be?" he asked.

"Thank you for the offer. But it isn't necessary. I know you'll be busy here," she said sadly.

"Is there anything I can do for you?" he asked.

"No, I'll be fine. I just need to get there so I can take care of Kelly. I can't imagine how she feels right now." Sammy began to cry again.

"I can't either," Jake said as he wiped his eyes. "I'm so sorry, Sammy."

"Me too, Jake. Me too," she said between tears.

They arrived at the local airport with only a few minutes to spare. Jake dropped her off curbside.

They kissed good-bye. Through Sammy's grief, she was still able to kiss him passionately, with love, with grief, with every ounce of life she had in her.

"Sammy…" Jake said as he held her.

"What?" she asked. Her eyes were red and swollen. She could barely look him in the eyes.

"I love you," he said.

"I love you too," she said as she started to pull away.

"Wait," he said, "I don't want to regret this morning ever. I can't let you leave this way. Will you marry me? Will you come back and marry me? We can figure out where our lives will take us, but I want us to do it together."

She looked at him; different tears flowed from her eyes. Her heart suddenly ached for a very different reason. She kissed him again.

"Yes," she said with a smile.

"Yes?" he asked.

"Yes. I will marry you."

"Okay, I'll see you soon," he said as he kissed her again.

"Okay, I'll see you soon," she repeated as she hurried to the check-in counter.

***

As the sun set on the horizon, Sammy looked out the airplane window. She glanced down at the mountains below, wondering what Greg's final thoughts were. She looked at her bare ring finger on her left hand, rubbing it absentmindedly.

She took turns quietly crying for Kelly's loss, then Maxie's loss, then her own loss. Greg was such a kind man, a good friend, a wonderful husband. She knew he was a good father. Sammy spent most of the day crying, grieving.

She told herself that when her plane landed she needed to be strong for Kelly, her friend who was always strong for her. Sammy was going to take care of Kelly. This was the last task of her dragonfly summer, she swore it. No more changes. She didn't like these changes anymore.

She had to be strong.

The pilot announced that they'd be landing soon. The local time was 6:40. The local temperature was a cool one hundred seven degrees.

CHAPTER 21

The month of August moved at a snail's pace—a hot, sticky snail at that. Sammy watched as Kelly did whatever she could to survive each day. With a three-month-old depending on her, Kelly had to keep moving, keep doing the next thing.

It was an endless string of hot days with baby bottles, spit-up, naps, and diapers, and not necessarily in that order. It was an odd blessing that Kelly had stopped nursing Maxie a few weeks before the plane crash.

Sammy, along with Kelly's mom, Ellen, and Greg's mom, Betty, formed a band of women whose purpose was to help Kelly and Maxie get through the first few weeks after Greg's death.

Ellen and Betty had both been widowed for a few years. Ellen rose to the occasion to help her daughter and granddaughter.

Betty, on the other hand, was suffering the loss of her son and required more energy than Kelly could muster. Sammy took it upon herself to do the best thing for Kelly and care for Betty.

Sammy cried herself to sleep almost nightly at the pain she saw her friend and Betty go through. When Sammy wasn't crying for Kelly or Betty, she cried for Maxie, the sweet baby who would never know her father.

In this way, the days of August dragged on. Greg's brother, who lived in town, handled the funeral arrangements as well as the legal and financial details. Luckily, Jake was able to find answers to most of Kelly's legal questions.

As Labor Day approached, the country was getting ready for a long holiday weekend. The band of women prepared to break up. Kelly insisted that Ellen go home to Florida. They would see each other again at Thanksgiving, if not sooner. Ellen reluctantly agreed to leave over the holiday weekend.

Although Betty lived in the Phoenix area, Greg's brother promised to take better care of her and to work on scheduling Betty's visits with Maxie instead of Betty dropping by daily.

As soon as Ellen left, Sammy packed up enough of Kelly's and Maxie's things for them to spend a few days with her at her house. Sammy wanted to get Kelly away from her home—her and Greg's home. Maxie had a lot of baby gear, but Sammy looked forward to seeing it all strewn about her house.

***

One morning, shortly after Maxie went down for her morning nap, Sammy coaxed Kelly into joining her in the pool. The two women silently floated on rafts listening for the slightest sound from the baby monitor.

"Seems like we haven't talked in ages, huh?" Kelly asked as she lay in the sun with her eyes closed.

"Yeah, well it was hard to talk with The Moms around," Sammy said.

Kelly laughed. "You make them sound like a rock band or something."

Sammy laughed too. "That's quite a visual."

"Isn't it? Oh, it feels good to laugh," Kelly said as she started to cry. She hopped off her raft and plunged underwater.

She came out of the water still crying. "I miss him so much. I was mad at him that morning. I didn't want him to get in a small frickin' plane and leave us. I told him I was worried.

He reassured me that nothing would happen; he wouldn't let it. I wish I would have been nicer or that I could have somehow talked him out of going. I dream about that morning over and over again. Why did this happen?" Kelly asked as she sobbed.

Sammy, already off her raft, was hugging her friend as she cried. "I don't know Kelly. These accidents never make sense. There's never a good time to die."

Kelly laughed through her tears. "That's all you got? 'There's never a good time to die'?"

"I know, I'm sorry. I got nothing good to say. It's shitty. If I could do anything for this not to have happened, I would. I would trade my life for his in a heartbeat to spare you this pain," Sammy said.

"But I would feel just as much pain at losing you too, Sammy. Don't you know that?" Kelly asked.

"Yeah, I know that. And Greg knew you loved him. It doesn't matter what you two said or didn't say that morning. He loved you and Maxie and knew you two loved him just as much. That love will never die," Sammy said. All she could do was hold Kelly while she cried. Nothing she could say would make her feel better. She needed time and space and maybe some distance.

"What can I do to make you feel better?" Sammy asked when Kelly finally stopped crying.

"I wish I knew," Kelly said as she swam to the pool steps.

"Do you feel up to taking a trip? Getting away for a while? I know it's only been a month, but I think a change of scenery and temperature would do you and Maxie some good," Sammy said, joining Kelly on the steps.

"What did you have in mind? Loon Lake?" Kelly asked.

"No. That place is far too isolated to do you any good. I was thinking more along the lines of Kathy's place in Napa Valley? Your brother could pick us up in San Francisco and he could even spend a few days with us at Kathy's. It would be a good distraction for you," Sammy said.

"That'd be nice. I've been cooped up in our house most of the summer keeping the baby out of the heat," Kelly said. "But what would people think of a new widow going on a vacation so soon after her husband's death?"

"Since when do you care what other people think? And, more importantly, it isn't a vacation, really; it's more a time for healing. You need to go someplace and rest. I know The Moms did their best to care for you, but be honest, they were exhausting weren't they?"

"You have no idea," Kelly said. "Well, I guess you do. You said that there's a cook there, right?"

"Yes, every meal would be planned and prepared by someone else, how wonderful is that? You can take Maxie on strolls through the hills and vineyards. You can rest or workout while she naps. I can babysit her if you want to go out to dinner with Tim or something. We can visit with Dana and see all the cool stuff she's done. We can even drive to the coast too, take Maxie to the beach."

"Is it okay to travel so much with a baby?" Kelly asked.

"Of course. Gabby said this is the best time to travel with a baby, and she should know after having three of them. She pointed out that Maxie doesn't move. She stays where you put her essentially. Why not put her on a plane and in a car on the way to a vineyard?" Sammy answered, trying her darnedest to convince her friend.

"That's true. I never thought of that," Kelly said. "Maxie did just have her four-month check. She doesn't need another well check for two more months," Kelly said, sounding almost convinced. "How long were you thinking?"

"Well, not that long," Sammy answered with a laugh, "but however long it takes to make you feel ready to come home to a life without Greg."

"I'm not sure I'll ever be ready for that," Kelly said.

"Then maybe we never come home," Sammy said.

"Did I tell you that Greg's partner is buying the firm?" Kelly asked.

"No you didn't. But I figured he probably would," Sammy said.

"It shouldn't take long for it to be a done deal," Kelly said.

"Well, then, what do you say? Let's get out of this heat?" Sammy asked.

"Napa Valley, here we come," Kelly said, feigning enthusiasm.

***

It didn't take long for Sammy and Kelly, along with little Maxie, to be on their way. Aunt Kathy was thrilled to have them and couldn't wait to get her hands on Maxie. Sammy knew that her aunt and life on the vineyard would help ease some of Kelly's pain.

Tim and his partner, Henry, picked up the women and Maxie at San Francisco's airport and drove them to the vineyard. It was a jovial drive and Sammy could see Kelly relax more with each mile driven.

Tim and Henry entertained the women with hilarious stories about their lives, their friends, and their jobs. Sammy found simple relief in being with happy people. She was thankful for their effect on Kelly.

As they neared Hidden Peaks Vineyard, Sammy's excitement grew. She looked forward to seeing her aunt and Dana. She was also curious to see what changes the two had made to Escondido. Sammy happily told Tim and Henry all about it, making them eager to see the place too.

Sammy noticed how the change of seasons made Napa Valley look so different from when she was there months before. So close to harvest, the vines were heavy and thick with grapes. She knew from talking to Kathy, that if they were there through harvest, it would be a magical time for all.

Kathy insisted it was the perfect place for Kelly to be after losing Greg. Kathy felt the harvest of the grapes was essentially the end of their "earthly lives" and the beginning of their new spirit as wine. It was all very symbolic to Kathy and she told Sammy as much.

When the group pulled up the dusty road, they all had similar reactions to Sammy's and Dana's at the start of the summer. And Aunt Kathy burst out of the front door to greet them, just as she had four months earlier. Except this time, Kathy floated toward them in a lacy, pale-yellow dress that made Kathy look ten-years younger and somewhat like an angel.

Sammy quickly climbed out of the car to hug her aunt. Her company was not far behind. Sammy reintroduced Kathy to everyone; she had met Kelly on several occasions and Tim and Henry a time or two. But when Kathy met Maxie, it was love at first sight.

"May I hold that babe?" Kathy asked, restraining herself from grabbing the snuggly infant.

"Of course," Kelly said, carefully handing Kathy her precious bundle.

"Oh sweet girl. Hello, beautiful," Kathy cooed, looking up at Kelly. With tears in her eyes, Kathy said to Kelly, "She is so gorgeous. What a precious gift you've been given. Kelly, dear, I'm so sorry for your loss. My heart aches for you and your daughter. I'm so happy y'all are here, though." She hugged Kelly with her one free arm.

Kelly choked back tears.

"Don't say anything," Kathy whispered in her ear. "I'm just thankful y'all came here to heal. I think it's a good, healthy place to heal that broken heart of yours."

Kelly smiled weakly and mouthed, *Thank you.*

Sammy heard this exchange and quickly wiped her own tears away before Kelly could see them.

"Come in. Come in," Kathy commanded. "Leave your bags right there. My fellas will be right out to get your things and put 'em in your rooms."

The group followed Kathy and her precious bundle into the ranch.

"Sammy, wait 'til y'all see the gorgeous rooms Dana's put together. She'll be round in a minute. She's out having a vineyard lesson right now. She'll be back in soon."

"A vineyard lesson?" Sammy asked.

"Yup. Marcus, Hank's main man, has been giving Dana vineyard tours and lessons in the raising of grapes. It's fascinating stuff, and I wanted Dana to learn as much as she could about everything while she's here," Kathy said.

Maxie made a disturbing little noise in her diaper, making everyone chuckle. Kathy giggled as she happily handed Maxie back to her mother.

Kelly quietly asked where she could change Maxie's diaper. Aunt Kathy directed her to a small sitting room. Kelly ducked away to take care of Maxie, with Tim and Henry in tow.

"Here comes Dana now," Kathy said as she saw Dana come to the back entrance.

Sammy met Dana at the door and was surprised by what she saw. Dana looked healthy and stunning with about ten pounds of curves on her previously thin body. She also had a sun-kissed tan and her long blonde hair was pulled back in a lose braid. Her cowgirl boots were well worn, indicating the workout they and Dana had gotten.

But the most significant change that Sammy noticed was the genuine sparkle in Dana's eyes and the wide grin on her face. Dana glowed.

"Sammy, how I missed you," Dana said as she entered the room and hugged Sammy.

"I missed you too. You look amazing," Sammy said.

"Thank you. I feel like a different person from the one you left here months ago," Dana said. "It's been magical."

"Good, hopefully Kelly can benefit from some of that magic," Sammy said.

"You bet she will," Dana and Kathy said in unison, making all three laugh.

"Where is Kelly?" Dana asked.

"She's changing Maxie's diaper. I can't wait to see what you've done to Escondido," Sammy said.

"You haven't told them yet?" Dana asked Kathy.

"Nope, I wanted to save the tour for you. It's your masterpiece. Y'all should be the one to show it off," Kathy said with pride. "Wait till ya see it, Sammy."

"Dana, you look beautiful," Kelly said as she came in.

"Kelly, so good to see you." Dana greeted her with a hug. "And so nice to see you again, Little Maxie. My, you have grown. You were a tiny little bug when I met you last."

"She looks so grown up," Dana said. After an awkward pause, Dana added quietly, "I'm so sorry about Greg. You've been in my prayers every night."

"Thank you," Kelly said kindly. "Let me introduce you to my brother, Tim, and his partner, Henry."

They all exchanged greetings and handshakes.

Sammy enjoyed watching Dana's reaction. She wasn't sure if she'd ever told Dana that Kelly's brother was gay.

But Tim and Henry made a striking pair. Both men were tall, trim, and very good-looking, though opposite in coloring. Tim had the same tones as Kelly: sandy-blond hair and bright-green eyes with beautiful olive skin. Henry was tan with sun-bleached blond hair and piercing brown eyes that twinkled.

Dana couldn't take her eyes off them. "I'm sorry for staring. But you guys are frickin' beautiful."

The group erupted with laughter.

Tim blushed and said, "Why thank you, Dana. Sammy said we'd like you."

Sammy interrupted, "Dana, I'm dying to see what you've done with Escondido. Can you please show us now?"

Kathy answered, "Yes, Dana, please let's go. I'm sure these folks all want some food and drink, and likely that baby needs something soon." Kathy looked to Kelly for agreement.

Kelly answered, "She'll be fine for another hour or so. She's such a good baby." Kelly looked down at her sleepy daughter with love.

"Okay, good, let's go," Dana said as the group headed out to Escondido.

As they walked across the courtyard, Kathy pointed out all the amenities and changes they made over the last few months. The courtyard was beautiful, with stones and a man-made stream that connected the water features. The ponds, waterfalls, hot tubs, and swimming holes were hidden among plants, trees, rocks, stepping stones, and bridges.

"Kathy, it's beautiful. Everything is so private. I love it," Sammy said.

"Yes, it has lots of little spots for couples to swim, snuggle, and relax," Kathy said.

"Well and not only couples," Dana corrected.

"Yes, of course not. Dana's been soaking her weary bones most nights and mornings since the tubs have been working," Kathy added.

"It's true. I've been taking full advantage of this space this summer. It's been great for my soul. Something about the trickle of water and soaking my body," Dana said.

"There's a bigger swimming pool for actual lap swimming and sunbathing down the walkway there if any of y'all want to swim or sun." Kathy pointed the way. "There's a new workout facility down those paths too."

As they continued to meander toward Escondido, Dana asked, "Kathy, will you tell them about Escondido's theme?"

"Oh yes. So when it came to decoratin' Escondido, as Sammy knows I wanted to pick a theme for the six master suites. I really wanted to do the seasons, but there were too many rooms. And then I thought about doing a different wine in each room, but the rooms would be too similar," she explained as she opened the door to Escondido.

When they entered the guesthouse, she continued, "Then I thought about the actual making of wine and all the essentials needed to create a quality bottle of wine. So the six themes were born from that magical process."

"That's intriguing," Sammy said.

"Isn't it?" Dana asked.

Kathy continued, "So the six rooms start with the Terroir Room; 'terroir' is French for 'soil.' The soil is very important in wine-making, as the grapes express where they are grown. Y'all can taste the slight mineralogy in a good wine."

Sammy smiled. "Kathy, I'm impressed. You sound like you know what you're talking about."

"Well, I hope so. Been listenin' to it for years," she replied with a grin.

"The second room is Sol which is French for 'sun' and the room represents the importance of sun and shade in the growin' of grapes," Kathy said, gesturing for them to sit on the denim sectional as Mateo entered with a platter of cheese and crackers.

"Thank you, Mateo," Kathy said as he placed the platter down in front of the group. Kathy introduced her young helper to the group. Mateo nodded shyly and silently poured each some wine and set out plates and other necessities.

"Tell 'em 'bout the other rooms, kiddo," Kathy told Dana.

The group enjoyed the wine and snacks as Dana continued. "The third room is the Cloud Room. It essentially symbolizes the unique properties of these microclimates found above the fog-line here in the hills. At this altitude, the nights are warmer and the days are much cooler than down in the valley floor. The key is to keep the grapes cool while still getting them maximum sunlight." Dana said all this with a certain air of confidence that Sammy appreciated.

"Marcus told me that when the grape vines are forced to struggle a little to survive, they may produce a smaller crop, but the crop will have more color, flavor, and aroma," Dana added.

The group all nodded with enlightenment at Dana's narrative.

"The fourth room is the Trellis Room. The trellis is important for the growth and support of the vines, branches, and shoots. And then the last two rooms represent the last two important elements in the wine-making process."

Sammy noticed Dana's enthusiasm and interest in everything she said. As Sammy looked to the others in the group, she noticed how enthralled they were with Dana. It was exciting to witness.

Dana continued. "The fifth room is the Oak Room, which represents the barrels in which wine ferments. The use of small oak barrels adds complexity and depth to the flavor of wine. It's fascinating. The old Napa Valley wineries used to use large redwood vats that produced quantity—not quality—wines. But Hidden Peaks and many other wineries use the smaller oak barrels and newer technologies like the stainless steel tanks."

With each new fact Dana revealed, Sammy was further impressed with her friend.

"The last room is the Glass Room which represents both the wine bottle and wine glasses," Dana concluded.

"What about the rooms down here?" Tim asked as he surveyed the bare walls.

"We haven't quite finished everything upstairs yet," Dana explained. "But when we do, we'll start down here. What's going to be fun about the downstairs is that it'll capture the history of wine-making in Napa Valley as well as Hank's family history here. Hank will likely tell you about his family history here in Napa Valley, which is a wonderful story, right Sammy?"

"Yes, it's cool. It'll give you guys a different perspective of Hidden Peaks, and Hank too," Sammy said.

"But the downstairs will reflect all the influences in Napa. We want to include a bunch of stuff; from the Native American history to the Chinese laborers, the Gold Rush and Prohibition, construction and the Golden Gate Bridge, which we discovered one of Hank's great uncles worked on the construction of it," Dana said with excitement.

Kathy interrupted, "Yes, yes, this room is going to have loads of stuff in it and I expect Dana to do a bang up job making it look elegant. Why don't we show y'all to your rooms so you can rest and refresh before dinner. Dana can you show 'em to their rooms? I need to go tend to a few things."

"Yes, of course. We'll see you in an hour or so for dinner," Dana replied as Kathy said her good-byes and excused herself.

Dana led Sammy and the gang up to the second floor to their rooms.

From the moment she completed the Sol Room, Dana had taken it as her own. She explained how she loved the feeling it bestowed on her every morning and the buttery yellow walls made her smile. The room was bright, with numerous leafy plants and two large bouquets of fresh-cut sunflowers.

She led the men to the Oak and Terroir rooms, giving them their choice. Both rooms were earthy, elegant, and masculine at the same time. Terroir Room was adorned with unique rock and mineral pieces, such as the slate tops on the dressers and tables. One wall had large photos of the mountain caves and the rock wall that meanders across Napa Valley, both of which were constructed by the Chinese laborers of the 1870s.

The men chose the Oak Room, filled with wood and leather, for its rustic woodsy feel. The gorgeous oak-four-poster king-size bed was the centerpiece of the room. A detailed crown molding circled above. One wall was floor-to-ceiling bookcases in a deep rich wood. Henry revealed that it reminded him of his grandfather's study in Seattle.

Sammy mentioned how beautiful the room was and that the Hidden Peaks wine barrels were the perfect bedside tables.

Dana had a charming white crib with white bedding and mosquito netting draped above it for effect added to the Cloud Room so Maxie and Kelly could stay in the room together. Dana even found an old white pedestal sink that she had converted into a unique but functional changing table. Sheep skin rugs and a variety of white fabrics and materials made the Cloud Room a relaxing and soothing room to be in. Sammy agreed that it was perfect for Kelly.

Sammy was excited to see which room she would get, and she was not disappointed in the Trellis Room. She thought it looked like sleeping in a garden. The headboard of the bed was a beautiful metal trellis that was adorned by something she felt was very fitting for her at the time: *dragonflies*. The walls were the palest blue, allowing the green, brown, and metallic pieces to really pop.

Furthermore, she was thrilled to find in her bathroom, not a shower curtain but an actual trellis covered in real ivy. Behind it was a Jacuzzi tub and waterfall showerhead. She looked forward to soaking in the tub.

Dana let the guests all settle into their rooms, to unpack and unwind before dinner.

Sammy made sure Kelly had everything she needed in her room.

"Thank you for talking me into coming here, Sam."

"I'm so glad you decided to join me. Isn't it fantastic?"

"Yes, it's pretty remarkable. I really like this room. It's so soothing. Each room is so different and they have such different vibes, don't they?"

Sammy snapped her fingers. "*Vibe*, that's exactly the word I was looking for. Like Dana's sunny room, it makes you want to work and get things accomplished. Doesn't it?" Sammy asked.

"It does," Kelly agreed. "And the Oak and Terroir rooms are mature and studious, I thought."

"They are," Sammy agreed. "I think we got the two relaxing rooms, don't ya think?"

"Yes. Mine is very relaxing, almost soothing or healing. Your room is more inspiring I think, kind of dreamy like you."

"Ya think? Huh, maybe that's why I liked it so much. Dana did a good job selecting rooms. Wanna look at the Glass Room with me?" Sammy asked.

"Of course," Kelly said as she laid Maxie down in the elegant crib.

The two women tiptoed to the last room. When Sammy opened the door, both women gasped in awe. It was a sophisticated room of mirrors and glass. A gorgeous crystal mobile hung in front of the window. The late afternoon sun hit it just right shooting drops of rainbows in every direction. It was breathtaking. Above the bed was a chandelier made from different colored wine bottles. It was stunning.

Sammy had a sudden vision of sharing this room with Jake. *The things we could do in here*, she thought. Her face burned with heat.

"Dang, Dana's got some talent," Kelly said in admiration.

Sammy came out of her daydream flustered. "Uh-huh. She sure does. It's beautiful." Her thoughts came into focus. "I had to quit reading her blog over a month ago before she revealed the bedroom themes. I wanted to be surprised, and I'm so glad

I waited. These rooms are wonderful."

They tiptoed back out and into Kelly's room.

"I really want to take a quick nap. Will you wake me up in a half hour?" Kelly asked.

"Yes, of course. Do you want me to watch Maxie?" Sammy asked.

"No, she should keep napping too. I'll wake her when I get up and make her a bottle then."

"Okay, sweet dreams," Sammy said as she shut the door behind her.

She heard Kelly reply, "How can I not have sweet dreams in this room?"

Sammy took advantage of the next thirty minutes. She quickly called Jake and told him all about the beautiful rooms. She even shared her little daydream with him. He promised he would make that dream come true someday. The minutes went by quickly as the two lovebirds shared stories about their days and spoke of their longing to be together.

CHAPTER 22

Tim and Henry stayed on for a few days, just long enough to entertain everyone. They took daily excursions around the vineyard. The middle of September brought busloads of tourists to town, so the group happily stayed confined to Hidden Peaks.

The harvest or "crush" was underway in the vineyards, which kept Hank busy and preoccupied. Kathy explained how they hoped for cool mornings and hot afternoons through Halloween. Letting the grapes hang on the vine as long as possible allows the flavor to develop to its fullest, resulting in a better vintage.

Since it was a wonderful summer weather-wise, not too hot or too wet, it turned out to be a perfect growing season and one of the best that Hank had ever seen. Kathy said she loved this particular "Harvest Hank" while mentioning that some years he was quite the bear.

The gang participated in a night-time harvest, picking grapes from midnight until four in the morning. They mostly watched the experienced workers quickly snip the heavy clusters with ease. It was an exhilarating night to watch the process up close and personal. By sunup, the grapes were in the press and the juices were flowing.

Marcus gave Dana and the group play-by-play details on the process. But he couldn't allow them to waste too much of his time. While harvest is exciting to watch and be a part of, it's hard work, fast-paced, and stressful. The group enjoyed watching the grapes go from vineyard to cellar.

Tim and Henry were sad to leave the excitement of the vineyard. But they looked forward to returning in two weeks to collect Kelly, Maxie, and Sammy for their return trip to the airport. The women had decided that two weeks was the perfect distraction.

Once the men left, Dana and Kathy had much work to attend to. Sammy and Kelly didn't mind one bit. They indulged in long walks with Maxie in her stroller, through the busy vineyard and down the quiet paths that ran through the ranch.

***

With each passing day, Sammy longed for Jake. Absence was certainly making their hearts grow fonder. She often snuck in an intimate call to him in the morning or afternoon. It was an exciting time in their relationship—they were newly in love.

They talked on the phone nightly, each recapping the events of the day and talking about their future together. They kept their engagement secret—only speaking of it to each other late at night. These late-night conversations filled Sammy's dreams while she slept.

She was happy to be at Hidden Peaks with Kelly, Dana, and her aunt. But her mind continued to drift back to her days and nights with Jake. She missed him. She yearned to be back at his cozy lodge to watch the weather turn and the leaves change color.

***

One morning, Sammy made a point of finding Dana in her office early before her day could begin.

"Hey stranger, what are you up to this morning?" Sammy asked, startling Dana.

"Oh hi, Sammy. I'm comparing small appliances for the kitchen. Sounds so uninteresting, doesn't it? But I love it. What's up?" Dana asked.

"I wanted a chance to talk. It seems you've been so busy and we haven't had any time to talk, just the two of us. Is there anything wrong?" Sammy asked, plopping down on Dana's extra office chair.

"No, nothing's wrong. I'm sorry, I've been keeping out of your way intentionally," Dana said.

Sammy was stunned by her honest answer. "Why?"

Dana looked up at Sammy and said, "Honestly, I feel really guilty. I was so childish about my divorce and indulged in such pity parties for myself, and here is poor Kelly and her real, unimaginable loss. I feel awkward and uncomfortable around her. I know I shouldn't, but I do. As you can see, I still have a confidence problem."

"Oh, Dana, you shouldn't feel that way at all. Kelly is one of the most understanding people I've ever known. She was on your side as soon as she found out about…George." Sammy still found it hard to say the words.

She quickly continued, "And you should be very confident. What you've done with these rooms here is amazing. They are each gorgeous, inviting, and unique. I think it's fantastic what you're learning here too. I'm blown away by it all."

"Thanks, Sammy," Dana said, "that means so much to me. Let's get some coffee."

Dana and Sammy headed to the kitchen where Dana fixed them both a cup of coffee. They settled down on the denim couch in the adjoining room.

"Sammy, I have to thank you again for everything. I can't imagine what I would be like if I were still back at Loon Lake and had been there all summer. Sounds like I missed some fun, burning down the forest." Dana chuckled.

"So now I burned down the forest?" Sammy asked in mock surprise.

"You know what I mean."

"Yes," Sammy said with a smile, "I know what you mean. It was quite a night, though. It's bizarre how the summer turned out. I was shocked when Gabby showed up. I can't believe she's getting divorced now too. I worry about getting married someday."

"No, Sammy. Believe in marriage. Believe in love. I do. I didn't before I came here, but I do now. After seeing Uncle Joe lose my aunt and seeing the support and love my parents showed each other, I believe. After watching Kathy and Hank act like newlyweds and lovebirds, I believe. I know I will love again and I think I will marry again. So if I believe, you should too," Dana said.

"Wow, I'd say you had a summer of dragonfly changes," Sammy said.

"A summer of what?" Dana asked.

"Changes in perspective, in self-realization. The kind of change that comes from emotional and mental maturity," Sammy said shyly behind her coffee cup.

"Yes, I'd say you're right. How about you? Did you have a summer of changes?" Dana asked.

"Mmm, a little, I guess. Nothing major, except maybe your brother," Sammy said.

"What about my brother?" Dana asked.

Sammy could tell he must not have mentioned the marriage proposal or else she would have certainly said something.

"I feel very strongly for him, that's all," Sammy said.

"Yeah? Is that what you call it? *Feel strongly for him*?" Dana teased. "He feels strongly for you too."

"I know he does." Sammy looked at Dana. "I miss him a little." She tried to change the subject.

"You'll see him soon, won't you?" Dana asked.

"Yes, I suppose I will. I just don't know when," Sammy said. "Cass's babies will be baptized in a few weeks. I was wondering if I should ask him to come out for that. I was going to ask him one night, but he was going on and on about how much work was needed at Vince's place. He didn't think they'd get what they needed done before the first snow. What do you think?"

"You should definitely invite him. He has to be there, don't ya think?" Dana asked as if there were no other choice. "Who cares about the first snow? Plus, I talked to Vince a few days ago and it sounded like things were moving along."

"That's kind of what I was thinking," Sammy said. "So, how's Vince doing then?"

"He's hanging in there. I think this big project is keeping his mind off of his mom. As far as the work goes, he said the big guest cabin is already framed and the exterior could be finished before the first snow. The construction crew is moving really fast and the permit process has been remarkably quick too. He's pretty excited as far as all that goes. I think he made the right choice. But we'll find out next summer, huh? I guess he's had a summer of…What kind of changes did you call it?"

"Dragonfly changes," Sammy said. "You're right—he's definitely had that kind of summer."

"I've missed you, Sammy. I really enjoyed our drive out here and those first few weeks together. I have such fond memories of that time. I will never forget it; everything was so unknown," Dana said.

"And now? Where do you go from here? What's next?" Sammy asked.

"Ah, the next year is up to Kathy, I think. You need to talk to her about that," Dana said vaguely.

"What do you mean?" Sammy asked.

"Ask her," Dana said.

"I will," Sammy answered. "And soon."

"Good, we need your input. She was supposed to talk to you days ago," Dana added.

"Okay, now I'm beyond curious," Sammy said, sounding frustrated.

"Good. Let's go see if we can find her," Dana said.

"Well, okay, then," Sammy said. She scribbled a note for Kelly and the two set out to find Aunt Kathy.

And find her they did. She was sitting in her "office" outside the dining room, with an open laptop, her notebook, and an array of colored pens.

"Good morning, girls," Kathy said as she saw the women heading her way.

"Good morning, Kathy," they replied.

"What's up?" Kathy asked. "Where's Kelly? How she holdin' up?"

"I heard her and Maxie up early this morning, so I can only assume and hope for Kelly's sake that they both fell back asleep and will sleep a bit more this morning," Sammy said as she sat next to Kathy.

She continued, "I think she's doing much better. Her looks of anguish are getting fewer and farther apart. I know she misses Greg so much and I can tell when she looks at Maxie her heart breaks for that baby. I think she's also sad for Greg that he doesn't get to see Maxie grow up. But I've told her he *does* see her every moment of her life. But, of course, it's not the same thing."

"Do y'all think her comin' here was a good idea?" Kathy asked.

"Most definitely. She's been able to heal, escape, and *breathe*," Sammy said.

"Good. That was my hope," Kathy said. "There were some things I've wanted to talk to you about but we haven't had much one-on-one time. Ya got some time to chat right now?"

"Of course. I'm all yours," Sammy said with concern.

"Oh, dear, there's nothin' to worry 'bout. It's just my old hare-brained ideas have been actin' up again and I wanted to talk to you and your level head about a thing or two. Dana's been a wonderful soundin' board, but much too agreeable, I'm afraid. No offense, dear," Kathy said to Dana.

"None taken," Dana replied without skipping a beat.

Sammy laughed and said, "Aunt Kathy, you got me more curious than a cat under a Christmas tree."

Kathy laughed her hearty laugh. "That's my girl! Ya sound just like me. Come, let's go to one of my new favorite spots. Wait till ya see what just arrived yesterday."

She led them down a winding path to a clearing under a large shade tree. At the base of the tree was a man-made trickling stream and pond complete with waterfall and water lilies. It was a pleasant little oasis.

"Look here, these are the two swings I had commissioned from that sweet craftsman up north that we stopped at after Bigfootin'. I remembered that old wooden swing in front of Jake's lodge last summer. I described it to the craftsman and asked if he could make two for me. They turned out better than I expected."

Sammy was surprised and so moved by the coincidence of it all. It was one of those moments when she believed in heavenly intervention.

"Look at the detailed carving on the swing. Simply gorgeous," Kathy said as she gently slid her fingers over the sculpted wood.

Upon closer investigation, Sammy gasped as the fine hairs on her arms tingled. "There are dragonflies carved in here. They are beautiful," she whispered. "Did you ask him for those specifically?"

"No, I didn't. I asked for something to remind me of a lake in Minnesota. I wanted to remember that time together with my girls. I know it was only a brief weekend trip with you girls last summer, but it was so special to me. You were all so happy that weekend and somehow finally at peace," Kathy said dreamily.

"Sit on 'em. They're pretty comfy too," Kathy said as she sat and swung like a kid. She giggled with delight.

Sammy and Dana joined her. The three happily swung, sipping their coffees as they listened to the birds and the sounds of harvest and wine-making off in the distance.

"Kathy, so what's up?" Sammy asked, breaking the silence.

"Well, it's nothing serious, so don't worry 'bout that. I wanted to tell y'all 'bout my business ventures and see whatcha thought. So, it was my good pal Linda in Shelter Cove who suggested the whole B and B thing to me. I liked the idea, but was never crazy about it," Kathy said.

Sammy mentally agreed that that line of hospitality wasn't exactly Kathy's style.

"But, I definitely liked the idea of a retreat house. When y'all get to be my age, you look back on your life and think 'bout what ya did well and what ya know. Now it's time for me to pass on my expertise and knowledge to someone younger with more energy and passion," Kathy said.

"You're nuts, Kathy. You have more energy than anyone I know," Sammy said.

"That might be true, but my interests are definitely shifting," Kathy said thoughtfully. "My experience in real estate amounts to a hill of beans in this economy. No one cares about what I know, so that can't be my legacy."

Sammy didn't know how to argue that one.

"But takin' care of you girls, helpin' y'all heal—I was good at that," Kathy said.

"You were *great* at that," Sammy interrupted.

"Helpin' sweet Dana here, that felt right. Y'all bringin' Kelly here to heal, that felt right to me too," Kathy said. "This is a place to heal, rest, and renew one's faith and hope in life. *That* is what I want my legacy to be: to help others."

"That sounds perfect for you. I completely agree. I think you're doing it and can continue to do it. Where do I fit in?" Sammy asked.

"Well, ya don't really. I just wanted your input and advice. See, there's an ordinance here in Napa Valley about what kinds of activities a winery can and can't take part in. Any activity has to have at least fifty percent of its time givin' to marketing of wine—that is, the education and development of customers. It's a way to make sure wineries here don't go into the party business or some such thing. And that kind of constraint doesn't exactly fit with what I want to do," Kathy explained.

"I've been learning all I can about wine-making, so I can cunningly include aspects of wine-making into Escondido, even if it isn't verbally expressed. Through their surroundings, visitors are educated," Dana chimed in.

"Ah, interesting," Sammy said. She noticed Kathy smiling and nodding at being in cahoots with Dana.

"Anyway, that's why I snagged those two properties earlier in the summer. In case I needed either for this retreat center I'm cookin' up in my mind," Kathy said.

"I like that: a *retreat center*," Sammy repeated.

"Yes and both properties are perfect for such centers. I'm not sure what to do with either just yet. But what I was getting' at, was I wondered if you think Gabby would be interested in helpin' me with such a task?" Kathy asked.

Sammy looked as if she was clobbered on top of the head with the idea. "That is a *fantastic* possibility." Sammy proceeded to tell the women about how wonderful Gabby was with the little impromptu art class and that she longed for something bigger and better. If anyone could do it, Sammy knew Gabby could.

"But what about the boys?" Kathy interrupted.

"That's up to her. Matty starts high school next year. It might be a good time for a move. He'll be starting in a new school anyway: it might work to start here. But which property? Both are so far from here. What would you do?" Sammy asked.

"Details. Details," Kathy teased. "No, those are good questions. As of now, Dana's agreed to help in any way she can. If I could talk Gabby and the boys into moving out next summer, Dana could move there for a while and help keep 'em company and start up the place."

"You'd do that?" Sammy asked.

"Of course," Dana said. "What else have I to do? What an experience that would be. And I loved your sister. She was so sweet. It would be fun to work on it with her and Kathy remotely."

"So, sounds like you think I should ask her…" Kathy said questioningly.

"Yes, I think you should ask her," Sammy said. "I think her and the boys would be perfect on the large ranch property. It was not as remote as the other property. It would be better for the boys, I think. Oh, but the little one has the pond, and I bet the boys would love to boat on it and fish in it."

"Yes, I get torn between the two places too. But I was thinking the horse property would be big enough to fit them and the retreat center too. Might even get some horses. I still have some thinkin' to do about it. Gabby said her and the boys were goin' to the twins' baptisms in October. I'm gonna talk to her then." Kathy sounded utterly convinced of her decision.

"Good idea," Sammy said. "I can't wait to find out what's gonna happen. What a wonderful opportunity for her."

"I hope she sees it that way too," Kathy said. "But I also know my dream may not be her dream and that's okay. I'll just have to find some other poor sucker." She looked directly at Dana when she said it.

"You know I'd do it in a heartbeat," Dana said.

"I know, dear. I got my eye on you for somethin' else, though, too," Kathy teased.

"She says this to me all the time," Dana told Sammy.

"Kathy, that's terrible. Don't tease her that way," Sammy scolded. "She's always been like that though, Dana. Gotta love her."

Dana smiled.

"Well, that was my big secret. I know you and Kelly are leavin' in a few days. There's one last thing I want y'all to do before ya go, but I didn't know if Kelly would be up for it," Kathy said.

"Get it? Up for it?" Kathy repeated as she nudged Dana lightly with her elbow.

"Yeah, I got it," Dana said as she lovingly rolled her eyes.

"What'd I miss?" Sammy asked.

"My friend in town has a hot-air balloon and she offered

to take you and Kelly up for a sunrise ride. Do you think Kelly'd want to go?" Kathy asked.

"Yes, I know she'd love to," Sammy said without hesitation.

"Even after the plane crash?" Dana asked.

"Yes, we saw a balloon outside of San Fran on our drive here, and she said she'd always wanted to go. Her brother even asked her the same thing, like about the plane crash, and she said it was a completely different scenario. She isn't afraid of a balloon ride at all. I'd love to surprise her with it if we could," Sammy said.

"It's a done deal, then. I'll call my friend and double check her availability for tomorrow morning. I can watch Maxie. Dana, you want to give 'em a lift into town and take some photos?" Kathy asked.

"I'd love to," Dana said.

"Perfect. I'll make the call when we get back to the house. We should probably go check on Kelly, huh?"

"Yeah, we should," Sammy said as the three got up and headed back up the path.

***

The next morning, the women were off on one of their final adventures in Napa Valley. Sammy didn't tell Kelly where they were going or what they were doing. Dana and Sammy rode along quietly as Kelly mumbled under her breath about being up before the crack of dawn and, worse still, before Maxie.

Sammy knew Kelly was just being Kelly, giving someone a hard time was the same as showing them love.

They arrived at the launch site just as the balloon crew had the balloon spread out and the fans in place to begin inflation.

"What in the world?" Kelly asked in awe.

"Want to go up in a balloon this morning?" Sammy asked excitedly.

"You know it," Kelly answered with delight.

The three women greeted the pilot and obediently listened

to instructions and information.

Within the hour, the pilot, Sammy, and Kelly—the only passengers—were in the small balloon, gently lifting off.

Back on the ground, Dana snapped away, capturing their assent in photos.

Sammy assumed that Kathy must have told the pilot their back stories. The pilot seemed to respect the women's privacy and kept the chit-chat to a minimum, allowing Sammy and Kelly to soak it all in.

As they gently rose higher and higher off the ground, Sammy began to feel free and weightless. The views were overwhelming: crystal-clear air in every direction. She could see the mountains in the distance and the land below. Every object and shadow was clear, not distorted like when looking through a scratched airplane window.

Sammy was so immersed in her own inner peace and joy that when she looked at Kelly's tear-streaked face she was surprised.

"Hey, what's going on in there?" Sammy asked cautiously.

"I feel him, Sammy," Kelly whispered. "Or it could be the lack of oxygen," she added with a smile. "But I feel Greg with us. I miss him so much. Sometimes, I don't know how I'm going to raise his daughter without him. How can I make her remember him?"

Sammy wondered the same thing many times. She looked out at the limitless sky. "We know there are stars out there right now, right? We just can't see them."

Kelly laughed and nodded as she wiped away her tears.

"Kids have this wonderfully innocent way of knowing Santa Clause, the Tooth Fairy, and the Easter Bunny without every really seeing them, right?" Sammy asked.

Kelly nodded again, looking down at the passing landscape.

"We even believe in God without really ever meeting Him or seeing Him in person, right?" Sammy asked.

Kelly shook her head and whispered, "Yes."

"That's how. You talk about her daddy. You tell her

stories about her daddy, your husband. You let her know he is watching her, like Santa and his elves. He'll know when she loses a tooth, just as much as the Tooth Fairy will. He'll celebrate every birthday with her. She will believe," Sammy said. She couldn't hold back her own tears. She wished Kelly and Maxie didn't have to remember him, but they did.

"Wow, damn, she's good, isn't she?" Kelly asked the eavesdropping pilot.

The pilot nodded in silence, her own eyes wet with tears.

Sammy placed her hand on Kelly's. "And I'm here to help you every step of the way. You aren't alone. You know that, right?"

"I know that," Kelly said. "This view is amazing. Isn't it? I wonder if this is what angels see."

"I hope so, Kell," Sammy replied.

The women rode in silence the next ten minutes, soaking in the scenery and weightlessness of it all. Again, Sammy felt free and alive.

She caught herself wishing she could share this moment with Jake and the irony of her wish resonated with understanding. Kelly would always wish to share moments with Greg like Maxie's first step, first word, or first day of school.

Kelly interrupted Sammy's thoughts. "Thank you for dragging me out here to Napa Valley, Sammy. I really did need to get away."

"You're welcome," Sammy replied.

"But I don't think I'm ready to go home to Arizona yet. I think I'm going to go stay with Tim and Henry for a few weeks, and my oldest friend from high school, Nancy, lives in the area. I'd like to visit with her a bit too," Kelly said.

"That sounds like a great idea," Sammy said. She knew she would miss Kelly dearly, but she knew Kelly was right. Kelly wasn't ready to go home.

"I've been thinking that I might even go spend some time in Florida with my mom after this too," Kelly added.

"I think if you can take as much time away as you need,

that's the best thing to do. Surround yourself and Maxie with people who love you and who can help you," Sammy said.

"I'm gonna miss you," Sammy added as she put her arm around Kelly's shoulder and squeezed.

"I'm going to miss you too, Sammy. I really will. Maybe you can come visit me in Florida," Kelly suggested.

"Maybe," Sammy said. "But I have to go to Cass's in a few weeks for the twins' baptisms and then back here for New Year's for Kathy and Hank's ceremony."

"And what about Jake?" Kelly asked.

"I don't know. Strangely, we haven't talked about when we'll see each other again. But I'm going to invite him to Cass's and Kathy's. So hopefully, I'll see him soon," Sammy said.

They enjoyed the remainder of the balloon ride. The pilot showed them a few points of interest. Sammy took notice that Kelly looked happier as the moments passed. She knew it would be a long time, if ever, before Kelly was her old self. But she knew Kelly was strong and would survive.

As the balloon approached the landing site, the women could see Dana's SUV waiting below. Within minutes, they could see her blonde little frame waving to them.

They landed with barely a bump. They thanked the pilot for the adventurous ride. The women helped the crew pack up the balloon and capped off the morning with a sparkling white wine toast.

As Dana drove them back to the vineyard, Sammy and Kelly told her all about the balloon ride. They failed to tell her about the emotional journey they'd gone on. It was their intense, emotional ride that Sammy knew they wouldn't share with anyone else. This was a new phase in her friendship with Kelly, sharing Kelly's most painful moments and respecting her privacy.

***

Departure day finally arrived. Tim and Henry turned up to collect the women and Maxie. They were thrilled that Kelly and Maxie were staying with them.

Sammy was sad to leave Kathy and Dana. She knew she would see her aunt and Hank at Cass's in a few weeks. She also knew she would likely see Dana at New Year's. But she was still sad to leave them and the magic of the vineyards. She'd used the word "magical" many times while she was there, but there was no better word that suited the place.

She was curious to see how Kathy's retreat center would unfold and what the future there held for Dana and Gabby.

After a flurry of bear hugs and good-byes, the gang left the vineyard in a hurry to get Sammy to the airport.

Sammy and Kelly were at a loss for words. Sammy had a lump of sadness in her throat. She really didn't want to leave Kelly. She felt guilty, as though she was abandoning her friend.

Tim and Henry filled the silence with entertaining small talk.

"Are you sure you're going to be okay?" Sammy asked Kelly as they neared the San Fran airport. "I don't feel right leaving you here."

Kelly smiled at Sammy. "You are the best friend a woman could ever ask for. I will be fine. You need to go and do what you need to do. Don't worry about me. I just need more time. I certainly don't expect you to put your life on hold to become my babysitter."

"Are you sure? I feel so bad," Sammy said helplessly.

"Don't. It's been almost two months that you've been waiting on me hand and foot. You've been amazing. You need to get home and figure out what the hell you and Jake are doing," Kelly scolded with a smile.

"That's true," Sammy agreed.

As they drove through the airport entrance, Sammy couldn't help but cry openly. She was doing a lot of that lately, but her heart was so raw when it came to Kelly and her situation. She was really going to miss her friend.

"Hey, snap out of it," Kelly said. "We'll be okay."

"I know. I know," Sammy said as Tim pulled into the departures area.

Tim hopped out to drop Sammy's bags with the curbside attendant.

Sammy hugged her friend and gave a sleeping Maxie a kiss on her button nose. After another flurry of hugs and good-byes, Sammy waved to her friends as they pulled away, leaving her on the airport curb. With a heavy sigh, she turned to the attendant to check in.

***

The flight home to Phoenix filled Sammy with a feeling that resembled excitement. It wasn't full-on excitement, as she really felt she had nothing to come home to. But it was relief and contentment with a dash of hope, that now nothing would stand in her way to see Jake.

His resort and guest cabins were finally closed for the season. He'd been busy helping Vince get ready for winter. She was going to invite him to Cass's in a few weeks, but she wanted to see him before that.

As the pilot announced their landing, she wished she were landing in Saw Mill instead of Phoenix. Her heart ached to see Jake. She knew what she needed to do next.

When she arrived at the baggage claim area, Sammy couldn't believe her eyes. She was sure she was dreaming.

Jake was standing with his back to her in front of her designated luggage carousel. Her heart skipped a beat. She stepped closer, sure she was mistaken.

As though he felt her there, he turned and looked directly at her, just like he had done months ago in the Saw Mill airport.

She was mesmerized and consumed with her desire and love for him *again.*

He greeted her with that "first kiss" kind of kiss. This time she was sure she felt it in her soul.

"Hiya," Sammy said breathlessly.

"Hiya," he said back. "I missed you." He gave her another small, gentle kiss.

"I missed you too. What are you doing here?" she asked awkwardly.

"Well, I figured if we're getting married, I needed to at least see what your life is like here. Don't ya think?" he asked.

"Yeah, I guess that would be a good idea," she agreed casually, trying to mask the immeasurable happiness she felt.

He collected her bags and suggested, "Let's get you home."

She leaned into him. A long, tender kiss was her only reply.

The End

ABOUT THE AUTHOR

JOAN GABLE is the author of the Loon Lake Series (*Summer of Firefly Memories* and *Summer of Dragonfly Changes*) and *My Christmas Curse.* She lives in Arizona with her husband, their two young daughters, and their attention-starved cat.

CPSIA information can be obtained at www.ICGtesting.com
Printed in the USA
LVOW04s1548120914

403825LV00015B/1033/P